Dope Girl Magic 3

**Lock Down Publications and Ca$h
Presents
Dope Girl Magic 3
A Novel by *Destiny Skai***

Dope Girl Magic 3

Lock Down Publications
P.O. Box 944
Stockbridge, Ga 30281

Visit our site at
www.lockdownpublications.com

Copyright 2020 by Destiny Skai
Dope Girl Magic 3

Lock Down Publications
Like our page on Facebook: Lock Down Publications @
www.facebook.com/lockdownpublications.ldp
Cover design and layout by: **Dynasty Cover Me**
Book interior design by: **Shawn Walker**
Edited by: **Kiera Northington**

Destiny Skai

Stay Connected with Us!

Text **LOCKDOWN** to 22828 to stay up-to-date with new releases, sneak peaks, contests and more…

Thank you!

Submission Guideline.

Submit the first three chapters of your completed manuscript to ldpsubmissions@gmail.com, subject line: Your book's title. The manuscript must be in a .doc file and sent as an attachment. Document should be in Times New Roman, double spaced and in size 12 font. Also, provide your synopsis and full contact information. If sending multiple submissions, they must each be in a separate email.

Have a story but no way to send it electronically? You can still submit to LDP/Ca$h Presents. Send in the first three chapters, written or typed, of your completed manuscript to:

LDP: Submissions Dept
P.O. Box 944
Stockbridge, Ga 30281

DO NOT send original manuscript. Must be a duplicate.

Provide your synopsis and a cover letter containing your full contact information.

Thanks for considering LDP and Ca$h Presents.

Previously

Tori paced the living room of the old house she and Kilo once shared. Old memories of her and her husband flooded her mind. So many great things happened at that address, including the conception of Capone. On the tragic side, it was where the tragedy that claimed Kilo's life took place.

"Kilo, baby, the closing for this house is taking place as we speak. I'll never let go of the memories we created here. Especially, our handsome ass son. I promise to be the best mother I can be."

The sound of a car pulling up interrupted her thoughts. Tori looked out the window and saw he was on time, as expected. Her heart began to race. The palms of her hands became sweaty. Tori wiped her hands along the side of her jeans as she struggled to keep her composure. "You can do this. You can do this," she repeated over and over again, as she opened the door and stood in the frame.

Diesel walked up to the door and gave Tori the biggest hug. It had been weeks since he'd last seen his daughter. "I'm so glad you called me."

"Come in." Tori stepped back and let him in. She closed the door and did an about-face. "Have a seat."

Diesel sat down and crossed his legs. "It's so good to see you, baby. What was so urgent that you needed me to come over? You know I'm here for you, no matter what it is."

Tori sat down in the single fold-out chair in the middle of the floor. "You know, I wish I could believe that, but I don't."

Diesel was puzzled about her response. "What do you mean? I've been by your side since the day your mother had you."

Tori shook her head. "Have you really?"

"Yes. I have. The only thing I'm guilty of is being an overbearing father and that's only because I love you. I've loved you since the day I knew your mother was expecting you."

Hate and anger wrapped around Tori's heart like a valve with intense pressure. "Somehow, I don't believe you."

"You should."

"At this moment, I'm going to forget about the lies that are spewing from your mouth like a venomous snake. I'm older and I know better. I'm going to get to the reason I brought you here."

"And what's that?" Diesel ignored her evil words in order to get down to the nitty gritty.

"Just like you, I've been keeping a four-year secret from you and it's time to come clean. Unlike you, I need to clear my conscience."

"And what would that be?" Diesel was skeptical about what his baby girl had to tell him.

"Lala, come out!" Tori screamed. Lala walked out with Capone in her arms.

Lala placed him down beside Tori. "Here you go."

Before he could say anything, Tori began to talk. "I would like for you to meet your grandson."

Diesel's eyes widened in surprise. "My who?"

"Your grandson." Tori pulled her son close to her. "When I went off to college, I was pregnant. My professor raised him so I could finish school. This is me and Kilo's son."

"Wait, what?" Diesel scratched his head. "My grandson?"

"Yes. I had a baby while I was away," Tori snapped.

"Why didn't you tell me?"

"For what? So, you could talk me out of it?" Tori was angry all over again.

Diesel contemplated about his response. The accusations she spat were true, but he wouldn't admit to that. His guilt wouldn't allow it. "No. I would've wanted to be there for you." Diesel sat upright, "What's his name?"

The toddler spoke up on his own. "My name is Capone."

"Come here." Diesel extended his arms.

Capone was as friendly as they came. "Can I, Mommy?"

"Yes," she replied.

Capone walked over and stood in front of his grandfather with a curious eye. "What's your name?"

"Grandpa Diesel."

8

"Hi, Papa Diesel," Capone smiled. He was the happiest kid anyone could ever meet. Diesel hugged him tight.

Tori gave them all of two minutes together, before she interrupted their session. "Lala, take him in the back."

"Okay," Lala replied. "Come on, Capone. Let's go."

When they left the room, Tori laid it out on the line. Her eyes roamed the room before she began to speak. "Do you know Kilo bought this house for me?"

"No, I didn't know that," Diesel answered quickly.

"I know you didn't." Tori had the meanest mug plastered on her grill. "When Kilo was killed, that was the worst day of my life. I wanted to die right along with him, because I knew there would never be another man on earth that would love me the way he did. But you took that away from me."

Diesel appeared shocked, but he knew exactly what she was talking about. "What are you talking about? I didn't take him away from you."

Tori grunted and rocked in her seat. "Stop lying to me," she screamed.

"I'm not," he rebutted quickly.

"You are." Tori jumped from her seat and pulled out the signature gold Desert Eagle that once belonged to Kilo. "You killed the love of my life."

Diesel held up both hands. "No, I didn't. Put the gun away. Please."

"No. You broke my heart and now I'm going to bust yours." Tori's finger rested comfortably on the trigger.

"Tori, please. I'm your father, don't do this," he pleaded.

"Fuck that." Tori put a round in the chamber. "Lala, come back out here."

Lala closed the door where Capone was watching cartoons and entered the bedroom. "You ready?"

"Yes." Tori stepped to the side with her gun still aimed. "Sit in this chair. And don't try anything or you will die here today."

Diesel sat down in his appointed seat without a fight. Tori kept her gun aimed at him, while Lala tied him up. In his heart, he felt like Tori wouldn't pull the trigger, but his mind said otherwise. He hoped his love for her outweighed the hate she had for him. When Lala was done, she looked at Tori.

"You want us to leave now?" she asked.

"Yes," Tori replied. Lala grabbed Capone and they left out the back door.

Tori sat down on the sofa. She was distraught and upset about everything she learned about her father. Her behavior was hysterical and unattainable. However, she tried to keep it together for the sake of the truth.

"I'm going to ask you some questions and I need you to be honest with me." Tori was ready for him to lie at any moment. "Again, I'm going to ask you a series of questions and you better be honest."

"Okay." Diesel nodded.

"Did you kill Kilo?" Tori's heart raced with anticipation.

"No."

Tori rubbed her temple. "Why are you lying?"

"I'm not."

"That's a lie," snapped. "I spoke with Sherrod, right before I killed him, and he told me he had an order from you to kidnap and kill Kilo."

Diesel knew his words wouldn't hold water when it came to his daughter, but he knew he had to be honest. "Tori, I swear, I had nothing to do with his death. On everything I love, I only told them to kidnap him and bring him to me. I knew he wouldn't come willingly. I had to make him come to me and that was the only way. Tori, I swear, all I wanted to do was talk to him about making you go to college. By the time we spoke, it was too late to call it off. They were already there. I couldn't stop it."

Tori sat in silence as she cried. No matter what Diesel said, it was his fault Kilo was dead. "You killed my husband. We had just gotten married at the courthouse the day you had your fake ass goons come here. You ruined my life," she screamed.

"I'm sorry, baby. That wasn't my intention." Diesel stated honestly.

"No. You keep that sad ass apology. You purposely ruined my life and now I'm going to ruin yours and your bastard child's." Tori aimed her gun at Diesel and pulled the trigger. *Boca!*

***

"Did you hear that shit?" Jarvis asked, while looking over in the passenger seat at Moon.

"That sounded like a gunshot," Moon replied, as he stared at the front door.

"Yeah, but now my question is, who pulled the trigger?" Jarvis was skeptical about he'd just heard.

"Shit, I'm out here with you." Moon stroked the barrel of his gun. "We know Tori's in there, but I know Diesel would never kill his daughter."

"Just like she won't kill her daddy." Jarvis rubbed his head. "It's somebody else in that house. We just don't know who it is."

"I agree. Them muthafuckas just killed somebody." Moon sat his gat on his lap.

"Well, we sitting right here until she comes out. I'm still snatching that bitch up just as soon as she's alone." Jarvis pulled out a cigarette and lit it. As they lie in wait, Jarvis peeped a familiar truck pull up. On edge, he watched closely as a familiar face stepped out of the vehicle. "What the fuck's going on?" Jarvis mumbled.

Destiny Skai

Chapter 1

Summer 1995

The living room was filled with marijuana smoke and the sound of "One More Chance," by the Notorious BIG filled the ears of the occupants. Women and men were rapping and sipping from red cups filled with alcohol. Others played dominoes and spades. Eazy was seated at the spades table with his partner, Bianca, talking mad shit to every loser they put out the seats.

"Get y'all monkey asses up," he chuckled. "Can we get some real competition at the table?" Eazy was tipsy and loud.

Bianca matched his energy, as she sipped from her cup. "Y'all heard my partner, get your asses up. Who's next?"

Byrd and Fabian sat down to the table. Fabian picked up the deck of cards. "We about to get both of y'all asses off the table and I'm the dealer."

Eazy chuckled. "Boy, you gone need Jesus to come down and shuffle these cards in order for you to win."

Fabian shuffled the deck several times before sliding it in Eazy's direction. "Nigga, I'm God. Now cut the deck, sucka!"

"Run it, sucka!" Eazy grabbed his empty cup and leaned back in his seat. "Chasity," he shouted over the music. "Come fix me another drink."

Chasity passed the weed to Byrd's wife, Michelle, and stood up. "I'll be back." Taking the cup from his hand, she looked him in the eyes. "Make this your last drink."

Eazy's top lip curled, as he snarled in anger. "I'm a grown ass man, so watch who you talking to like that. When I tell you to do something, just do it. I don't need all that slick shit from you."

Chasity rolled her eyes and turned on her heels. "What the fuck ever."

"You heard what the fuck I said," Eazy snapped and picked up his hand. Chasity returned with his cup and shoved it into his hand, spilling some of the liquid onto his hand and clothing. "What the fuck is your problem?"

13

The room became silent when Eazy shouted and rose to his feet.

"You're my problem." Chasity placed her hand on her hip. She too was tipsy and high. "I'm tired of all this shit."

Eazy felt disrespected, so he reached back and popped his wife in the mouth. "You better sit yo' ass down somewhere, before I beat your ass in here." Chasity stumbled and grabbed her face.

Diesel appeared out of the blue and jumped in between them. He put his hand on Eazy's chest. "Come on, bro, don't do this in front of everybody."

"Fuck that! If she wanna be disrespectful in front of these muthafuckas, this is where she gone get it at," Eazy barked with anger in his tone.

Chasity reached over Diesel's shoulder and tried to swing on Eazy, but she missed. "You wanna hit me in front of these people? Watch I call the police on your ass."

"Do it, bitch, and watch I bury your ass alive." They were one set of people Eazy didn't fuck with. Nor did he take being threatened lightly.

"Calm down," Diesel pleaded with his brother. "Sit down and finish playing cards. I'll take care of her."

"Take that bitch home before I fuck her up." Eazy sat back down at the table.

"Keep disrespecting me, Eazy. I'm the mother of your kids. Your wife. Are you stupid?" Chasity's eyes were full of tears.

"Chasity, be quiet and let's go. You had too much to drink and you not gone win this fight." Diesel pushed her towards the door.

Eazy took a deep breath and picked up his cards. Fabian glanced over at him to make sure his day-one was straight. "You good now?"

"Yeah. I'm good." It was funny how quickly his mood changed, as if nothing just happened. "Bianca, let's run these niggas off the table."

"With pleasure," she smiled.

***

Diesel pulled up in the driveway of Eazy's house. Chasity opened the door and jumped out the front seat with the quickness. Unsure of what she was doing, Diesel gave chase. Chasity leaned forward in the grass and coughed harshly. When he realized she was throwing up, Diesel kept his distance and waited on her to finish. Chasity wiped her mouth and stood up.

"You good?" Diesel asked.

"Yeah. Open the door."

Diesel unlocked the door and escorted her inside. Chasity walked down the hallway with her brother-in-law in tow. Once inside the bedroom, she flicked on the light and flopped down on the bed.

Diesel grabbed her arm. "Get up. You need to shower, so you can go to bed."

Chasity pulled away from him. "I am."

"Well, get up then."

"No. You can leave," she debated.

"Get up now!" Diesel raised his voice and she automatically rose to her feet.

"Fine."

Chasity walked into the bathroom and closed the door. Slowly, she removed her clothes and stepped inside the tub. The knob was cold to the touch as she turned it on and so was the water that hit her skin. Once the water was warm enough, she washed her face and lathered her body with body wash.

After spending a good fifteen minutes in the shower, she stepped out and put on her robe. When she opened the door, to her surprise, Diesel was no longer sitting on the bed. Chasity exited the room and went into the living room where he was seated. He looked up when he heard movement.

"You feel better now?"

"Almost," she smiled and walked towards him. Chasity stood in front of Diesel and opened her robe. "But I think you can help me with that."

Diesel sat there with his eyes glued on the brown-skinned beauty in front of him. Chasity's skin was flawless. Her C-cups sat pretty, but the best sight was her bald kitty. He cleared his throat. "Close your robe and go to bed." Diesel tried to stand up, but she pushed him back down.

Chasity licked her soft, full lips and placed her fingers between her legs. "Don't you want to make me feel good? My pussy's so wet right now and I could use something nice and hard right about now." Moving her fingers, she closed her eyes and moaned.

Diesel salivated as he watched Chasity pleasure herself. The once-limp rod in his pants was now throbbing and ready to bust through his zipper. No longer able to keep his composure, he unzipped his pants and pulled out his piece and stroked it. Chasity opened her eyes. Excited about the sight of his long, thick chocolate dick, she climbed onto his lap and eased down on it.

Chasity held the back of the sofa, while rolling her hips in a circular motion. Diesel palmed her ass as he grunted from the grip of her nookie. Their bodies were in tuned with one another. Sexy pants and moans filled their lungs. "Diesel, you feel so good. Just like I knew you would."

Diesel didn't respond. He let his tongue do the talking for him, as he took one of her breasts into his mouth. Chasity felt all sort of tingles running up and down her spine. With ease, she bounced up and down on his shaft. It was a moment she had been dreaming about for a while. Her marriage with Eazy had hit a rough bump in the road and it was time for a new driver. At night when they lie in bed together, it felt like she was living with a stranger. Bianca and Diesel's marriage seemed so perfect and she wanted the same for herself.

Chasity placed her hand underneath Diesel's chin and moved his head. Affection was what she wanted, so she placed her lips onto his and slid her tongue into his mouth. He was game and kissed her back. In between the lip lock, she mumbled, "Diesel, fuck me please."

Chasity raised up from his lap, so they could get up and switch positions. Lying down on the sofa, she opened her legs and welcomed Diesel inside the place that belonged to her husband.

16

Approximately forty minutes later, their session had come to an end. Diesel stood up and put his pants back on. Chasity put on her robe and sat down on the sofa. "How do you feel?"

The reality of their actions had finally kicked in. "What the hell did we just do?"

"We just had mind-blowing sex, in case you didn't notice," she smirked.

"Yeah we did, but it was wrong," he finally admitted.

Chasity stood up and walked over to him, placing her hand on his chest. "But didn't I make you feel good? I know you made us very happy and I can't wait for us to do it again."

"Chasity," he paused when he felt her hand massaging his dick through his pants.

"This dick belongs to me and Bianca now. So, don't you forget it, okay?" Chasity kissed his lips once more. "Now go back to the party before Eazy gets suspicious. I'll see you later."

Diesel grabbed his keys and left. When he arrived back home, Eazy and Bianca were still at the table whooping ass, but the crowd had died down.

Eazy looked up at him. "She didn't give you a hard time, did she?"

Diesel's mind went back to the hard-on she gave him. "Nah. But when she wake up, her ass gone have a hangover."

Eazy shook his head. "Thanks, bro. I appreciate that."

"It's all good. No thanks needed."

"Well, it's been fun, but my ass is going to take a shower." Bianca stood up. "You want to join me?"

"I'll be up in a few. Let me walk everybody out," Diesel replied.

"Goodnight." Bianca immediately left the room.

Once everyone had left, Diesel fixed another drink, so he could get his second wind and second nut. Then he went into the bedroom, ready for a round two.

Destiny Skai

Chapter 2

Honcho waited on Lala to arrive with Capone before they set out on their mission, leaving Fabian on babysitting duty. The couple rode in silence until they reached their destination. Honcho turned off the car. "You ready?"

"As ready as I'm going to be," she said sweetly.

"Come on."

The two got out the car and walked up on the porch. Honcho stood off to the side, while Lala knocked on the door. There was no answer, so she knocked harder.

"Who is it?" a woman shouted.

"Your neighbor."

The door opened and the woman had a questionable look on her face. As long as she lived in the neighborhood, she had never seen the woman before. "Hi, how can I help you?"

"Are you Michelle?" Lala asked.

"Yes."

Lala stepped to the side. Honcho approached the door with his gun aimed at his victim's stomach. "Back up," he demanded.

A look of terror flashed over Michelle's face, as she backed up into her home. "Take whatever you want, just don't hurt me."

Lala closed the door and locked it.

"Who's in here with you?" Honcho looked around the living room.

"Nobody. I'm alone. My husband isn't here," she babbled.

"Sit down." Honcho kept his gun on her, as she followed his instructions. "As long as you cooperate, I won't kill you. Baby, keep your eyes on her while I check upstairs."

Michelle's eyes grew wide. Then she panicked. "No. Please. My kids are upstairs taking a nap."

"That's lie number one. I asked you who was here," Honcho snapped, while removing a zip tie from his pocket. "Tie her up."

Lala grabbed her by the arm and pulled her up. "Turn around." Quickly, she restrained Michelle and pushed her onto the sofa.

Michelle sat on the couch crying and praying that the nightmare unfolding before her eyes would be over soon. The second she saw Honcho return, she questioned him. "What do you want from me?"

"I want you to sit back and relax," Honcho replied.

"Please tell me what's going on," she pleaded. "Is this about my husband?"

Lala stood a few feet away. "You're going to find soon enough, so be quiet."

***

Diesel's scream was music to Tori's ears. The single bullet to his kneecap was enough to let him know she meant business. After all the pain he inflicted on her over the years, she was finally getting revenge. It was time to pay the piper. Tori stood in front of her father with a sinister grin.

"As much as I hate to admit it, that felt good. You took so much from me and now it's my turn."

Diesel grunted. He couldn't believe Tori actually pulled the trigger on him. "So, this is what our relationship has come to? You want to kill your father?"

"Kids kill their parents every day." Tori shrugged. "Besides, you killed my mother, and I will never forgive you for that. You took away my son's grandmother. She missed me getting married, graduating and going through labor. No matter what the two of you went through, I never chose a side, because I considered your feelings. But not once have you considered mine."

"Baby, that's not true. Do you really think I'm that cold and evil to take away your mother? Why do you think that?" Diesel pleaded with tears in his eyes.

Tori wiped the mist from her eyes with the back of her hand. "I've been reading her diary. In one of her passages, she wrote that she had been having dreams about you killing her with bad dope."

"That's not true. Bianca was sick. She said a lot of crazy things."

"You keep saying that, but you were her enabler. You knew she had a problem and you still allowed her to get high on your watch, under your roof. That's not love." Tori grew angrier and more emotional by the minute. "The one thing I hate the most is the fact that my whole life was built on a lie. There is so much I didn't know, all because you thought it was best to keep it a secret."

"Dammit, Tori, I did it to protect you."

"From whom?" she screamed. "You? My mother? Eazy? Or the fact that all y'all were sleeping together and that's where the beef started?"

Diesel's heart began race and thump hard against his chest cavity. The information she dropped on him had to fall from the mouth of his enemy. "Who told you that, Eazy?"

"No. He didn't have to. I read it in her diary. The one you gave me," she hissed. "She also said it was your fault because you had an ongoing affair with Chasity."

Diesel held his head low. Had he known Bianca spilled their deepest, darkest secrets in that book, he would've destroyed her things. "I'm sorry, Tori, but there are just some things you wouldn't understand."

"Well, at least I know why you didn't want me with Kilo." Tori raised her gun once more. "I'm not letting you walk out of here, so you might as well tell me what you did to my mother."

"I didn't kill her."

"Stop lying to me!" Tori squeezed the trigger, blowing out his other kneecap. *Boca!* Diesel tried his best to keep from yelling. So, he rocked back and forth, squeezing his eyes shut. Blood ran down his legs from his fresh wounds.

***

Eazy glanced in the rearview mirror looking at his victim. The fear in the man's eyes said a thousand words. Just as he was about to say something, his phone rang. It was the call he had been waiting on.

"Yeah."

"We in here."

"Go ahead. You on speaker." Eazy held his phone up in the air, so his victim could hear.

Honcho put the receiver to Michelle's mouth. "Say hello to your husband."

"Byron, is that you?" Michelle whimpered through her tears.

Byrd damn near lost his marbles when he heard his wife's voice, who was clearly in distress. "Michelle, baby, are you okay?"

"Yes. Please do what they say, baby. I'm so scared," she begged.

"I am. Where are the kids?"

"They're upstairs taking a nap. Is this going to be over soon?" All Michelle wanted was for the modern-day Bonnie and Clyde to leave their home.

"I hope so. Just do whatever he says. I love you." Byrd did his best to keep his composure. The last thing he wanted to do was to put more fear in her heart.

"Enough of that. Do what you supposed to do, and your family can walk." Eazy moved his arm before Michelle had a chance to respond and put the phone to his ear. "If you don't hear from me in the next thirty minutes, rock them all."

"A'ight." Honcho ended the call.

Byrd had never been so scared in his life. "Come on, Eazy, man. They innocent. They don't have nothing to do with this."

Eazy looked back at the guy he once considered a friend and shook his head. "Whether they live or die is in your hands. You control their fate, after all is said and done."

Byrd was prepared to do anything to save his family. Even if that meant turning on the family he built with Diesel. Eazy walked around to the passenger side of his truck and pulled Byrd from the backseat. It was hard for him to maneuver with his hands tied behind his back.

Eazy pushed Byrd through the front door and locked it. Byrd and Diesel locked eyes and Eazy laughed. "I brought your snitch."

"Fuck you talkin' about a snitch?" Despite the pain he was feeling, he needed to know what the fuck was going on.

"Oh, he didn't tell you." Eazy pushed Byrd onto the floor. "You didn't tell your boss man you been talking to them folks?"

"What folks?" Byrd snapped. "You know damn well I don't fuck with twelve."

"That's not what I saw," Eazy instigated.

Diesel looked down at Byrd. "What the fuck he talking about?"

"I swear, Diesel, I don't know man." Byrd's voice cracked.

"But I do." Tori pulled her phone from her pocket and scrolled through the gallery. "Let me show you."

Tori put the screen directly in front of Diesel's eyes, so he could get a good look. The video she played for him was the recording she took of him several weeks back of him at the gas station talking to Detective Andrews.

Diesel's eyebrows grew crooked. Then he looked down at his right-hand man. "You need to tell me why you talking to a fuckin' detective in this video."

"I didn't say shit to him. He was just fucking with me, that's all." Byrd nodded his head slowly. "Come on. D, you know me, man."

Diesel didn't know what to believe. It was hard being that he just watched the video with his own two eyes. "Nah, I can't say that I do. People surprise you every day. As you can see, my own daughter shot me twice and she ain't trying to take me to the hospital." Then he looked up at Tori. "I underestimated you."

"Yeah, you did," she agreed with a slight nod. "And now that I have Byrd here, let's see if we can get to the bottom of this."

"The bottom of what?" Byrd questioned.

"Did he kill my mother?" If anyone knew about Diesel's dirt and secrets, it was Byrd.

"No. He didn't." Byrd didn't hesitate in answering the question.

"I think you're forgetting what's at stake here." Tori looked at Eazy. "Can you make that call please? Put it on speaker."

Honcho picked up the phone. "Yeah."

Tori moved closer to Eazy. "We need a little persuasion to get Byrd to talk. Where's his beloved wife?"

"Right here. How much persuasion we talking?"

"Enough to make her scream." Tori looked Byrd in the eye as a loud thump, followed by Michelle's scream blasted through the speaker. "And if that's not enough, you know what's next. A bullet. So, I would advise you to make the best decision."

"Okay. Okay. Just leave her alone, please." Byrd was on the floor begging. Then he looked up at Diesel. "I'm sorry, man. I'm prepared to die with you today, but I can't let them kill my wife and kids."

Diesel looked into his daughter's dark eyes. He didn't recognize the vicious woman standing in front of him. Her eyes resembled venomous slits. Then he thought back to the snake he killed in his backyard. Then it all made sense. His enemy was his very own daughter.

"Tori, this is between me and you. Please let Byrd and his family go," her father begged. "I'll tell you what you want to know."

"I need to hear it first." Tori rocked on her heels and waited for the story to begin. "And I want the whole truth and nothing but the truth."

"Okay," he agreed.

"I'll call you back." Tori hung up the phone with Honcho.

Diesel's eyes were locked in with Tori's. "You sure you want to hear this? Cause I'ma give it to you raw and uncut. Can you handle the truth?"

"That's all I ever wanted from you," she admitted.

"Okay." Diesel took a deep breath and relived the night of Tori's sweet sixteen birthday party, after catching Kilo in her bed. Eazy couldn't wait to hear the details of that night. If it wasn't for Kilo, he would've put Diesel down that night for threatening his son.

                        ***

"What the fuck is wrong with you? Did you know she was fucking that nigga?" Diesel paced the floor while shouting at Bianca.

"Yeah. I did know that. What's the problem?"

"She's sixteen and has no business having sex."

Bianca giggled and flicked the ashes from her cigarette into the ashtray. "Did you forget what we were doing at that age?"

"I don't give a fuck about what we did. This is my daughter we're talking about. That shit ain't cool, Bianca."

"No shit, stupid. That's my daughter too. You can't stop her from having sex. Neither can I, so get over it. Just be glad she not out here fucking any and everybody. Kilo is her boyfriend."

Bianca sat the cigarette down and opened the dresser drawer. Inside was an eight-ball of pure, uncut powder. That instantly set him off. Diesel snatched the clear plastic bag that housed the product.

"This why you don't give a fuck about nothing. You too busy getting high to realize what Tori is doing is wrong."

Bianca stood up and attempted to take her happy medicine back. "Give me my shit. I don't wanna talk to you."

"You don't have a fuckin' choice. Now sit the fuck down before I knock you down."

Bianca backed up and opened the drawer once more. This time she pulled out a small handgun and aimed it at her husband. "If you put your hands on me again, nigga, I will kill your motherfucking ass. Now play with me."

Diesel remained calm. A huge part of him knew she wouldn't pull the trigger, but a tiny part of him said not to push her. Bianca was high and he didn't want to underestimate her. "You're not going to shoot me, so put that up before you hurt yourself."

"The only person I want to hurt is you."

"Why? Because I don't agree that Tori should be having sex or messing with Kilo?"

"You and I both know we can't stop her from seeing him."

Bianca waved the gun in the air. "This isn't about Kilo. It's about Eazy and the hatred you have towards him. From what I can see, Kilo loves Tori and you need to accept that fact."

"Fuck Eazy. It's your fault all of this went down in the first place."

"Yeah, blame me, since that's easier than accepting your role in all of this. At one point in time, the two of you were inseparable.

You allowed pussy to get in the way of that. No one is to blame except you. All this shit is your fucking fault, Diesel, so get over it!" Bianca screamed with tears in her eyes.

"I didn't make you fuck that nigga."

"Well, if you hadn't fucked his girl, I wouldn't have fucked your brother. That's called karma."

"That ain't my brother."

"Well, step-brother, if that makes you feel better. At the end of the day, you are the one to blame." Bianca wiped her eyes. "Do you know why I despise you so much? I lost my son because of you." Her voice elevated. "I hate you. I fucking hate you. I can't stand seeing your face. You didn't protect me. You wasn't there when I needed you that night, because you was laid up with that bitch, Chasity. Now give me my shit, so I can get high and forget about the misery I'm living in, being here with you."

Those words hit Diesel in the chest. It made him weak because a lot of what she spoke on was the truth. "Damn, you don't love me anymore?"

"No. I haven't loved you since the day I lost my son." Her response was harsh and nonchalant.

Afraid of the answer that was to follow his next question, he took a deep breath, preparing for the painful truth. "You keep saying your son. Was that even my son?"

"No. He wasn't your son."

Diesel's heart stopped beating for a split second. Deep down inside, that was always a question he had pushed to the back of his mind. But he was too afraid to ask back then. Diesel wanted to hurt her badly, but it wasn't worth it. Bianca wasn't worth seeing him shed a single tear. She made it clear she no longer loved him. The sad and crazy thing was he still loved her, despite her indiscretions.

Diesel left the room fuming. His blood was boiling and Bianca had managed to pump his heart full of hatred in a matter of seconds. On his way down the steps, he bumped into Byrd.

"Why the evil look in your eyes?" Byrd asked him out of curiosity.

"It's time for that bitch to go. She just disrespected me for the last time and there's no coming back from this." Diesel went out into the garage and popped the hood on Bianca's car. She never went anywhere, so the car just sat and collected dust. The battery cables were covered with corrosion. Diesel removed one of the cables and scraped it clean with a knife. Carefully, he mixed the battery acid into the dope and tied the bag.

"It's over for you, bitch! So, enjoy your last time getting high," he mumbled.

When he came back, he was fuming and Bianca was still complaining about getting high.

"You said a lot of hurtful shit just now, but I'm going to give you a pass. I've done a lot of shit I'm not proud of, but at the end of the day, I never intentionally hurt you the way you did me."

Diesel tossed the powder on the bed. "Smoke your life away. Destroy yourself. You love this more than me anyway."

"You goddamn right. The drugs never lied to me."

Diesel didn't reply. He just walked away and went into his bedroom.

***

Tori stood with a blank stare on her face. She couldn't believe the words that came from his mouth. The heinous act he committed against her mother. Her heart broke all over again just like it was her birthday. Uncontrollable tears cascaded down her face, as she struggled to catch her breath.

"Tori, say something please." Diesel knew his life was over. All he wanted to do was make peace.

Eazy stepped over to Tori and hugged her tight. "I'm right here just like I've always been. You're still my daughter." Eazy glanced over at Diesel. "And for the record, Bianca lied to you. That wasn't my son and she knew that. She said that to get back at you after all those years. If you wasn't so busy fucking my wife, you would've knew that."

Tori stepped from Eazy's embrace with the meanest, coldest scowl on her pretty face. Her hand still housed the cold piece of steel. "I'm going to do something you didn't do for my mom or Kilo. Do you have any final words before you leave here?"

"I've loved you here on earth and I will love you in death. I'm sorry I hurt you and took away the ones you truly loved. But the one thing I won't apologize for is being an overprotective dad and shielding you from the things you wouldn't have understood. One day, you will have a daughter and you will understand. I love you, Tori. You'll always be Daddy's little girl." Diesel closed his eyes. He couldn't look into his daughter's eyes as she pulled the trigger.

"I love you too."

The last thing he heard was multiple gunshots before falling out the chair. As he laid on the floor gasping for air, Tori and Eazy lowered their guns and watched his chest rise and fall for the last time. Then, Byrd met the same fate.

Outside, Jarvis stared at the house when he heard what appeared to be more gunshots. "Yo, some shit is going down in that bitch. Diesel in that muthafucka and so is Eazy. Them niggas hate each other. But what I can't figure out is why the fuck Eazy got Byrd."

Moon scratched his head. "That's a damn good question."

"Somebody ain't walking out alive. I bet you that."

"Oh, I know," he agreed.

"And I ain't moving until I know who it is." Jarvis was determined to get to the bottom of what had just popped off.

Chapter 3

Tron walked out of the bathroom after cleaning up the gash Fresh left on the side of his head. He had a headache out this world. Flopping down on the sofa, he poured a shot of moonshine and took it to the head. It was the strongest shit he ever swallowed. "Yo, where the fuck you get this nasty ass shit from?" Jeff laughed, while taking a pull of the weed. "That's an old man remedy. I bet that headache subside in a few minutes." "I hope so." Tron laid across the sofa and tried to relax. "So, you gone tell me what happened or nah?" "Yeah," he sighed. "Last night I was at the corner store getting me some wrap and shit. I'm on the phone, so I wasn't paying attention to my surroundings." Jeff interrupted him first quarter. "Now you know better than that shit." "Yeah, I know. My ass was on the phone, that's the problem. But anyway, I get inside the car and the next thing I know, this nigga hit me with the butt of his gun." Jeff automatically stopped tending to his weed and focused on what his boy was telling him. "What nigga?" "That nigga Fresh." "What y'all beefing or some shit?" "Nah," Tron sucked his teeth. "That nigga think I did something to Dazzle." Before responding, Jeff thought back to the day Dazzle was at the house and Tron wouldn't open the door. He saw the scratches on his neck, but he didn't say anything because he already knew they were fighting. "Like what?" "He said he couldn't find her. I told the nigga I don't know where she at." "What, she missing?" Jeff relit the joint. "That's what he said, but knowing Dazzle, she probably out here being a hoe." Tron was still salty about her moving on. Therefore, he wasted no time bashing her whenever he got the chance. "You know that's not true."

"I don't know shit."

"Well, have you tried to call her? Or at least see where your son at? She might be missing for real, bro." Out of all the years he'd known Dazzle, he knew she took motherhood seriously.

Tron remained silent as he picked up his phone and called Dazzle. Her phone rang until he caught the voicemail. He tried again to no avail. Then he decided to call her mother's house.

"Hello."

"Hey, Ms. Shalonda."

"Who is this?" she snapped.

"This Tron. I'm looking for Dazzle. I've been trying to call her so I can see Jamir, but she not answering her phone."

Just hearing his voice set her off. Instead of cursing him out in front of her grandson, she got up and went inside the bathroom.

"Ms. Shalonda?" he called her name when the phone went silent.

"I'm here." She closed the door behind her. "Tron, let me tell you something right now. If you did anything to my daughter, I'm going to kill your ass and I mean that. You know I don't play about my child."

"What you talking about?" Tron asked.

"My daughter is missing. I haven't seen or heard from her. And that's quite strange, because I always talk to her. But all of a sudden, you out and she disappears."

Tron could hear the anger and frustration in her voice. That confirmed Fresh's story about Dazzle being missing. "Ms. Shalonda, I swear, I didn't do anything to her. I'm just trying to see my son, that's all."

"Oh, you definitely did something to my baby. Don't think she didn't tell me about you and raggedy ass, slutty ass Tweety." She had been waiting to confront his ass since he first went to jail.

"I know I wasn't the best boyfriend, but—"

Ms. Shalonda cut him off. "The absolute worst. She couldn't have prayed for worst."

Tron shook his head. "I know, Ms. Shalonda. At the end of the day, I'm human and I still love her. Just know I wouldn't physically hurt her," he sighed in defeat. "Do you have Jamir?"

"Yes, I do and you can't see him until I find my daughter. I need to know you wasn't behind this." Without warning or a goodbye, she ended the call.

Tron threw the phone by his feet. "Fuck, man!"

"What happened?"

"She missing for real. Her mama said I can't see my son until she knows I had nothing to do with her disappearance."

"So, what you gone do in the meantime?"

"Shit. I can't do nothing."

"You wanna look for her?"

"Fuck her. She took my son away. I hope they never find bitch and if they do, I'm gone kill her ass." Tron lit a cigarette to calm his nerves.

"I'm confused. You just said you love the girl."

"I do. This bitch playing house with my son, and her nigga tried me. I owe both of them bitches a bullet."

Jeff loved Tron like they shared the same DNA, but he was dead ass wrong. "Bro, you moved on with Tweety and you got Mya. Let that shit go and let her be happy."

"Damn, bro, who side you on?"

"The right side. If you want to be out here with your kids, let that shit go. You can't kill the mother of your child. That's crazy. You forced that girl to move on."

"Yeah, a'ight." Tron nodded his head and let everything Jeff said go in one ear and out the other. Dazzle and her nigga had to die and that was the bottom line.

***

Terrell pulled Marsha into a tight embrace, as he roughly gripped her ass. "I'm so happy to see you. I've been thinking about you all day," he breathed heavily in her ear.

"I see," she giggled. "I've been thinking about you too. Did you miss me?"

"Of course, I did."

Marsha stared into his eyes. "Well, show me."

Terrell pushed Marsha against the credenza. She placed her hands on the wood and anticipated what was to happen next. Eagerly, he loosened the button on her jeans and pulled them down to her feet. "No panties again, I see."

"Not at all," she smiled.

"Just how I like it." Terrell unbuckled his pants and stepped out of them. His rod was at semi-attention. Rubbing it against her lips, he coated his meat with her juices and plunged inside the goodies from behind.

The sudden penetration took her breath away. Marsha gripped the wood and leaned forward. Terrell squeezed her hips and went deep. Each thrust was fast and hard. He had no mercy when it came to beating Marsha's back out and that was what he liked about her. His wife was another story. Sex with her was mediocre. All she wanted to do was missionary, and suck his dick like it grossed her out. Whenever he got rough with her, she would complain about the pain. Terrell would shake his head and think to himself, *what grown ass woman can't take some dick, and cries?* And that was the reason he was cheating with Marsha. She knew how to take dick and swallow it like a grown ass woman. None of that kiddie shit.

Terrell grunted like Tony the Tiger and hammered away like it was the last nut he would catch in life. Periodically, he delivered heavy smacks to her voluptuous ass. That ignited a fire in Marsha's ass, causing her to throw it back aggressively.

"Fuck me, daddy. Just like that. Get this pussy," she shouted, stroking his ego.

That was an instant turn-on for him. It made him feel like the king of the jungle. "You love this dick, don't you?"

"Yes, daddy. I do." Marsha bit down on her bottom lip.

"Throw that pussy on daddy then." Terrell grabbed a handful of her hair and wrapped it around his hand. "Oh yeah, she biting."

The warm erotic friction against her clit summoned Marsha a heavy, creamy orgasm. Her breathing increased as her body ejected its juices onto his dick. The gushiness excited Terrell too and his nut followed suit. "Where you want this nut at, baby?"

"Put it on my ass."

Terrell pumped a few more times before pulling out and ejaculating onto her cheeks. "Damn," he sighed. "You know how to suck a nigga dry."

"I didn't suck you dry yet." Marsha kneeled down in front of Terrell with hunger in her eyes.

"We can do that later. I need an intermission." He grabbed Marsha by the arm and pulled her up to his level. "I have something I need you to do for me. But first, I need to know if I can trust you."

"Of course, you can trust me. You know that already. What do you need me to do?" she asked.

"Follow me. I'll show you." Terrell put his pants back on, so did Marsha. He then led the way to where he held his victim.

Marsha froze when she saw a woman being restrained. "What the hell do you have going on in here?"

Terrell turned and looked back her. "This is what I need help with."

"To do what? What kind of kinky shit you got going on in here?" she put her hands on her hips.

"Relax, there's no kinky shit going on."

"Well, why is this woman tied up?"

"She took something from me and I'm going to get it back," he turned back to Dazzle. "Isn't that right?"

Dazzle didn't say a word. She simply stared at the woman in the room, hoping and praying she would talk some sense into his head.

"What did she take from you?" Marsha had a million questions and quite frankly, she was ready to leave.

"That's all you need to know."

"I'm not killing anyone. As a matter of fact, I think I should leave. I'm not about to risk my badge for something I know nothing about." Marsha took a step back.

Terrell turned on his heels and shot her an evil stare. "You're here now and you will get involved. You said I could trust you. Now trust me when I say you will not lose your badge. All I need for you to do is watch her until I come back."

Marsha didn't want to do it, but at that point she had no choice. Therefore, she agreed to be the babysitter. "Fine. And this better not blow back in my face."

"Trust me, it won't. I'll even pay you for your troubles."

"Okay." Terrell pulled out Dazzle's phone. It was show time.

Chapter 4

Tori's emotions were all over place as she sat on the floor staring at Diesel's dead body. So many thoughts were running through her mind. The things Diesel revealed to her sent her off into a rage. *How could he kill her mother? How could he be so cold and lie to her with a straight face?* Then she realized one important fact. She was just like her father. A cold-hearted killer.

"Tori, you need to get out of here. I'll clean up this mess." When she didn't reply, Eazy walked over and placed his hand on her shoulder. "Tori!"

"Yeah," she shook her head and looked up at him. "What did you say?"

"I said, you need to leave. I'll clean this mess up," he reiterated.

"Okay." Tori pulled out her phone and called Honcho.

"Hello," he answered on the second ring.

"It's done. Give her that bag of money and let her know if she talks, she's dead. Her kids too."

"Once I leave here, I'm headed that way."

"Okay." Tori hung up the phone and got off the floor. She then walked towards Diesel and removed all the money he had in his pockets. "Make this look like a robbery gone bad." Then she kissed his forehead. "I'll see you on the other side. I know I'll be joining you for all of my sins."

Before she could utter another word, her phone rang again. When she looked at the screen, she damn near jumped for joy. "It's Dazzle." She quickly answered the call. "Where have you been? Are you okay?"

"She's okay for now." The male voice on the opposite end of the phone startled her.

"Who is this?"

"You don't recognize my voice?" Terrell asked with a sinister laugh.

"No. I don't. Now who is this and why do you have her phone?"

"It's me, Terrell. Or should I say Detective Andrews?"

The name instantly clicked. He was the one that helped her get the video of Byrd at the gas station. "Whitney's uncle?"

"The one and only." He grimaced.

"Why do you have her?"

"It seems your friend has gotten herself into a little trouble and needs you to bail her out."

Tori stood back on her legs. "What kind of trouble?"

"One hundred thousand dollars' worth of trouble."

"Stop with the riddles. What are you saying right now?" Tori displayed a lot of hostility in her voice.

"I caught your little friend with a kilo of coke and for one hundred thousand dollars, I can make it go away. If not, I'm sure the feds would be interested in your little operation."

"What? You've got to be kidding me," she huffed.

"Nope. You have two hours to get me the money, if you want her back." Terrell rubbed Dazzle's face. "And, if you want to see her alive."

Tori couldn't believe her ears. If it wasn't one thing, it was another. Nonetheless, she had to get her girl back. "First, I need to know she's alive. Let me talk to her."

Terrell put the phone on speaker. "Say hello to your friend."

"Tori, please help me," Dazzle cried.

"I got you, sis, I promise. Just stay strong. This will be over soon."

"That's good to hear. Now get me my money," he barked.

It took everything in her body to stay calm. "Where do you want to meet?"

"I'll call you back in one hour with the details." Terrell hung up the phone.

Eazy stood with a raised brow. "What's going on?"

"Dazzle was kidnapped, and he wants one hundred thousand dollars to get her back." Tori sent a quick text.

"What are you going to do?" he questioned.

"I have to get her back."

"You can't go alone."

"I'm not. Fresh is going with me."

"If you need me, I'm here." Eazy didn't feel comfortable with the situation, but he knew she could handle herself.

"I got it. I need help with this mess right here." Tori kissed Eazy on the cheek. "I'll call you later. I'm about to meet up with Honcho."

"Be safe."

"Always."

Tori left out the house in a hurry and jumped into her car. The sound of her phone made her hesitate. When she looked at the screen, she saw it was Jude. It was bad timing, so she sent him to the voicemail. Her mind and heart raced as she flushed it down the road. Not once did she look in her rearview to see that she was being followed.

***

"It's about that time, my boy. You ready to snatch this bitch up?" Moon asked.

"I've never been more ready in all my life. I'm ready to fuck his most precious jewel before I knock his socks off and hers too. Once we get her, she gone tell us what the fuck was happening in that goddamn house," Jarvis stated, while keeping his eyes on Tori.

"You still on that, I see." Tori was a bad bitch in his eyes, but he couldn't pull himself to rape no female that wasn't willing to give up the goods. It didn't matter how fine she was.

"Hell yeah. Those two niggas hate each other, so I know they wasn't having a kumbaya moment in that bitch. Unless some shit went down, and they done fucked around and killed Byrd."

Jarvis lit his sixth cigarette and took a pull. His nerves were bad, but he ignored them. The only thing on his mind was avenging his family's death. He was determined to take Diesel out.

Making sure that Tori wasn't aware she was being followed, he kept a car between them. The longer he followed her, fear began to slip away, and excitement took its place. Finally, her car turned off into an apartment complex. The tail had officially come to an end.

Jarvis grabbed his heat from underneath the seat. "Get ready to jump in the driver's seat so I can snatch her ass up."

Moon nodded.

Tori pulled into a parking spot, but she didn't get out. Jarvis pulled up in an empty spot two spaces away. His eyes were glued on his prey. Jarvis put his hand on the door and pulled the lever.

"Wait." Moon stopped him.

"What?"

"Look up."

Jarvis frowned when he saw Fresh and Milo approaching Tori's car. He punched the steering wheel. "Damn!"

"So much for that plan," Moon stated.

***

Fresh and Milo climbed into the car and closed the door. "What's up, Tori? How you been?" Milo asked.

"I've had better days. I'm glad to see you made out to this side." She glanced at him in the rearview mirror.

"It's good to be home. They fucked up my paperwork, so I had to wait to be released." Milo rubbed his beard.

"Well, that's behind you now."

"Hell yeah," Milo replied.

"So, what's up, Tori? I heard the urgency in your voice," Fresh asked in an even tone.

"Dazzle is alive," she blurted it out.

That news alone made Fresh happy. "Where is she?"

"I don't know, but she was kidnapped and there's a ransom."

"By who?"

Tori broke down the conversation she had with Terrell, including the one hundred thousand dollars to get her back. Fresh was fuming as he listened to the details. Especially when he found out she was crying.

"I'm killing that nigga when I get her back. I don't give a fuck if he law enforcement or not," Fresh ranted.

Tori shook her head. "I just have to go home and get the money, so that when he calls, we're ready."

"Nah, I'll pay it. Go to my house so I can get it."

***

One Hour Later

As promised, Terrell called Tori back at the exact moment he said he would. "Hello." She picked up.

"Meet me at the Extra Space Storage on Dixie Highway in twenty minutes."

"I'm on my way right now."

"Oh, and none of that funny shit. Let's make this as painless as possible. I would hate to send you to prison."

Tori hung up the phone in his ear. "He is really pushing his fucking luck."

"What he said?" Fresh asked.

"Not to pull no funny shit or he gone send me to prison."

"After this he better hide, because I'm gone rock that bitch to sleep. I swear." Fresh threatened with an ice-cold stare.

"I'm with that, but we have to smart about killing a cop," Tori added.

Milo leaned up from the front seat. He was fresh out the chain gang and ready to drop a body. "Nah, sis, we got this. You just chill. That's what you got hittas for you, feel me? Besides, my trigger finger itchy. I ain't clapped a nigga in years," he chuckled.

"Well, you about to get your chance," Fresh exclaimed.

The last ten minutes of the ride was in silence. Fresh was thinking about Dazzle. Milo was thinking about busting his cherry on his first kill. Tori was thinking about the car that was following her earlier. Immediately, she thought it was Jude. While en route to meet Fresh and Milo, he had called a few times. Soon enough, she would get the answer to her question.

The lights at the storage building were dimly lit when she pulled in and the gate was already open. That was surprising, being that it was normally closed. Tori drove inside and looked down each aisle until she saw a dark-colored car parked beside an outside unit.

"That's got to be him."

As they got closer and pulled up in front of the vehicle, Tori turned off the lights. Fresh was taken back to the video he saw at the hotel. "This the same car I saw on the tape at the hotel."

The trio got out the car and left the doors open. Terrell could be seen getting out, as well as a passenger. It wasn't Dazzle.

Tori stopped in front of her car. "Where is Dazzle?"

"Where is my money?" Terrell asked.

Fresh held the bag up. "Right here. Now where is my girl?"

"Let me see it."

Fresh unzipped the bag and pulled out a stack of bills. "Now for the last time, where is my girl?" He then pulled out his gun and pointed it at the crooked cop.

Marsha pulled her gun out as well. "You don't want to do that."

Milo pulled his gun out on Marsha. "Neither do you."

Terrell could see that things were about to unravel, so he had to take control of the situation. "Everyone, calm down. There will be no bullets flying tonight." He walked over to the storage until and raised the door. Dazzle stepped out slowly, as Terrell held her arm. "Throw the bag over here and I'll let her go."

Fresh threw the bag and Dazzle ran straight into his arms. He looked at her and instantly became angry when he saw the blood on her shirt. "What the fuck this nigga did to you?"

"Just get me out of here, please," she begged.

"Get in the car. Tori, let's go," Fresh demanded.

Once they were inside things took a turn when they heard a gunshot. Tori looked up and saw that Fresh was unloading his clip in Terrell's direction. Terrell and Marsha took cover until the bullets stopped. That was when they returned fire. Tori slammed her foot down on the gas and went into reverse. Milo leaned out the window and returned fire to slow them down, so they could escape. Tires screeched as Tori floored it out of the storage unit. That wasn't a part of the plan and now she had to worry about Terrell retaliating.

***

Later on that night, Tori found herself on Jude's doorstep. Seeing the way Fresh was invested and loved Dazzle made her miss the touch and affection of a man. She cursed Diesel for his responsibility of taking away the only man she ever loved and father of her child. There wasn't an ounce of doubt when it came down to the love he had for her. Jude, on the other hand, was a totally different story. She wasn't too sure of anything and he possessed traits that were red flags, but she placed those signs to the back of her mind.

The door swung open and Jude stood there in a pair of boxer briefs, with a less than pleasant look on his face. "I've been calling you and for some strange reason, all I've gotten was your damn voicemail. Where were you?"

"I know. I'm sorry." She hung her head low. "It's just that I've been going through so much and didn't want to burden you with my problems."

Jude ran his hand across his face with a sigh of irritation. "I get that, Tori. Life happens, but that's no excuse to shut me out. I mean damn, you acting like I'm not your man or some shit."

Tori took a deep breath and exhaled. "So, you're going to make me stand outside the door and talk to you or you gone let me in?"

Jude hesitated at first. He was upset with Tori, but at the same time he loved her. He needed her.

"I mean, unless you have company or some shit." Tori looked him in the eyes and folded her arms across her chest.

"Nah, I don't cheat." Jude opened the door wider, while stepping to side so she could enter.

Tori stood by the wall and waited on him to lead the way. They headed to his bedroom. Jude climbed back into bed and laid on his side. Tori sat down beside him. He was anxious to hear what she had to say. "Let's talk. What's going on with you?" he asked.

Tori debated on how much she should tell him. True enough, she wanted to be honest with him, but there were some subjects that were off limits. Realizing she was having a hard time speaking, he pushed the envelope.

"Tori, listen to me. I know I've shown my ass a time or two when it came to you, but that's because I love you. And when I love, I love hard. I'm not trying to be a jealous boyfriend, but there are just some things that triggered me. For instance, your brother-in-law. I know I shouldn't have reacted the way I did and I'm sorry. That will never happen again. I promise."

Tori nodded her head.

Jude needed to look into her eyes, so he reached out and placed his hand on her chin. Now face-to-face, he continued. "It will never happen again, okay?"

"Okay."

"I love you, Tori, and I'll do anything to make you happy. I don't want you to push me away by keeping things away from me or avoiding me." Jude sat up and placed a tender, yet seductive kiss to her lips. "Let me love you, Tori. Teach me how to love you."

Tori's heart melted and she felt like putty in his hands, but that wasn't enough to just lay her entire heart on the line. Because not too long ago, he was an angry bird and suddenly became a teddy bear in a matter of seconds.

"A few days ago, my friend went missing without a trace. My father wants me out the drug game, thinking I should work a nine-to-five. I'm missing my mom like crazy. I just feel like my world is in shambles."

Jude hugged her tight and rubbed her back. "I'm so sorry, baby. You should've come to me. That's what I'm here for, but you have to trust me. Don't disappear on me and avoid my calls. I was starting to think you wanted to call it quits." There was a pregnant pause in the room and it was disturbing to him. "Do you want to be with me?"

Tori thought for a split second before responding. "Yes. It's not that I don't want to be with you. I've just been going through some personal matters, that's all."

"I've missed you," he admitted.

"I miss you too and I promise, things will be different on my end as well."

"I'll be patient and more understanding."

"Thank you," she smiled. Tori placed her hand inside his boxers and stroked his dick. "Now, let's get to the make-up sex."

Jude couldn't argue with that. He removed his boxers, while Tori got undressed. He tried to get up, but Tori pushed him back down. "I'm in control tonight." Turned on by her aggressiveness, he laid back and allowed his lady to take the lead.

Tori grabbed ahold of his dick and stroked it before straddling him. Placing the mushroom tip of his head against her lips, she eased down until he filled her up, inch by inch.

"Damn, I missed you." Jude smacked her ass.

"Mmm. Sss. I missed you too," she hissed while rolling her hips.

Jude couldn't resist touching her. Placing both hands on her waist, he assisted with the pace of her grind. Tori put her hands on his chest and moved her body up and down, slightly bouncing on his dick. Leaning forward, she parted his lips with her tongue. They engaged in a passionate lip lock. Tori sucked on his tongue and bounced a little harder.

Still on his back, Jude planted his feet on the bed and returned some hard pumps. Tori moaned loudly as Jude fucked her back. She needed to take back control. Tori sat up and planted her feet on the bed and bounced while on her toes.

"Yeah. Fuck, daddy, just like that." Jude enjoyed the sight of his dick going in and out of her womanly folds. He placed his thumb on her clit and rubbed it gently.

Tori damn near lost it when he hit that spot. "Jude. Baby, shit," she moaned. "You about to make me cum."

"I know. Keep going." Jude moved his thumb faster. The pressure made Tori scream out in erotic pleasure. It was hard to keep steady with her knees buckling, but she managed to stay on top until she creamed all over his dick.

After a heavy climax, Jude put Tori in the doggy style position. It was time to teach her a lesson. With his hands on her hips, he pounded away. Heavy smacks filled the room. Jude grabbed her neck and squeezed firmly.

"Don't you ever disappear on me again," he grunted. Tori couldn't respond. She was too caught up in the moment. Jude squeezed a little tighter. "Do you hear me?"

"Yes. Yes. I hear you."

"You belong to me now." Jude spit down the crack of her ass and stuck his thumb inside. The penetration from both holes made Tori cum again. She bit down on the pillow.

Tori lowered her body. Now she was flat on the bed. He was wearing her ass out. While positioned back to chest, he continued to deliver back shots. Putting her leg up, he went deeper, harder and faster. Jude bit and licked on her neck. His pelvis smacked against her ass.

"This pussy so good," he grunted. "It's so good, I can't pull out." Jude slow-stroked her from the back, until he released his semen inside her body. He was determined to make sure Tori didn't leave him. Even if he had to put a baby in her ass.

Chapter 5

Lowell Correctional Institution

The intercom in the dorm sounded off and all the ladies quickly grew silent. "Walker, come out to the sally port so you can go and see your counselor." All of the ladies started to clap and scream because they knew what time it was. Chasity hopped off her bunk and put on her sneakers. "A bitch about to sign these papers," she screamed happily.

"Damn right, bunkie, tomorrow is the big day. You been waiting a long ass time for this day," Shell yelled.

Chasity left out the dorm and walked down the cold hallway in her prison blues and a huge smile on her face. Over the years, she gained twenty pounds, but she still looked good. The extra weight just so happened to go to all the right places.

Mr. Williams sat behind his desk, talking on the phone. He waved for Chasity to enter. She closed the door. "I'll call you back when I go on my lunch break." He put the phone back on the receiver. "Ms. Walker, how are you today?"

"Better, now that I'm about to sign these papers." Chasity sat down in the chair.

"Good. I just need you to sign these release papers." Mr. Williams handed her the documents.

Chasity rushed through each paper, placing her signature on the highlighted lines. "I can't believe this day is finally here."

"It's a blessing and you deserve it. Do you need to make a phone call to your family?" he asked.

"As a matter of fact, I do." Chasity had been waiting to make one phone call in particular and now was her chance.

"Hello."

"Hey husband," she smirked. "Are you happy to hear from me?"

"Now you know damn well I'm not your husband anymore, Chasity. What do you want?" Eazy replied.

"I just wanted to let you know I'll be home soon."

"I don't care. You not coming here." He knew her time was winding down. He just didn't know when. That part of his life was over. When he divorced Chasity, he cut all ties with her.

"Yes, I am. It's time for us to fix our family."

"It's too late for that. Now, if you don't want anything else, I'm hanging up."

"I'll see you soon." Chasity spoke to the dial tone because Eazy had already hung up. She put the phone back on the receiver. "Thanks. I appreciate the phone call."

"You're welcome. You be good out there and don't come back."

"Trust me, I'm not. I've given this place too many years of my life. I lost my kids and my husband in the process."

Back inside the dorm, Chasity started to pack up the things she was keeping and gave away the items she no longer had use for. Her girlfriend, Blake, walked up to her bunk as she finished up. "So, you leaving me, huh?"

"You know I can't stay."

Blake leaned down and whispered in her ear. "Meet me in the shower so I can eat it one last time before you leave me."

"I guess I can since I'm about to be in the free world getting some dick." Chasity laughed.

"Stop playing with me and get up. I wish you would give my shit up and I'm about to come home."

"I'm coming."

Chasity went inside the shower and took off her clothes. Blake was ready. She had the towel on the tile for her girl to lay on. It would be their last time together, so she was ready to go all-in, until Chasity walked through the gates the next morning. Blake was masculine, yet fine. She had a washboard stomach and rocked braids in her hair. Her eyes were light brown and her complexion was a rich, honey color. Blake was definitely easy on the eyes.

Chasity got down on the floor and laid back with her legs open. The sudden flick of Blake's tongue, followed by her sucking on her clit, sent her body into a frenzy. Blake's tongue was powerful, and she definitely knew her way around the vagina. Chasity's eyes rolled, as she watched the ceiling as if it were a television screen. Her hands stroked Blake's scalp when she felt her fingers slip in and out of her wetness. "Damn. Shit," Chasity mumbled.

Blake continued to feast with satisfaction, hearing Chasity's moans. "I'm gone suck the lining out your pussy all night," she promised.

Chasity closed her eyes and reminisced about her original release date, which was four years ago.

"Good evening, Ms. Walker. I'm Federal Agent Tillman and this is my partner, Agent Ross."

Chasity rolled her eyes and sucked her teeth. She had no idea what the feds wanted with her, but she was about to find out. "And how can I help you?"

"How does early release sound?" Agent Tillman asked.

"It sounds like I have to work for it."

"Of course you do, but it's a simple task," he assured her.

"I'm listening." Chasity sat back in the hard chair and folded her arms across her chest.

"We've been investigating your husband, Eric Kingsley."

Chasity frowned. "You mean, ex-husband."

Agent Tillman nodded his head. "Whatever the case may be, but anyway, according to a few sources, he's responsible for being the head of distribution of cocaine."

"What does that have to do with me? I'm locked up, remember? I don't know what he's doing," she lied.

Agent Tillman paced the floor. "See, I highly doubt that. The two of you were married. This isn't new to him. He's been at it for years. We just haven't been able to catch him in the act or build a case solid enough for the charges to stick."

"I'm sorry, but I can't help you." Chasity stood up and walked towards the door.

"What about your son, Kilo Kingsley? I can just go and pick him up. How do you feel about sending letters back and forth to each other from one prison to the next? I can guarantee he'll do at least fifteen years in prison for possessing a kilo of cocaine."

Chasity stood at the door with her eyes closed after hearing her son's name.

Agent Ross laughed. "That's cute how you named your son Kilo, just like the dope, huh?"

Agent Tillman laughed as well. "Hmm. The family heirloom, cocaine."

Chasity returned to her seat. "If I help you, promise me you'll leave my son alone. He's a good kid."

"Of course. All we want is your husband."

Chasity was always taught to never be a snitch, but that shit went out the window the moment they threatened to lock up her son.

A few tears escaped Chasity's eyes. The pain of Kilo and the pleasure of the orgasm she was feeling had her mind gone.

***

Sinaloa, Mexico

"Hurry up and load the truck. We have deliveries to make," Lance shouted at the workers. Ever since he'd proved his loyalty to Charro, his status upgraded and now he had full control over one of the warehouses. The men scrambled to finish loading the product that was stored in crates.

"What's up, my boy?" Emilio walked in, wearing a Kool-Aid grin on his face.

Lance and Emilio slapped hands and G-hugged. "Shit, getting to the money. What's up with you?"

"Check this out." Emilio lowered his voice. "I just left Charro. He asked me how things went in the states."

Lance lowered his eyes with a questionable stare. "What did you tell him?"

"I told him that everything went smooth," Emilio answered truthfully.

"You didn't tell him I wasn't present, did you?" Lance liked his partner, but if he had to kill him, he would and without hesitation.

"Of course not. I covered you for sure."

"Thanks, man. I appreciate that." Lance placed his hands in his pockets. "I was just doing the best thing for the business."

"I get it, but now you owe me one." Emilio chuckled. "You know Charro is crazy as hell, but I got your back."

"Thanks again."

"Well, I'm about to head out. I have some business to take care of. If you not busy, come by the house so we could have a few drinks."

"I'll let you know."

"Adios, cabrón."

"Fuck you." Lance laughed it off and got back to work. Once all of the deliveries were made, he decided to call it a night. He was drained and would have to take a raincheck on hanging out with Emilio.

Lance unlocked the door and walked into the Mediterranean-styled house quickly and quietly, like a mouse. Making his way into the kitchen, he fixed a glass of Hornitos and went out on the balcony. It had been a long day. All he wanted to do was have a drink, shower and go to sleep.

The darkness in the sky and complete silence put his mind at ease. It allowed him to think in peace. He went from living a perfect life to living in hiding and off the radar. It certainly wasn't what he bargained for. Lance took out his phone and thumbed through the photos. His heart ached, looking at his loved ones. All he wanted to do was go back to the life he once lived. A single tear cascaded from his brown eyes, but he quickly wiped it away.

"I didn't hear you come in, papi," a soft female voice whispered from behind, catching him off guard.

Lance dimmed the light on his phone and put it in his pocket. "I just got in."

Araceli stood in front of Lance, dressed in sexy black lingerie. Her olive colored skin glistened against the lightening from the full moon. "I've been waiting for you."

"Oh yeah?" he asked flatly.

"What's wrong?"

"I'm just tired. It's been a long day." That was only a smidgen of the problem.

"I can make you forget all about it." Araceli got down on her knees and unbuckled his pants. Once she freed his wood, she wrapped her small, pink lips around the head and slurped him up slowly.

Lance held his glass in his left hand, which was the dominant one. However, over the years he'd managed to utilize them both equally. Using his right hand, he placed it on top of Araceli's head and guided her pace. When it came down to sloppy-toppy, she was good at it. A certified head doctor. Araceli massaged his balls gently, as she deep throated every inch. He could feel her tonsils graze the tip of his head. It excited him. Lance downed the rest of his liquor and sat the glass on the small table beside him. Now utilizing his left hand as well, he used them both to force her head down further.

Araceli choked a little, but she kept bobbing her head up and down. Lance thrusted his hips, pushing his dick further inside. Araceli gagged viciously. "Choke on that dick," he mumbled.

A tremendous amount of spit covered his piece, making it slippery. Lance pulled her hair, so she could come up for air. Her mouth glistened with his pre-cum. "Swallow it." Araceli swallowed every drop and went back to sucking until he busted a nut, trickling down her throat.

Lance looked down at her. "Bedroom."

After multiple rounds of sex, Lance laid on his back staring at the ceiling. Araceli laid up under him, trying to pick his brain. "What's going on with you, Lance? It seems like your mind is elsewhere."

"It's nothing. Go to sleep."

"I can't sleep. We need to talk," she sighed.

From experience, Lance knew what that meant, and he was hoping she wasn't about to pull the pregnancy card on him. For months they used condoms, but that stopped a few weeks ago. The pullout method wasn't guaranteed, but he didn't purposely bust in no other place, except for her mouth.

"About what?" he asked.

Araceli sat up and faced him. "I'm. I'm—"

Here we go, he thought. "Not pregnant, I hope," he blurted out.

"Geesh, don't sound so insensitive."

"Is that what it is?" All he wanted was for her to get to the point. "No." Araceli paused. "Lance, I'm in love with you. I know it's only been four months, but I've fallen in love with you."

Lance was baffled. He didn't feel the same way about her. All they did was have sex. They never went out on dates. He didn't want to mislead her. Lance sat on the edge of the bed with his feet grounded on the wooden floor.

"Can you please say something?" Her voice cracked.

"What do you want me to say? That I love you back" Lance stood up and started to get dressed.

"Where are you going?"

"I'm going home."

"Lance, please don't leave."

"Araceli, you know I don't want a relationship. We discussed that from the beginning. You agreed to our terms."

Araceli started to cry. "You want me to apologize for the way I feel about you. Well, I can't."

"And that's why we have to stop. I'm sorry, but I'm not in love with you. My job won't allow me to establish a relationship with any woman. Please don't call me again. It's over." Lance grabbed his keys and headed towards the door. Araceli gave chase, while speaking loudly in Spanish.

As he reached the door, she grabbed him from behind and held onto him for dear life. "Lance, please don't leave me."

"Araceli, it's over." Lance gave her back the spare key she gave him and walked out of her life forever. He didn't lie to her, but he also didn't tell her the truth. The fact of the matter was his heart belonged to one woman and he had hopes of getting her back one day.

Chapter 6

Several weeks had passed since Diesel and Chasity first slept to-gether. What started off as a one-time fling, turned into a full-fledged affair. The two would sneak off and have sex whenever they had the chance. This particular day, Chasity was at her brother Justin's house, watching her niece. Since she couldn't get away, she had Diesel to come over. Upon his arrival, Chasity let him in.

"Jenna, go to your room and don't come out."

"Okay," she replied, as she left the living room. Chasity followed her niece to her room and locked the door from the outside with a key.

Diesel was on the sofa shirtless. "We don't have much time, so let's make this quick."

"Come on."

The two went into the spare bedroom, closed the door and got busy. Justin wasn't due back home until that evening, but she couldn't chance being caught by him. He would certainly disapprove of her behavior. The last thing she needed was their business going beyond the four walls.

On the home front, Diesel's marriage appeared to be picture perfect, but her marriage remained the same. All she and Eazy did was argue. And quite frankly, she was tired. He was an excellent father, but he could've used help in the husband department. Eazy took care of home, but he spent a lot of time away. Chasity enjoyed the perks, but she wanted him home more.

The headboard knocked hard against the bed. Diesel had Chasity pinned to the bed, breaking her off proper. It felt like her insides were being rearranged by the way he manhandled the vagina. Grunts and moans echoed in the room. The two were so caught up in the moment, they never heard the door open.

"You no good ass nigga," Bianca screamed.

Diesel jumped off Chasity with the quickness. When he looked in his wife's direction, he was staring down the barrel of Eazy's gun.

Eazy possessed a menacing scowl, as his finger rested on the trigger. "Give me one good reason why I shouldn't blow your fuckin' brains out."

It felt like time was at a standstill. Diesel could see his life flash before his eyes. "I'm sorry, bro."

"Baby, please. Don't do this," Chasity whimpered, while trying to cover up her nude body.

"Shut up, hoe!" Eazy spat. All he saw was red.

Bianca lost it and delivered multiple blows to Diesel's face. He tried to block them to no avail. "How could you do this to me? All I've done was be faithful to you."

Eazy was on the opposite side of the bed, beating Chasity's ass with a closed fist. Her body collapsed to the floor, but that didn't stop the slew of punches he delivered to her face and body. All she could do was ball up on the floor and pray he didn't kill her.

"I'm sorry! I'm sorry!" she screamed from the pit of her stomach.

"What the fuck going on in here?" A voice rang out.

When Eazy turned around, he saw Justin. He stood there with the strangest look on his face. Eazy was prepared to beat Justin's ass too if he interfered. "I'm about to kill yo' muthafuckin' sister. That's what' going on."

"For what? What happened?" Clearly, he could put two and two together, but he needed confirmation on what he was witnessing. Just in case his eyes were playing cruel trick on him.

Bianca stopped hitting Diesel and looked at Justin. "I'll tell you what's going on. Your trifling ass sister fucking my husband in your house."

Justin hung his head in disappointment. "Chasity, is this true?" She wiped the blood from her mouth and nodded her head in embarrassment. He couldn't believe what he was hearing. "So, you was fucking in my house while my daughter here." Justin felt bad for Eazy and Bianca. "Listen, brother." he placed his hand on the arm Eazy held the gun in. "Think about what you about to do. If you kill her, you'll go to prison. What's going to happen to Kilo and Honcho? They need their father out here with them."

Eazy thought long and hard about his boys. His brother-in-law was right. If he killed Chasity, he was definitely going to prison. He could flee, but eventually he'd be caught. The thought of leaving his kids behind leveled his thinking. Relaxing his arm, he tucked his gun away. Then he looked at Diesel.

"You can keep the hoe, 'cause I don't want her. Cheating pussy ain't no good." Then he looked down at Chasity, who was huddled in the corner. "Don't bring your ass back to my house. I'll send your shit here and I want a divorce."

"Eazy, please," Chasity cried.

Ignoring her cries, he headed towards the door. "Let's go Bianca."

Before walking off, Bianca took another swing at Diesel. "And don't bring your ass home either."

Eazy and Bianca ended up at his house, where they sat on the patio, drinking and smoking. To say they were heartbroken was an understatement. They dedicated their lives to their spouses and all they got in return was betrayal.

Bianca sat with tears pouring down her face. "I can't believe he did this to me, to you and our families. What am I supposed to tell my daughter?"

Eazy took a pull from his blunt. Slowly, he inhaled until he filled his lungs, before exhaling slowly. "Don't tell her anything yet. Our kids are innocent in this. They won't understand."

"I feel so stupid. How could I have not known he was cheating on me?" Bianca was beyond hurt. Her life always revolved around Diesel.

"You're not stupid. You just wasn't paying attention. But me, I paid attention to everything. I noticed the sneaky conversations she was having, the need to babysit her niece and visit her brother often, without our kids. I started to follow her. Then one day, I saw Diesel's truck there. I called him to see if he would answer, but he didn't. Then I tried Chasity. She didn't answer either." Eazy passed the blunt to her. "When I spoke with him later, he lied about his whereabouts. That was when I knew."

"I was too busy taking care of my household, that's how he was able to do me dirty right under my nose." Bianca sniffled and wiped her face with her shirt.

"One day, I slipped the key from her key ring and made a copy. I was ready to confirm what I already knew in my heart. The reason I took you is so you could see it with your own eyes. I needed you to trust my word and not his."

"I would've believed you."

"Seeing is believing."

For the next few hours, they sat out back talking, drinking and smoking. At 2:00 am, they called it quits and went inside. Without a doubt, they were drunk. Bianca grabbed her keys and purse.

"What are you doing?" Eazy asked.

"I'm about to get Tori and go home." Bianca's words slurred.

"No. That's not a good idea. Besides, she's asleep. You can sleep in the guest bedroom."

"Are you sure?"

"Come on now. You know you can stay here."

"I need some water." Bianca stumbled into the kitchen. She leaned against the counter, while Eazy fixed a cup for her. Bianca gulped down the water in a matter of seconds and sat the cup down. "I'm so hurt," she mumbled. "That ungrateful motherfucker!"

Eazy wiped her tears. "It's going to be okay. We'll get through is. Time heals all wounds."

Bianca hugged Eazy. "I hope so." When she released him, she looked into his eyes. "They really did a number on us."

"Yeah, they did," he agreed.

In the midst of gazing into one another's eyes, their lips connected, and their tongues collided in a sloppy kiss. Eazy picked Bianca up and sat her on the counter. Moving between her legs, he hiked up her dress and pulled off her panties. Eazy freed his dick from his boxers and plunged inside of her wet, slippery tunnel. Bianca wrapped her legs around his waist. Feeling good, she thrusted her hips forward. Eazy's dick felt so good gliding in and out of her gushy goodies.

The next morning, Eazy woke up with a pounding headache. He felt a leg on him and mumbled, "I know I didn't let this bitch back in the house after what she did." When he pulled the blanket back, his eyes widened in surprise. "Oh shit, Bianca. Wake up!" Bianca was slobbing her ass off when he woke her up. "What?" she said in a groggy tone.

"Get up before the kids see us like this." Bianca took a look around the room and then down at her naked body. "Shit!"

***

Two months had passed since Eazy and Bianca slept together. Their communication was slim, but it was time to put an end to all of that. Bianca arrived at his house and they sat down on the sofa.

"How have you been?" she asked.

"I'm good. How about you?"

"I can't complain." Bianca's heart started to race when she thought about the reason for her visit.

"Well, what's going on? I haven't seen you since that morning. I don't want you feel no type of way. We were drunk and hurting. Things just went further than expected."

"I know. It's not your fault. We both were under the influence, but it was consensual sex. That's all that matters." Bianca fiddled with her fingers before she looked into his eyes. "I need to tell you something."

"What's that?"

"I'm pregnant."

"You think it's mine?"

"I don't know. But I have a doctor's appointment to find out how far along I am. If I am, would you want me to get rid of it?"

Eazy sat in silence for a moment before answering her question. "No. I wouldn't. I don't believe in abortions."

"Would you go to the appointment with me?"

"Yeah." No matter the circumstances, he would definitely be there for Bianca and the child if it was his.

A few days later, Eazy accompanied Bianca to her visit as promised. That was when he found out she was four months pregnant and there was no way possible he could be the father. From that moment on, Bianca decided to make things work with her husband, and Diesel moved back home.

Chapter 7

One week later

The streets were silent since Diesel's murder hit the airwaves. It was like the president died and the nation lost their leader. All of his spots had been shut down like a ghost town. Tori took a break from her own organization so she could lay her father to rest. They respected her decision and waited on the word to move.

Tori spent her entire morning finalizing the arrangements for Diesel's funeral. Jude was right by her side, serving as her support system. Opening up the car door, Jude helped her inside and closed it. Then he went over to the driver's side.

"Where to next?"

"I need to pick up his tuxedo and go by his attorney's office." Tori's eyes were hidden by a pair of sunglasses.

"Baby, how are feeling? I'm worried about you." The concern in his voice was heavy.

"I'm fine."

"You keep saying that, but not once have I seen you cry and that scares me." Jude reached over and grabbed her hand. "I'm here for you. So, don't feel like you can't talk to me. I love you, Tori. You're my world and I would die if something happened to you."

"I guess it just hasn't registered yet. It doesn't seem real. Maybe reality will settle in when I dress him personally."

"You sure you can handle that?" Jude was uncertain about her completing that task without having a mental breakdown.

"Yes. I'll be fine. He's my father. I have to dress him. It's only right. I didn't get the chance to do that with Kilo."

"Okay. I'll be here every step of the way." Jude released her hand and pulled off. The sound of Kilo's name made him unsure of himself. It was like he was in competition with a ghost. There he was in the flesh, and she failed to love him properly. All because she couldn't let go of her dead husband.

After picking up the tuxedo, Jude drove Tori to the attorney's office in Boca Raton. "You can drop me off in the front."

"Call me when you on the way down, so you don't have to walk."

"Okay."

Tori stepped from the car and walked into the building. Then proceeded to take the elevator to the sixth floor. Her heels clacked against the floor, as she made her way down the hallway and through the double glass doors. As expected, she saw Jenna sitting in the lobby with her bastard son and talking to Mr. Goldstein. His head swiveled in Tori's direction.

"Good afternoon Ms. Price." He grabbed her hand and kissed it. I'm so sorry for your loss."

"Thank you."

"Shall we get started?"

"Yes indeed."

Tori followed behind Mr. Goldstein and so did Jenna. He had been the family attorney for as long as she could remember. Tori sat on one side of the table and Jenna sat on the opposite side with Torin Jr. on her lap.

Mr. Goldstein opened the folder in front of him and removed some paperwork. "A few weeks ago, Mr. Price had me to change his will."

Tori had no idea what she was in for, but she hoped like hell he didn't leave everything to his concubine. She looked like she would take his belongings and give it to the next nigga. Tori would prefer he left it to his illegitimate son, instead of the tramp ass mammy.

"The will goes as follows. Torin Jr., is to receive one million dollars on his twenty-first birthday. Tori, as of today, you have inherited thirty million dollars, the mansion in Boca Raton, his vehicles and all real estate properties."

"What?" Jenna shouted. "That's it? He didn't leave me anything?"

"Let me double check." Mr. Goldstein pushed his glasses back and looked at the paperwork once more. "Oh, I did leave out one thing. The house in Weston, you may continue to live in. Once he turns twenty-one, that deed will automatically convert into his name."

"I can't believe this," Jenna ranted. "How am I supposed to take care of my son? This is bullshit. We were getting married and I live in that house in Boca."

"I'm sorry, but as of today you no longer reside there. And because you were not married, you're not entitled to his estate. However, you do have possession of the property in Weston." Mr. Goldstein did his best to explain the situation to her. "Now, there is a letter he asked me to read in the event that something happened to him."

He cleared his throat and continued. "If you are hearing this letter, that means my time on earth has expired. For weeks, I've felt my life coming to an end, so I made some changes to my dying declaration. I won't be here in the physical form to care for my kids, but I will in my absence. My dearest Tori, no amount of money will bring back your mother or Kilo. But it makes me feel better to know I left you with everything I owned. No matter what we went through, I never stopped loving you. Not even for a second. You were my first and only child for years. You hold a special place in my heart. Even as I rest at my final destination.

"Torin Jr., my second namesake, on your twenty-first birthday you will be a millionaire. You won't understand why I set this up as you grow up, but once you become a man, you will see why I made you wait. This is to ensure no one spends what solely belongs to you. Make me proud, son. I'll be your guardian angel forever. I love you.

Tori, my last wish is for you to forgive me. If you could find it in your heart to love your brother, please take care of him for me. But that's up to you. You've had me for twenty-four years. Torin won't get that opportunity. Look out for him. Love, your father."

When he was done reading the letter, Tori was in tears. Diesel knew he was going to die all along. But the craziest part was the confession he slipped in there. Mr. Goldstein passed her a copy of the documents and she quickly left the room. There was no way she could sit in there any longer.

***

The day had finally come for Diesel to be laid to rest. Tori spared no expense when it came to his homegoing service. She put him away nicely and put his plot right next to her mother at the cemetery.

Tori was dressed in a black Versace pantsuit with gold trimmings and buttons, with a pair of gold stiletto heels. Those were Diesel's favorite colors and designer. Adding the finishing touches to her makeup, she put on her necklace and a pair of earrings. Once she was dressed, she walked downstairs. The limo was scheduled to arrive at any moment. Standing in the living room of her father's house, which now belonged to her, brought back so many memories.

"The limo is here, baby. You ready?" Jude asked sweetly.

"Yes."

Eazy and Tori's clan, stood outside, along with Diesel's workers. She was surprised to see Jenna standing out there. Tori could see the black horse and carriage from where she was standing, followed by two black limos.

"Let's get this show on the road," Eazy stated, while staring at Jenna and the child beside her.

They all walked towards the end of the driveway. "Mommy, can I ride on the carriage?" Torin was excited about seeing the horse.

"No, baby. You're going to ride with Mommy," Jenna replied.

"I don't want to." He stomped his foot.

Tori watched as he had a fit. Then she walked over towards them. "You can ride with me. Would you like that?"

"Can I ride with my sister, Mommy?"

"Sure." Jenna smiled. "Thank you."

Tori nodded and grabbed his hand. Capone had her other hand, as they walked towards the carriage. The kids sat between Tori and Jude, as they made their way to the church.

The service was beautiful and packed to capacity. It was like the entire Broward County showed up and out for the legend. Diesel was dressed to the nines in a custom gold and black Versace jacket, black slacks and matching shoes. His body rested peacefully in a glass casket trimmed in gold. When it was time to view the body, Tori didn't get up. She just sat there in a daze, as everyone walked past and took their final glance at his shell. Just when she thought everything was going smoothly, loud screaming erupted. It was Jenna and she was acting like a plum fool.

"Noo! Diesel, wake up, baby! Please don't leave me." Jenna threw herself on top of the casket and grip the bars on both side. "What am I supposed to do without you? We need you."

The funeral home workers had to pry her hands off the casket. Her actions instantly made Torin cry. Tori was about to grab her baby brother and console him, but Jude grabbed him first. Placing him on his lap, he dried his tears and calmed him down.

Diesel's service had finally come to an end. The pallbearers, which were Diesel's workers, carried the casket down the aisle and out the door. Tori and the rest of the crowd followed behind them. As they walked down the steps, the sound of fireworks erupted. When the first body dropped, they knew those were gunshots.

***

Michelle sat on her sofa smoking a blunt. The kids were away at her parents' house, so she could pack their things. After Byrd's murder of Byrd and her near-death experience, there was no way in hell she was going to continue to reside in that home. With the money she received from Honcho, the money Byrd left behind and his insurance policy, Michelle could pick any state and start over.

Hard banging on the door frightened her, causing her to drop her blunt on the floor. "Shit," she screeched. "Who the fuck is this?"

Michelle checked the peephole before opening the door. The last time she opened the door blindly a gun was being pointed at her stomach. Cracking the door open slightly, she spoke. "Yes. How can I help you?"

"Are you Michelle Miller?" the woman asked.

"Yes, I am."

"I'm Detective Taylor and this is my partner, Detective Spencer. We have a few questions about your husband. May we come in?"

"Yes." Michelle opened the door, allowing them entrance inside her home.

Detective Taylor looked around the living room that was once immaculate. Now it was in disarray. There were multiple boxes scattered across the floor and a few suitcases stacked against the wall. "Going somewhere?"

It didn't take a college degree for Michelle to realize what the detective was insinuating. She placed one hand on her hip, then sighed with irritation in her tone. "As a matter of fact, I am."

"Where to?" she questioned with suspicion.

"I'm going to Naples to live with my parents." Michelle knew another question was coming, so she explained before Detective Taylor could utter a word. "The safety of my kids and myself are important to me. So, yes, I am leaving. I'm not gambling with my life like that. Whoever killed my husband might come for me next."

Detective Spencer joined in on the conversation. "Do you have any idea of who would want your husband dead?"

"No. I don't." Michelle moved closer to the sofa. "Have a seat. I know you'll be here for a while."

"Thank you." Detective Taylor replied, as she and her partner sat down on the sofa. "Mrs. Miller, let me ask you a question. Did you notice any strange behavior from your husband in the weeks leading up to his death?"

Michelle sat down on the love seat and crossed her legs. The questioning was a little off to her, so she needed clarity. "I'm sorry, what do you mean, strange behavior?"

"I mean, was he receiving any phone calls or threats? Has he had a recent fight with anyone? An argument or something?"

"My husband was a family man. He didn't have any enemies," she stated as if she believed her own lies.

Detective Ross leaned forward in his seat. The lines in his forehead were heavily wrinkled and his eyes had become slanted. His demeanor resembled someone who was running out of patience.

"Mrs. Miller, I'm going to cut straight to the chase and so are you. There will be no more games, because I feel like you know more than what you're leading us to believe."

Michelle sat in silence as her heart began to thump rapidly. Her nervousness was at an all-time high. Then finally she managed to get a few words out. "I'm telling you I don't know anything."

Detective Ross had enough at that point, and it was time to lay it down on the line. "I highly doubt that, but I'm going to give you a chance to be honest." He paused briefly before making his point.

"Your husband was found executed with a well-known kingpin. I've been with the department for years, and that's about as long as your husband's friendship with Mr. Torin Price Sr., or should I say Diesel?" Detective Ross rubbed his hands together. "Now, again, is there anything you've noticed out of the ordinary of his daily routine? Any threats that you know about?"

Michelle sat still, contemplating about her next response. It was obvious they'd done their homework and wanted answers. In her heart, she wanted justice for her husband and kids. She wanted them to pay for destroying her family and holding her captive in the comfort of her own home. Therefore, snitching on Honcho played out in her mind heavily. He didn't know it, but after staring at him for a while, she figured out his identity. Although she hadn't seen him in years, he was the spitting image of his father. The confirmation came when she looked at the phone screen and saw his father's name.

Just from being in their circle years ago, she knew the consequences of working with the police. She also knew if word got back to Eazy that she snitched on his son, he would reach out and touch her from anywhere. Even behind bars. Michelle thought a little longer before opening her mouth.

"I'm sorry, but that part of his life he kept from me. I don't know anything about the business he was involved in and that's the truth." The lie rolled off her tongue effortlessly.

Detective Taylor jumped in. "Are you sure about that?"

"Yes. I am."

Detective Taylor leaned forward and folded her hands together. "Or maybe you set him up? Maybe you wanted out of that lifestyle and decided it would be best to get rid of him and keep the money."

Michelle became aggravated after hearing the false accusations. "I love my husband. He meant more to me than anything in this world besides our kids. I would never hurt him."

Detective Taylor stood up and glanced over at Miller. "If you think of anything, give us a call. Oh, and don't go too far."

Michelle sighed with relief when they left. She couldn't finish packing fast enough. It was time to get away once and for all.

Chapter 8

As the gunshots continued to ring out, Tori looked towards the road and saw someone opening fire in their direction. On instinct, she snatched up Capone and Torin and hit the ground. Two of Diesel's men dropped the casket, drew their weapons and opened fire. Pandemonium broke out amongst the crowd and the attendees ran for their lives.

Tori screamed when she saw the chaos and her father's casket dropping before her very eyes. His perfect homegoing had been ruined. Jude pulled his gun out as he ran towards the road, blasting shots. The silver car sped off with a screeching sound. Seconds later, the police were in pursuit of the vehicle.

Tori held onto her son and brother until she felt someone tugging at her arm. When she looked up, it was Jude. "Come on, baby."

Quickly she rose to her feet and grabbed the boys by their hands, while ushering them towards the limo. "Tori! Tori!" Torin cried.

"Come on, baby, just walk. We have to get out of here." Tori felt his hand slip away. "Tor—" Her heart skipped a beat when she saw him on the ground. Dropping to her knees, she grabbed him. The wetness on his shirt grabbed her attention. Tori released a painful scream from her gut. "He's been shot!"

Jude rushed to her side and picked him up. "We gotta get him to a hospital."

Tori's nerves were a wreck and the tremble in her hands was uncontrollable, as she kneeled at his side. "I'm here, baby. You're going to be okay. Just relax, okay?" Torin Jr., kept his focus on Tori, as he cried from the pain.

Capone sat back with confusion on his sweet, innocent face. The lives of her loved ones flashed before Tori's eyes. It made her hold Capone tighter, and look at Torin Jr., differently. He was innocent in the bullshit Diesel and Jenna started, so it was unfair to hold him responsible. Tori looked into his eyes and knew she had to protect him from that moment on. It was what her father wanted. Therefore, she had to honor his last wish.

After their arrival at the hospital, Tori was able to reach Jenna through one of Diesel's workers. Torin's injuries were non-life threatening. By the grace of God, the bullet only grazed his arm.

Jenna frantically rushed through the hospital doors with a stricken look of panic plastered on her face. "Where's my baby? Where's my baby?"

Tori stood up and greeted her. "He's in pediatrics in the back. It was just a flesh wound, so he's going to be okay."

"Oh my God. I didn't know what I was going to do. I need to see him. What happened? All I heard was gunshots, so I ran," she rambled.

"I don't know. When I heard the shots, I just grabbed him and my son and shielded them until it was over." Tori thought back to that moment and realized that of it wasn't for her quick thinking, they would be having a different conversation.

"Thank you for bringing him."

"You don't have to thank me. I did what I was supposed to do."

Jenna stared at Tori for a brief moment. She could see a mixture of Diesel and Bianca in her. "Tori, I know you don't like me, and I understand why. I just need you to know I didn't purposely ruin your parents' marriage. According to him, it was already over. I was madly in love with him and I guess that made me dumb and naïve. Everything he told me, I believed until I got pregnant and he hid me for years. I wanted him to be honest with her, but he wouldn't. He said he couldn't leave you and mess up the family."

Tori wanted to be upset. At one point, she wanted to slap her for being so stupid for a man. But she knew Diesel could be charming and persuasive. Instead of voicing her opinion, she remained silent.

"All I want is for my son to be connected to his family. You're all he has." Tears rolled down her cheeks. "You don't have to say anything now. You can think about it and give me a call. Please."

"We'll talk," she promised. "In the meantime, go check on your son. I'll be right here when you come back."

"Okay." Jenna wiped her face and walked away to reunite with her baby boy.

***

Eazy paced the floor, scratching his head and yelling. "I want Tori with round the clock security. Do y'all understand that?" His group of men nodded with complete understanding. "Secondly, find out who the fuck is responsible." Eazy pounded the table. "I want every last one of them muthafuckas dead." Eazy looked up when he saw Tori walk into the room. Rushing in her direction, he hugged her tight. "Are you okay?"

"Yes. I'm fine."

"Where is Capone and your brother?" he asked.

"Capone just went upstairs, and Junior is with his mama. He has a flesh wound, so he'll be okay. They're staying at Diesel's house until we figure out who was behind the shooting." Despite her feelings towards Jenna, she wanted her and Torin Jr., to be safe. He was definitely going to need her because life without a mother was tough. Junior was already fatherless. She couldn't let him be a complete orphan.

"That's grown woman shit. I know how you feel about her, so I commend you for that."

"I'm just doing what I have to do." Tori shrugged her shoulders. "So, what's going on? Have you heard anything yet?"

"Not yet, but my soldiers are on it." Eazy caught a quick glance at Jude. He wasn't feeling his vibe, but he let it slide for the moment. "In the meantime, I'm providing you with around the clock security."

Jude stepped in as soon as those words left his lips. "There's no need for that. I'll take care of her."

Honcho rose from the seat he was sitting in. "Nah, we got her, bruh. This a family affair."

Jude wasn't backing down for shit. He needed them to know he could hold his own. "This my lady, so I'm her family now. It's my job to protect—"

"Nigga, we don't need yo' fuckin' help. You been in the picture thirty minutes and I don't trust yo' muthafuckin' ass." Honcho made it across the room quickly. The distance between the two closed up immediately. "As far as we know, you the ops."

"Nigga, I ain't the fuckin' ops," Jude snapped.

Eazy stepped in between them, closing up the space and opportunity for a fight. "Listen, right now we're at war. We don't have time for the back and forth. We all have one common goal in mind and that's to keep Tori safe. Everything else is irrelevant." He placed his hand on Honcho's shoulder. "Relax, son, it's going to be okay."

Honcho did like he was told and fell back. As he took a seat at the table, his eyes remained locked on Jude. He didn't trust that nigga for a second. Moving forward, he promised to keep his eyes on him at all times.

Eazy didn't like exchange of words between Jude and his son. Apparently, there was a previous run-in that he needed to be brought up to speed on. With a mean, yet serious look on his face, he spoke on the elephant in the room.

"It's obvious something has happened before tonight. Therefore, I need to ask you a serious question." Eazy looked Tori in the eyes. "Do you trust him?"

After what transpired after the funeral, it was hard to trust a single soul. Tori was already on high alert. The shootout only made it worse. Exhaling, she nodded her head.

"Yes." Truth be told, Tori wasn't sure if that was the correct answer. But she also knew it was best to keep your enemies close.

"Are you sure?" Eazy needed clarity. Especially after hearing the hesitation in her voice.

"Yes." Tori's response was quicker that time. Honcho's face held a grim expression, as he nodded in Tori's direction. His blood boiled at the thought of Tori being with Jude.

"Well, I'm still providing an extra man. I have to be sure Tori is safe and you're not completely outnumbered."

"Okay," she nodded her head. "I can use the extra security during the day."

Satisfied, Eazy turned back to his crew to execute a plan.

***

Back at Jude's place, an exhausted Tori laid out across the bed after taking a much-needed shower. Every inch of her body ached and sleep rode her eyelids. Jude sat beside his queen, while messaging her feet. "Do you have any idea who could be responsible for this?"

"No."

"Have you been beefing with anyone?"

"No."

"What about your father?"

"It's obvious that he was beefing with someone." Tori closed her eyes. The intense pleasure on her feet allowed her to relax. "I just don't know who that someone is," she yawned.

Jude watched Tori get comfortable. A million questions wrecked his brain, but there was one in particular that didn't sit well with him. "Let me ask you question."

"Yes." Her eyes remained closed.

Jude took a deep breath. "Why you never told me you had a son?"

Tori's eyes flickered open slowly. "I never told anyone about my son. My family just found out about him recently."

"How is that possible?" Jude displayed confusion on his face.

"When I went off to college in Atlanta, I found out I was pregnant. I didn't know what to do." Tori paused to maintain her emotions. "I couldn't have an abortion, so my professor offered to take care of him so I could focus on getting my degree. Once I got it, I brought him back."

Jude couldn't believe what he was hearing. Tori had managed to hide a whole son for four years. In his mind, there was no telling what else she was hiding from him. "Damn. I'm surprised you were able to keep that a secret for so long."

Jude continued to rub her feet until she fell asleep. She appeared to be out cold, but he had to make sure. "Tori," he spoke just above a whisper. "Tori." When he didn't get a response, he swiped her keys and left the apartment.

During his drive to his grandmother's house, Jude thought back to all of the time he spent with Tori. Every time he thought things were going well, she showed him he was wrong. It was bad enough he had trust issues. Now, Tori's secret was making it worse. And not to mention, the beef between him and Honcho. Not once did she step in to diffuse the situation and he had a problem with that.

Coming to a complete stop, Jude parked in front of the burned-down foundation he used to call home when he was a kid and killed the lights. It hurt his heart to lose the backbone of the family. His grandmother meant everything to him, and he wasn't going to rest until he found out who was responsible for her demise. Jude hadn't cried once, but the sight of the charred remains forced the tears to fall gracefully.

"I love you, Grandma," he mumbled. "If I was here, that shit wouldn't have happened. I'm going to find out who did this to you and set them bitches on fire."

After sitting in place for a good twenty minutes, Jude decided it was time to vacate the premises. He needed answers and there was only one person that could shed the light he needed. Pulling off, he cruised up the street and out the neighborhood.

As he drove to his next destination, he spotted a vehicle that appeared to be following him. Jude reached over into the back seat, pulled out his choppa and sat it in his lap. "Come on, bitch, so I can light yo' ass up." That was when it dawned on him, he was in Tori's car. Then he came to the conclusion that whoever was following him had to think she was driving.

Jude drove at a low rate of speed. He couldn't risk throwing them off. They could potentially be the same ones who shot up the funeral earlier that day. Calmly, he made his way to the street he was looking for and parked the car. As he watched the rearview, he saw the car pull in behind him.

Swiftly, he jumped from the car, while aiming the choppa directly at the window. The beam from the streetlight shined brightly and he could see it was the same silver car from earlier. Snatching the door open, he was surprised to see who the driver was.

"Nigga, what the fuck you doing following me?" Jude's bark was on one thousand.

Jarvis had his hands up. "Cuz, chill, man. I didn't even know that was you. I'm trying to get home."

Jude snatched Jarvis by the collar. "Get yo' ass out the car." He pulled him out aggressively.

Jarvis lost his footing and bumped into the front of the car. "Yo, what you doing?"

"Walk, nigga, befo' I kill yo' ass."

Jarvis stopped procrastinating and hustled to the front door. Once inside Jude delivered a powerful blow to the back of his head, causing him to fall. "What you doing following Tori's car?"

Jarvis rolled over onto his back. "Cuz, I just told you I wasn't following you. A nigga was trying to get to the crib."

"Nigga, quit lying. I been watching you in the rearview since I left Grandma house." Jude kicked Jarvis repeatedly in the ribs. Jarvis squirmed around on the floor.

A sudden scream startled Jude. "What are you doing to him?" Lisa screamed.

Jude stopped kicking Jarvis and looked at her with a menacing stare. "Mind yo' fuckin' business and get back in that room before you have an early delivery."

"Lisa, just go in the room and close the door," Jarvis groaned while holding his rib cage. "Come on, fam. What you doing?"

Jude stood over Jarvis with the same dangerous look. "Where you been all day?"

"I been out hustling. That's all a nigga can do right now."

"Nah, let's try this again." Jude aimed his gun at Jarvis. "Tell me right now. Did you shoot up Diesel's funeral?"

"What?" Jarvis' eyes stretched wide like the sun.

"You heard what the fuck I said. Did you shoot up that nigga funeral? And I'm not asking again. Ya' ass gone swallow these bullets next, along with your girl and the baby."

Jarvis knew he wasn't bluffing. He had to protect Lisa and their unborn child. Sighing heavily, he wiped his mouth. "Yeah. It was me."

"See how easy that was?" Jude raised his foot and stomped on Jarvis' head several times. "The next time I ask you a question, you answer me right away." Blood and spit traveled out his mouth sideways. His bones were sore to the touch. "Don't you get lost, I have a job for you to do."

Jarvis took short, quick breaths. "I'm not gone leave. I'll be right here. I swear. And while you over here kicking my ass, you need to look into that bitch. I think her pops killed Grandma."

Jude was on the verge of stomping him once more for disrespecting Tori. But when he heard there was a possibility Diesel killed his grandma, he froze. "How do you know that?"

"The only person I was involved with before I went into hiding was Diesel. This could've been his way of getting me back for leaving his camp."

Jude thought for a second, but something wasn't adding up with the math. "So, you want me to believe Diesel killed Grandma because you left his camp? Nigga, you was a corner boy. Not no damn lieutenant. All I know is you better put that one good ear that you have left to the streets and find out who did it." Jude raised his hand that clutched the choppa and aimed it at his very own ear. "Or you gone lose that one too."

"I'm on it. I swear." Jarvis breathed a sigh of relief when Jude left. His mind told him he needed to up and leave, but the way his funds were set up, they wasn't getting that damn far.

Chapter 9

The apartment was so quiet, you could hear a pin drop. Lala and Dazzle were at the table, separating dope and bagging it up accordingly. In spite of what Dazzle had just gone through, she wanted to be present on distribution day. She missed getting to the money with her girls and it was the perfect time for her express how she felt about the kidnapping with Terrell. That was something she hadn't spoke on as of yet.

Tori stood beside them, waiting on everyone to be seated. Jude was right there, positioned at her side. The same way Kilo used to be. Once they were all in place, she cleared her throat.

"First off, I appreciate everyone's condolences and concern, and for being present when it really mattered. The death of my father was a tremendous loss for me, but I know that I can't sit and sulk in my sorrows. As of today, we are back in business."

"Fuckin right." Ace clapped. He was happy to be getting back to the money. "We got you, sis. Don't worry about shit. Just consider me as your personal bulletproof vest."

"Thanks." Tori giggled softly, but she knew he meant every word he spoke. "I have a meeting set up with my father's crew. They need a new supplier, so I'll be extending my services to them. With us supplying them, we don't have to worry about fighting over territory because I'm stepping in, in place of my father. This will be a smooth transition and the opportunity to expand."

"And if it's not?" Fresh asked.

"You know what we have to do." Tori nodded her head. "They only get two options."

"That's what the fuck I'm talking about," Ace shouted about the possibility of busting his guns.

The meeting lasted approximately twenty minutes before Tori brought it to a close. "If no one has any questions or concerns, you can leave. Grab your bags on the way out."

Everyone in attendance left the apartment one by one after grabbing their work. Tori waited until the room was practically empty to address the next plan. "Honcho and Lala, are y'all ready to get on the road?"

Lala nodded her head. Honcho leaned against the counter. "We good to go. I just don't feel comfortable leaving you 'round this nigga." He held his peace until Jude left the room. "You need to be careful until we figure out what the fuck going on."

Tori knew his words were sincere, but he had nothing to worry about when it came down to Jude. She could hold her own. Besides, she didn't see him as a threat. He was crazy and jealous, but she felt he truly did care for her. "I'm going to be just fine. Stop worrying so much."

"Listen," he sighed. "At least take the security detail Pops put in place for you. I'll feel better knowing you have dudes I trust around you."

Tori leaned forward and kissed him on the cheek. "If it makes you feel better, then okay. I'll take it."

"Thank you. That's all I ask." Honcho grabbed the duffle bag from the table. "I'll be outside. I'm about to load the car so we can head out."

"Okay," Tori replied.

"I'll be out in a few minutes," Lala replied, while focusing all of her attention on Dazzle, until she heard Honcho close the door. "So, how are you feeling these days, Dazzle?"

"I'm doing better," she stated without giving her any eye contact.

"I've been calling and texting, but you haven't been responding to me. What's going on?" Lala was deeply concerned, being that they hadn't spoken since the last time she saw her. "I've been worried about you."

Dazzle's eyes fluttered before she finally looked into Lala's direction. Slowly exhaling, she spoke her truth. "Honestly, I just don't know how to feel. The guy that kidnapped me, his name is Terrell Andrews. You know, Terry's cousin."

Lala covered her mouth briefly and took a deep breath. The response truly caught her off guard. "Dazzle, I'm so sorry. I didn't know. This is all my fault."

"He's looking for you and he's not going to rest until he gets the answers he's looking for. I told him I didn't know who he was talking about," Dazzle truthfully stated.

"Fuck!" Lala hit the table. "So, he just let you go?" Dazzle huffed. "Not without a ransom."

"How much? I'll pay you back." Lala felt bad. If it wasn't for her, Dazzle would've never been caught up in her bullshit in the first place.

"It's all good. Fresh paid him." Dazzle placed both hands on the counter and rocked on her heels with her eyes closed. "I thought I was going to die. I thought I would never see my son again. You have no idea what I went through."

Lala stepped closer and put her arm around Dazzle. "Please don't be mad at me. I didn't mean for any of this to happen."

"We know," Tori answered, so Dazzle didn't have to.

Dazzle stood up and looked at Tori. "I never meant to tell on you. He took my phone and figured it out. It was like he knew who you were."

"Yeah. He does. Remember the girl Whitney we saw in the club? She used to live next door to Eazy," Tori purposely left out the part of her doing business with him.

Lala squinted her eyes. "Yeah. I remember."

"Well, that's her uncle."

Lala sucked her teeth. "I knew I didn't like that bitch for a reason."

"Yeah, 'cause you thought she fucked Honcho," Tori laughed.

"Quit lying, heffa." Lala's ears perked up when she heard the horn blow. "I gotta go. Honcho is ready."

"Be safe." Tori smiled before hugging Lala.

"I will." Lala hugged Dazzle. She could feel the tension in her shoulders but decided to let it go. "I'll call you once we get there."

"Okay." When the door closed, Tori looked at Dazzle. "You know you have to forgive her, right?"

Exhaling heavily, Dazzle batted her lashes. "Yeah, I know. I just need a little more time and I'll be okay."

"Good. Well, get out there. Your man is waiting on you and Ace is waiting on me. I'll see you later."

"Okay. I love you, sis."

"I love you too." On the way out, Tori grabbed her duffle bag, locked up the apartment and climbed inside the truck.

"Where to, Boss Lady?" Ace asked, while putting the truck in drive and pulling out the parking lot.

"We have to go to Dillard, Parkway and then Margate. After that, I need to go by my hair store." Crossing her legs, she looked over at Ace. "From now on, whenever Honcho goes out of town, you'll be my driver."

"I can do that."

"Also, I need a favor from you."

He could tell by her tone that it was serious. "What's that?"

"I need you to keep Tank under control. He's hotheaded and I want to make sure he doesn't put us in a jam. We don't need any additional heat coming this way."

Ace nodded his head. Tori spoke facts, so he didn't contest what she was saying. "You right about that. I can keep him on a tight leash. He'll listen to me."

"Okay." Tori was happy with his reply. All she needed was for him to uphold his end of the deal. Diesel was finally out of the picture and now she could run all of his territories. If anyone got out of line, they would be dealt with. Tori looked out the window and smiled because in a short amount of time, every hustler would bow down to the throne.

***

Tron sat on the sofa, twisting up a blunt and bopping his head to Tupac. "Aye, what time your girl coming through? I got niggas waiting on this work."

Tweety sat her phone face down on the coffee table. "She just texted me and said she was on the way." Tron continued to bop. "You know you can't be here when she comes, right?"

"I'll go in the room." He put the blunt to his lip and flicked the lighter.

"Tron, she can't know you're here." The nervousness in her voice was thick. "You know she'll cut me off if that happens."

Tron allowed the smoke to fill his lungs before blowing it out his nose and mouth. "Chill out girl, damn. She not gone see me."

Tweety got up and went into the kitchen to fix a glass of wine. Ever since Tron came home, she found herself drinking more. Her liquor intake had been so heavy, she decided to take a break that day and have some wine instead. Before sitting down, Tweety grabbed the blunt from Tron's hand and sat down.

"Damn, that's all you do is drink now." Tron shook his head.

Tweety twisted up her lips and rolled her eyes. "I wonder why."

"It ain't because of me. That's some shit you was doing before I came home." Tron refused to take responsibility for her uncontrollable drinking habit.

"If you must know, this is wine."

"It still has alcohol in it." Tron shrugged his shoulders. "But whatever floats your boat."

"You're the reason I drink so much. Every time I turn around, you have some shit going on."

"Well, stop turning around then." Tron smirked.

"Don't be funny, smart ass." Tweety sipped from her glass and sat it down. "You know, since you came home, you haven't done one thing you promised me. It's like you switched up on the one person that was there for you. I took your son in and your underage baby mama on the strength of love."

Tron sat there with low eyes, as he listened to her throw everything she did back in his face. No matter how he felt about it, she wasn't lying. Tweety dumped the ashes in the tray and passed it back to him. "I must be a special kind of fool to think you would be a man and stand on your words."

Tron wasn't in the mood to hear the truth, so he just sat there like a mute. Luckily, the doorbell sang, and he breathed a sigh of relief. *Saved by the bell*, he thought. Tweety stood up and eyed him with a look of hatred. She couldn't believe she ruined her friendship for something that wasn't promising in the end. Tweety waited until Tron closed the bedroom door before she unlocked the door.

Tori walked in, with Ace right behind her. "Hey, Tweety."

"Hey, Tori. I'm so sorry to hear about your father. I know that's hard on you." Tweety reached out and hugged her. "I wanted to show up for you, but I didn't want drama to pop off with my presence."

"It's okay. I understand." Tori turned towards her bodyguard. "This is Ace. He works for me." After the short introduction, Tori sat down, but Ace remained standing by the front door.

"Let me go and get your money. I'll be right back."

When Tweety left the room, Ace chuckled. "Aye, Boss Lady, your homegirl taken? She just my type." He loved a redbone since he was a dark-skinned, chocolate brother with waves and sparkling brown eyes.

Tori looked back at him with a disapproving stare. "Nah. She really not your type. Trust me on that."

Ace nodded his head. He wasn't sure what she meant by it, but he trusted her judgement. "I'll take your word for it."

"You should."

Just then, Tweety walked back into the room, carrying stacks of money. She sat them on the table. Tori counted out the money, then gave Tweety her cut. "So, everything is going smooth for you?"

"Yeah. It moves pretty fast, because I have a few homeboys that spend on a daily basis."

"That's what's up." Tori passed the money off to Ace. He shoved it into the bag he was holding and sat the bagged product that totaled up to half a kilo on the table. Keeping her eyes on Tweety, she shook her head. "Ace, can you step outside really quick I need to talk to her in private."

"No problem." Ace opened the door, stepped out and closed it.

"What's going on with you?"

Tweety rubbed her hands against her thighs. "What do you mean?"

"What's up with the bruises on your face?" Tori was genuinely concerned.

"Huh?" Tweety was dumbfounded.

"The bruises, Tweety. They're clearing up, but I can tell you recently had a black eye." Tori leaned forward and folded her hands. "You letting this nigga put hands on you?"

"Who?"

Tori huffed. She wasn't in the mood for the lies. "Come on, let's not do this. I know it's Tron and yes, I know he's out. You couldn't possibly think I didn't know."

Tweety hung her head low and put her focus on the rug underneath the coffee table. Nodding her head slowly, she admitted it without words.

Tori inched towards her and placed her hand on her shoulder. "This is not okay, and you can't think it is. I mean, have you really lost your self-esteem to where you feel like you need to scrape the bottom of the bucket? You deserve better than this. Dazzle did too and that's why she moved on."

Tears threatened to fall, but Tweety did her best to contain her emotions. But she was in so much pain, the water invaded her lids anyway. "How is she?"

"Dazzle is good. She's in a healthy and happy relationship. But we're not talking about her. I'm talking about you. Tweety, you lowered your standards to be with him. You saw firsthand how he treated her. You couldn't have thought he would treat you better than he did Dazzle. I mean, she had a baby with him, and he still didn't respect her. The shit he did to her was foul as fuck. How did you think he was going to treat you?"

Tweety just sat there and cried. She couldn't say too much because she knew Tron was in the other room listening. "I didn't mean to hurt her. It just happened."

"Girl, please." Tori rolled her eyes. "You picked the boy clothes up from her house and brought them to yours. You knew what you were doing."

"Well, I'm paying for it now." Tweety wiped her eyes. "I guess this is karma coming back on me."

"It doesn't have to be that way." Tori was tired of giving advice to a brick wall, so she rose to her feet. It wasn't like she was going to take her advice, so Tori decided to save her breath.

"Listen, I've known you for a long time and that's why I haven't thrown away the friendship. Some of the things you did were grounds for termination, but I'm not going to judge you. I just hope you wake up and make the best decision for you. This is no longer about Dazzle. She's happy where she's at and this guy is perfect for her and Jamir. Find your happiness. Stop letting that broke ass nigga beat on you. He just got out of prison, so I know he ain't taking care of your household."

Tweety sat there in silence as Tori got up and exited her home. As soon as she sat back and covered her face with her hands, Tron walked back into the living room. He walked up to Tweety and smacked her in the face, startling her. *Whap!*

Tweety dropped her hands and looked into the eyes of a monster. "What you hit me for?"

"You sitting out here, letting this dumb ass bitch talk about me. How the fuck you sit here and say nothing?" Tron backhanded her that time. "Stupid ass hoe. How you let a bitch come in here and disrespect yo' nigga like that?"

Tron was steady huffing and puffing when he turned his back on her. Tweety grabbed the glass ashtray from the table and slammed it against his head, causing him to stumble. Using the opportunity to get him back for all the beatings he subjected her to, Tweety grabbed the vase and broke it across his back. Tron was dazed. Therefore, he couldn't fight back. Tweety ran up on him and threw wild punches at his frame, while screaming, "This for beating my ass." Tweety was determined to teach him a lesson. For the old and new.

Chapter 10

After leaving Tori's spot, Jude slid through his old neighborhood, chopping it up with his boys. His last stop was making sure his trap spot was running smooth. Upon his arrival, the gang was there playing the Xbox with several females sitting around. That was the norm for them, so he didn't fuss about it.

"Fuck going on in here?" he joked, stating the obvious.

"Big homie, what's good?" Mike stood and dapped him up.

"Shit cooling. I see y'all in this bitch having a party."

"You know how we do. We party and get to the money." Mike chuckled, while sipping liquor from his red cup.

"As long as the money flowing, I'm Gucci." Jude sat on the sofa and fixed him a big cup of Grey Goose, while talking to his partner. A few minutes later, Toya, one of the chicks in attendance, approached him.

"What's up, Jude?"

"Sup, shorty?" Jude licked his lips, while staring at her thick thighs, being held up by a pair of tights. Toya's camel toe was poking out.

"Nothing much." Toya sat down in his lap. They had a few run-ins in the past. Nothing sexual, but that was about to change, because she was trying to be his lady. Running around with lame ass niggas was a thing of the past. She wanted the boss. Someone who would have her rocking designer and pushing a foreign whip. "I'm trying to see what's up with you."

"Is that right?" Jude caressed her inner thigh.

"Yeah. I mean, if you not scared to see what I'm talking about."

"And what's that?" he asked out of curiosity.

Toya leaned closer to his ear and licked it. "You can see what this mouth and pussy talking about."

Jude's dick jumped in his pants and he could feel it stiffening, slowly but surely. "Let's do that then." He looked at Mike and grinned. "I'll be right back."

"Handle yo' business, shit." Mike chuckled.

Jude and Toya walked to the back room and closed the door. Toya didn't waste any time removing her tights and top. Jude unbuckled his belt, dropping his jeans and boxers to his ankles. Then he stroked his rod slowly.

"Show me what that mouth do."

"I got you, baby." Toya got down on her knees and grabbed his semi-erect dick. She stroked it a few times before wrapping her lips around the tip and sucking slowly.

The sensation alone made Jude relax and lean back on the bed. He didn't know if it was the liquor or if she really knew how to work her jaw muscles. Whatever it was, he was enjoying it. Jude closed his eyes and enjoyed the ride. Loud slurping sounds filled his ears, and he could feel her saliva dripping down his dick. Toya bobbed her head up and down, while massaging his balls.

She was determined to suck him dry and plaster her name across his brain. One thing she was certain of was, niggas were suckers for pussy and head. She was equipped and talented with the use of both. So, there was no doubt she would have him eating out the palm of her hands over the next few days. All she had to do was work her magic.

Toya spent thirty minutes on her knees. Her jaws grew tired and Jude was nowhere near bussing a nut. That alone was discouraging. She didn't know what type of monster she was dealing with. Suddenly, Jude raised up on his elbows and placed his hand on top of her head. The head was good, but it was hard for him to buss off that way.

"Stand up," he demanded. Toya rose to her feet and looked into his dark eyes. "Put your hands on the dresser and lean forward."

Toya was prepared to follow any direction he threw her way. Jude stood behind her and smacked her ass. Spitting down the crack of her ass, he smeared it from the front to the back. Holding his dick in his hands, he slipped on a Magnum. There was no way he was hitting her raw. Jude then placed it against her opening and plunged in deep.

"Shit!" Toya squirmed from the thickness of his soldier.

Jude grabbed her hair and wrapped it around his hand. Aggressively, he delivered deep, hard pumps. Periodically, he would yank her hair, causing her head to jerk backwards. He wasn't sparing her at all. Toya felt like one of her important organs was about to rupture, due to his roughness. Her muffled pants quickly changed to moans, then grunts and ultimately ended with loud wails. Jude knew everyone in the house heard the noise. That didn't bother him though.

Jude yanked her hair harder. "Unt, unt! You supposed to be showing me what that pussy do. Now show me." With that being said, he stopped moving in order to allow her to put in some work. Smacking her ass, he kept talking shit. "Throw that shit back. Fuck this dick!" he demanded.

Toya lowered her body onto the dresser and threw the pussy on him as he requested. Her hands gripped the dresser so tight, until she was certain she would slip. One wrong move and she would be eating wood.

Jude frowned at her minimal movement. He wasn't happy with the lazy back shots. Placing his hand on the lower part of her stomach, he pulled her in his direction until he was seated on the bed. "Bounce on my shit until I bust or you ain't gone like what happens next," he threatened.

Toya was turned on by his aggressiveness. Spreading her feet apart, she slid down on his pole and bounced slowly. The more she got into it, the skin clapping grew louder and louder. "Jude. Jude," she moaned. Smacking her ass, Jude fucked her back until he released his nut into the latex cum catcher.

Jude snatched the rubber off and put his clothes back on. Toya stood a few inches away, doing the same thing. "You want to take down my number so we can link up again? I'm looking forward to another round of that good-good," she giggled.

Jude twisted the knob on the door, but before he opened it, he looked back and shook his head. "Nah. I'm good. I got a lady. Thanks for the offer tho'."

Toya was stunned. That wasn't the response she was looking for. A painful expression slid across her face. "So, you just gone play me like that? That's fucked up, Jude."

"How?" he shrugged. "You threw the pussy on me. I didn't ask for it."

Toya rocked on her heels. She was pissed. "Mr., 'I Got A Girl,' you didn't turn it down either."

"I'm a man and I had a few drinks, so it appeared to be appealing. Your talk game was harder than your sex game," he chuckled. "You need to work on that."

"Fuck you, Jude," she spat, with frustration lacing her tone.

"We already did that. I'm good." Jude opened the door. "Grab your shit and let's go."

Jude entered the living room with Toya behind him stomping her feet like a child. His boys were still entertaining the other females, but he was about to shut shit down. "Aye, y'all hoes gotta go. We have more important shit to do."

Toya grabbed her purse and stormed out the door. Her friend, Mika, shot Jude an evil look. "What you did to my girl?"

"Besides fuck the air out of her, I ain't did shit." Jude started to pick up the other purses sitting around and tossed them towards the door one by one. "Get out now and I mean that shit."

"You a rude ass bitch," Mika shouted, while heading to the door to retrieve her purse.

"I don't give a fuck. That ain't my lady." The rest of the girls got up and followed Mika out the door.

Mike was on the sofa cracking the fuck up. "Boy, you hard on them hoes."

"Fuck them bitches, bruh." Jude chuckled, as he sat next to Mike. "I have a job for you to do."

"Speak on it, shit."

"We need to eliminate some competition. I can't have nobody stepping on my toes as I rise to the top. Hit this shit on Saturday night. Take all the product and leave the rest to me. Just text me when the job done." Jude reached into his pocket and pulled out a piece of paper. "This the address. Be careful and don't get caught."

"Nigga, I'm a professional. I don't get caught," Mike boasted.

"I hope so." Jude rose to his feet. "I gotta head out and handle some business. I'll hit you up in a few days to touch bases."

"A'ight, cool." Mike scratched his head. He was missing some valuable information. "Aye, you gone tell me who shit I'm about to run up in?"

Jude stopped in his tracks without turning to face Mike. "That's not important. Just know it's a sweet lick."

Once he said that, he exited the house. Thirty minutes later, he was pulling into his designated parking spot. To his surprise, Tori was there, but she was still sitting in the car. Jude walked over and tapped on the window. Tori unlocked the door so he could get inside.

"What's up, baby?" Jude leaned over and kissed her on the cheek.

"Nothing much. Just tired." It had been a long, productive day and all she wanted to do was go home and get some sleep.

"Why don't you just come inside, so I can give you a nice massage?" he insisted.

Tori leaned her head against the headrest, while looking in his direction. "That sounds so good right now, but I can't. I have to go and pick up my son."

"Well, go pick him up and come back. He can stay here too. That will give us a chance to bond." He grabbed Tori's hand. "Since I'm in this for the long haul."

In her mind, she didn't know how their relationship was going to play out. Her heart wasn't in it the way his was. Besides, her guard was still up about him and she didn't want to bring Capone around him like that. "I appreciate the gesture, baby, I really do," she exhaled. "But it's too early for that right now. I mean, you just found out about him and I haven't sat down with him to explain our relationship. With everything that's been going on, I don't want to put too much pressure on my child."

Jude was disappointed to say the least, but he refused to give up on the chance to get closer to her. "Okay. I see what you saying. How about I take the both of you to Orlando this weekend? We can take him to Disney, or wherever you want to go." The look on her face said she wasn't having that either, so he had to do a little more convincing.

"Baby, I'm trying here. You've been through a lot these past few weeks and I think you need a chance to kick back, relax and not think about the business for the weekend. If you don't do this now, all you're going to do is burn yourself out."

Tori sat still for a moment and thought about what he was saying. Jude did have a point. Not once had she sat down and taken a break. "Okay. We can do that," she agreed.

"This will be good for us. Hell, I need a break too," he added.

"I agree. I just need to make arrangements for Capone. This will be our first trip out the area, and I think we should do it alone. You know." Tori placed her hand on his chest. "Have some us time. I'm thinking Jacuzzi."

Jude's eyes lit up. "Shiidd, that sounds good to me."

"I thought it would." She winked and kissed his lips.

"We'll leave out on Friday. I'll look for a suite with a Jacuzzi in it. We might not leave the room messing around with me."

"Hmm." She grinned.

"You bullshitting, we might get pregnant this weekend." Jude slipped her some tongue, but Tori couldn't enjoy it after hearing that last comment.

The following day, Tori paid a visit to her doctor to get a prescription for birth control. There wasn't a snowball's chance in hell that she was about to get pregnant.

Chapter 11

Jenna awakened from the thunderstorm's loud rumbling. Through the window, she could see the rain fall on the windowpane. On stormy days, she and Diesel stayed in bed, watching television or making love. Jenna missed him terribly. She was happy to have his replica in her life. Their son gave her the will to carry on.

Snuggled up under her was Torin, his arm wrapped up in bandages. Jenna had to count her blessings. If it wasn't for Tori and her quick reflexes, it probably would've ended with a fatality. It was bad enough she had to live without Diesel. Just the thought of her losing the one thing they shared, planted tears in her eyes. Hugging him carefully, she gently kissed him on top of the head.

"Mommy loves you so much. I don't know what I would've done without you. You're my world."

Jenna climbed from the bed and went into the bathroom to relieve her bladder. Sitting on the toilet, she wiped the tears away with her shirt. "Diesel, I miss you so much. Why did you leave me? I told you not to leave that day," she screamed. "But you didn't listen to me as usual."

Once Jenna was finished, she flushed the toilet and washed her hands. From the way her day was starting, she knew it was going to be a painful, dreary twenty hours. Stepping out the bathroom, she was startled by Tori's presence. She was sitting on the bed, rubbing Torin's head.

Tori looked up at her. "You okay?"

"No."

"Has he been in any pain?"

"A little bit. The medicine they gave him makes him sleep the majority of the day." Jenna joined Tori on the bed. "Thank you for letting us stay here. I know you don't have to."

Tori looked into Jenna's saddened eyes. The redness held a story of the pain in her heart. That was when she realized that maybe Jenna really did love her father. "I did it because I wanted to. The shoes you're walking in now, I've been walking in them for four years and I can promise you, it won't be easy. I'm sure you know that already."

Jenna nodded. "I do." For a few seconds, she just stared at Tori. She and Torin definitely shared features. "Can I ask you a question?"

"Sure."

"What changed your heart? Why protect us? For months, I've tried to talk to you and make peace. I know you hated me. You probably still do. I can't say I blame you."

Tori stood up and stared out the window. "All my life, it's always been me, my mom and dad. We were the perfect family in my eyes. If they had a fight or an argument, they never let me see or hear it. On my sixteenth birthday, all of that changed. I saw my mom disrespect my dad with words and violence."

Tori closed her eyes, as she relived one of the worst days of her life. "My dad was so mad that he ignored the fact that I was standing there. I watched him slap her to the ground. It shocked me because I never saw them act that way."

That was the second time Jenna heard that story. After the incident, she saw Diesel and he told her what happened. However, it wouldn't hurt hearing it from Tori's point of view, so she sat there listening attentively.

"I'll never forgive him for what he did to her." Tori turned around to face Jenna. "He killed my mother."

Jenna's mouth hung open. She couldn't believe what she was hearing. "Wait! Huh?" Her ears had to be playing a trick on her.

"He killed my mother," she repeated. "You asked why I had a change of heart, here's why. I lost my mother at a young age. She missed my high school and college graduation. She missed me get married and give birth to my son." Tori looked over at Junior, who was sleeping so peacefully. "He lost his father. He doesn't need to lose you too. That's not a good feeling. Trust me, I know. The love of a mother is everything."

"I'm sorry, Tori. I really am. I didn't know."

"I know you didn't. That's why I told you." Tori needed Jenna to know who she was truly crying over. To let her know she didn't know Diesel as well as she thought she did. "And for the record, I don't hate you. I don't know you well enough to form an opinion about you. All I knew was that you were having an affair with my dad and got pregnant. Did that bother me? Of course, it did. And look at how he presented it to me. On a special day I couldn't share with my mother or husband."

"Trust me. I understand. I told him it was a bad idea, but he promised to tell you about us. I begged him to on several occasions."

"It's not your fault. That was his job." Tori headed towards the bedroom door. "I'm leaving, but I'll be back later. I have two bodyguards downstairs for you. So, if you need to go anywhere, they will take you."

Jenna stopped Tori before she walked away. "Tori, I know this is probably not the right time to bring this up, but I'm going to need help taking care of Torin." She held her hands up in surrender. "I'm not asking you for a handout, but if you have work for me to do, I'll do it. I don't care what it is. I'll clean for you, wash your clothes. Just help me please."

"The last thing Torin needs is for you to be in the drug game."

"Tori, please," she begged. "I have to make money some type of way. I've never had a job, so I don't have any skills to find a job."

Tori closed her eyes and rubbed her forehead. "Okay. I tell you what. Diesel left me an apartment complex and the manager needs an assistant. I'll have her to train you in the next few weeks."

Jenna was so happy that she rushed Tori and hugged her tight. "I promise, you won't regret it. Thank you so much. You don't know how much this means to me."

"You're welcome." Tori was confused about how she was with Diesel and didn't have any money stashed away. "Let me ask you something. Did you put any money away while you were with him?"

Jenna was a little embarrassed, but she had to tell the truth. "No. Diesel controlled everything. Whenever he gave me money, I shopped with it. All I have left is two thousand dollars."

"When I come back, I'll bring you ten grand. Keep that for yourself. I'll handle Torin."

Jenna cried and hugged her again. "I don't know how I got so lucky, but I appreciate you more than you know."

Tori smiled and walked away. In her heart, she knew she was doing the right thing. Tori just hoped her mom wasn't frowning down on the decisions she was making when it came to Jenna and Torin. At the end of the day she had a conscience. And besides, ten grand wasn't shit compared to the millions she was sitting on. As long as Jenna didn't burn her in the end, she would have the support she needed for Torin. The day Jenna bit the hand that was feeding her, she would be joining Diesel. That wasn't a threat. It was a promise.

***

After the rain finally stopped, Jenna decided it was time to go and pay her father a visit. As she held Torin's hand, they walked down the stairs together. The living room was empty and so was the kitchen. "Well, where are the bodyguards?" she mumbled.

Jenna glanced at the front door and saw that it was unlocked. As she stepped out with caution, she spotted the familiar faces shooting dice.

"Blake, you is a cheating motherfucker! These dice must be loaded." Sonny snatched the dice and shook them in his hand.

"You just sorry, that's all." Blake chuckled. When he heard the door close, he turned in that direction. "Hey, Jenna, you need to go somewhere?"

"Hey, Blake. Yeah, I need to go to my father's house."

He looked back at Sonny. "Start the truck. Let me lock the door."

Sonny walked up and opened the door for Jenna. "How you doing today?"

"I'm good." Jenna put Torin inside before climbing in and giving him the directions.

On their way over, the truck was completely silent. There were no conversations whatsoever. Jenna just stared out the window. It was awkward riding in Diesel's truck without him present. That was going to take some getting used to, but she promised to take it one day at a time.

The moment the truck pulled up in the driveway and stopped, Blake hopped out and opened the door. Jenna stepped to the side, while Blake grabbed Torin. "We'll be sitting out here until you're ready," he assured her.

"Okay."

Jenna hadn't seen her father in weeks. A visit with him was long overdue. Pulling out her keys, she unlocked the door and let herself in. As usual, the house was immaculate. It had been the same way since she was a child.

"Dad!" she called out. "Where are you?" There was no answer. As Jenna walked down the hall, she could hear the water running. Once she realized he was in the shower, she headed back to the living room to sit down. While waiting on her father to get out, the front door opened and a woman walked in. Jenna was totally caught off guard. It took a minute for her to register who she was looking at in the flesh.

"Hey, niece." Chasity smiled as she walked over and stood in the middle of the floor. "Are you happy to see me?"

Jenna sucked her teeth. "Should I be?"

"That depends."

"On what?" Jenna was not in the mood for the aggravation.

Chasity looked at the little boy who was sitting beside her. Tilting her head to the side, she squinted her eyes. "He's handsome. What's your name?"

"Torin," he spoke softly.

Chasity looked at Jenna with daggers shooting from her eyes. "As in Torin Price?"

"Yep. He's a junior." Jenna popped her lips.

"You dirty slut," Chasity spat.

Jenna crossed her legs. "Oh, you're the fine one to talk. I wonder where I got that from. How quickly did prison make you forget about your sins?"

Chasity was heated. It had been years since she'd last seen Diesel, but she still held a special place in her heart for him. "How could you sleep with him and have a baby for him? You couldn't find your own man?"

Jenna laughed. "You mean like you? The last time I checked, your man was Eazy, not Diesel."

"That was always your problem," Chasity hissed. "Always in grown folks' business."

"Well, what was your problem? The last time I checked, you were supposed to be babysitting me and not sneaking your husband's stepbrother over here to fuck." Jenna continued to laugh and shake her head. "Now, that's some trifling shit for your ass."

"Yeah, you probably was watching us."

"And you would be correct." Jenna stood up, just in case Chasity wanted to try some slick shit. Auntie or not, she would beat her ass. "You remember that time y'all was in the living room? I was in the hallway peeking. When I saw that big, black d-i-c-k, I knew I had to get some of that. We been fucking for years too."

"You should be ashamed of yourself."

"Not at all. This is grown p-u-s-s-y and I was giving it to the man of my choice. I don't need your approval. You wasn't worried when you was fucking that lady husband, now were you?" Jenna was ready to lay it out on the table, but Justin walked in.

"What's going on in here?" he asked.

"A rude reunion." Jenna snapped. "Why didn't you tell me she was here?"

"I didn't think she would be here when you arrived," Justin admitted.

"What is that supposed to mean?" Chasity huffed.

Justin frowned. That was the one thing he was trying to avoid. A confrontation. "It means I didn't want the two of you getting into it."

"All this time you knew she had a baby with Diesel and you didn't tell me?" Chasity continued to carry on like Diesel was her husband.

Justin looked in his sister's eyes. "That wasn't my place to tell you. This is my daughter."

"Do you hear how crazy you sound? They should've put your ass in the nut house for what you did. Diesel is not your husband. He wasn't even your boyfriend." Jenna grabbed Torin by the arm. "Come on, baby, let's go. You let me know when she leaves. Until then, I will not be back." Jenna rushed out the door ignoring every word that came out of Chasity's mouth.

Destiny Skai

Chapter 12

Sinaloa, Mexico

The irritating sound of the roosters were a constant reminder that he was a long way from home. When Lance relocated almost a year ago, he found out his neighbor trained his roosters to partake in cock fights. That was one of the ways he made extra money. Lance walked towards the balcony and opened the blinds. His apartment was cold as ice, so he welcomed in the sun to warm his skin. Fixing a cup of coffee, he sat down at the table.

The day he had been waiting on had finally presented itself. The Federal Bureau of Investigations finally had enough evidence to build a solid case against the most notorious drug lord, Churro.

Tapping away at his laptop smiling, Lance checked his offshore accounts. He'd managed to move $800 million dollars undetected. That was more than enough to get away and start a brand-new life in any country he chose. Staring at the time, the takedown would be unfolding in less than thirty minutes. The life Churro built was finally coming to a close and he didn't have a clue. Lance had no sympathy for him, especially after he killed his nephew. The disheartening part about it was the fact that he paid all expenses and sat with his sister daily to comfort her. Only a person without a conscience could do that.

Using his left hand, he picked up his phone and dialed a number. The phone rang six times before someone answered. "Thank you for calling Simple Charters, my name is Angela. How may I assist you today?"

Lance stared at the fake driver's license and passport that sat beside him. "Hi, Angela. My name is Alexander Betts. I need to book a private jet to Ft. Lauderdale, Florida, immediately."

"The earliest I can book you would be Saturday at noon." Angela didn't bother to look at the calendar. Her biggest pet peeve were last-minute customers. It required too much paperwork at the last minute.

"No. You don't understand. My grandmother is on her death bed and I need to see her one last time before they pull the plug at eight o'clock tonight. Please help me," he sniffled as if he were crying. Lance was lying through his teeth. All he needed was a great escape back to the states and pronto.

Angela instantly felt bad for him. "I'm sorry to hear that, sir. Give me one second while I speak to my manager."

"Okay."

Angela placed him on hold and looked at the first available flight. She didn't need to speak to a manager. That was her way of making herself feel better after lying to him in the first place. After finding a flight, she took him off hold. "Mr. Betts, thank you so much for holding. I was able to speak to my manager and we can accommodate you tonight at six. Is that okay?"

"Yes. That's perfect."

"And are you traveling alone?"

"Yes."

"Okay. I'm able to book you on our Turboprop jet for four thousand dollars. Is that fine?"

"Yes." He nodded.

"What card would you be using today?" Angela politely asked.

"American Express." Lance provided all details she needed and sat the card down on the table. He counted his blessings as he thought about what might occur if he was stuck until Saturday.

"Take down this confirmation number. Let me know when you are ready."

Lance used his right hand to hold the phone and his left hand to write down the information. "I'm ready."

"Your confirmation number is CP nine-eight-seven, eight-five-two. You're going to board your flight at Bacubirito Airport. Please be there by five forty-five pm. Do you have any other questions for me?"

"No. That would be all."

"Thank you for calling Simple Charters, have a great day."

"You as well."

98

Lance hung up the phone feeling great. It was almost over. A text message came through his phone. It was Agent Smith, letting him know Churro's property and warehouses were about to be taken down at that very second. He knew Churro wasn't going down without a fight and FBI agents would be killed in the process. He had high hopes that Agent Smith would be one of them. It was 4:15 pm, so that left him less than two hours to get out of Dodge. Quickly, he packed away his laptop and every ounce of evidence that proved he lived there. Flipping open his wallet, he looked at the photo and took a deep breath.

***

A loud crashing sound echoed throughout the house as the front door came crashing down. "FBI, put your hands up."

Churro's men whipped out their firearms and started to shoot. The federal agents took cover and returned fire. From upstairs, Churro could hear the loud shots and grabbed his own arsenal weapon. Emilio was at his side, ready to protect him by any means necessary.

"Where is Lance?" Churro asked.

"I don't know."

"Try to call him," Churro demanded, while trying to figure out a way to escape.

Emilio took his phone from his pocket and dialed Lance's number. When he didn't pick up, he tried again. "He didn't answer. We have to get out of here."

"Fuck!" Churro ran to his balcony and looked over in his yard. He was disappointed to see it was swarming with the feds. "There's no way out. These cabróns are everywhere."

Emilio held his gun at his side and opened the door. "We have to make a way. Follow me."

Churro and Emilio moved down the hallway as the feds hollered throughout the house. All they had to do was make it to the third level to the hidden room and they were home free. Hopefully. They were able to pass through without being seen. Churro smiled when he realized they were less than ten feet away from freedom. "We made it." He closed the door behind them.

"Not so fast, amigo."

Churro turned on his heels when he heard a voice behind him. The sight of the FBI jacket ruined every ounce of hope he had of escaping. "Cabrón," he huffed.

Agent Smith trained his weapon on his assailants. "Put your weapons down."

"I don't think so." Emilio raised his hand slowly but froze when he saw multiple weapons being drawn on him. Agent Smith wasn't alone.

Closing in the space between him and his target, Agent Smith slapped the cuffs on Churro. "Do you how long I've been waiting to do this?" he chuckled. "To take down the biggest drug lord in Mexico."

"I'm sure you mean that in every aspect of the word." Churro chuckled and tilted his head to the side with a smirk. "But hmmm, let me guess. Would it be the moment you realized you were gay? I'm sorry to disappoint you, I'm not interested."

"You wish you were that lucky." Agent Smith pushed him down onto the sofa. Emilio kneeled down and placed his gun on the floor. There was no way out. It was over.

***

Lance was fully dressed and ready to head out. That was, until he heard movement inside his apartment. An eerie feeling came over here, so he picked up his pistol and twisted on the silencer. Creeping towards the door, he spotted two of Churro's men browsing through his things. There was no way he could let them leave. Lance took aim and fired two individual head shots into both men. Their bodies hit the ground with a loud thud. It was time to get ghost before anyone else made a special appearance.

Lance grabbed his bag and headed for the door. Before stepping out, he checked the left and right side of the hallway, just in case more were waiting. Instead of taking the elevator, he opted on the stairs. He was halfway to his car before a bullet whizzed past his head, shattering the glass in a van. Lance dropped his items on the ground and let off multiple shots in the same direction the bullet came from. Bullets slammed hard against the frame of some parked cars, along with the windows. He ducked for cover to keep from getting hit. As soon as the shots stopped, Lance grabbed his bag and jumped into the car. The second he started the car more gunshots rang out. Lance slammed on the gas and got the fuck out of Dodge. He only had twenty minutes to get to the airport and time was ticking.

Lance could hear screeching tires behind him. When he looked into his rearview mirror, he could see a van hot on his trail. Then suddenly the crashing sound of glass. The shooter had shot out his back window. Flooring it, he zipped through traffic trying to avoid them. Losing them was mandatory. He couldn't have a shootout at the airport. Lance knew the Mexican roads like the back of his hand, so he turned down a side street that led up to the docks.

"It's only one way out," he mumbled. Lance grabbed his second weapon and loaded the first one. It was time to get rid of them once and for all.

Stepping out the car, he closed the door and hid behind a dumpster. It wasn't long before the van pulled up behind it. Two men hopped out and approached the vehicle slowly with their hands on the trigger. Lance stood up and fired two shots into one of the men. His partner that stood on the passenger side shot in his direction, but he was able to duck. When he stood up, he ran towards his car. Just as he reached, the second shooter stood up and caught a bullet to the forehead. Lance jumped into his car and drove off.

It was 5:58 pm when Lance arrived at the airport. He provided the clerk the confirmation number and was escorted to the private jet that awaited him. Sitting down on the cushioned seat, Lance leaned back to relax. That was the longest shootout he'd been in and his ass was exhausted. The flight attendant brought him a pillow. "Do you need anything else?" she asked with a smile.

"I'm good. Thank you."

"We're set to arrive in the states in one hour and forty minutes. If you need anything, hit the button on the seat."

"Thank you." Lance rested his head on the pillow and closed his eyes. The moment he had anticipated for years was finally within his reach. It was time to settle the score once and for all.

Chapter 13

Fall 1995

Chasity rubbed her slender leg against Diesel's leg as they laid in bed together. Gently, she scraped her nail across his chest. "You always make me feel so good. I can just lay here with you forever." "Hmm, is that right?" Diesel stared up at the ceiling.

"Yes." Chasity grabbed the bottom of his chin and turned his head towards her. Leaning in she kissed his lips. "I'm in love with you, Diesel, and I want you to leave Bianca. I'm willing to leave Eazy for you."

There was so much doubt in his eyes. The fling they had was just that. It wasn't love. It was sex. "Chasity," he hesitated.

"Yes, my love?" she purred.

Diesel thought about his words. He didn't want to hurt her feelings, so he tried to choose them wisely. However, it wasn't possible to sugarcoat the way he truly felt. "I'm sorry."

"What are you sorry for?"

Diesel knew she wasn't going to take it well. "I can't leave my family. That just can't happen."

Chasity was disappointed by his answer. It wasn't what she was expecting at all. She sat up with tears in her eyes. What do you mean you can't leave your family? I'm asking you to leave Bianca."

Diesel ran his hand across his face. "She's a part of my family. We built a family together. I just can't up and leave her like that."

Chasity lunged a pillow at the wall, as she screamed. "And what about me?"

"This wasn't a part of the plan and you know that." Diesel got up and started to get dressed.

"That's it? You're just going to up and leave me like this?"

"Yes. I have to go."

Chasity jumped up and grabbed his shirt. "You can't leave me like this. I just told you I'll leave him for you."

"That's because he put you out already." Diesel pushed her hands away. "I still love my wife and I have to make this work with her. I'm not allowing another man to raise my child."

"Don't do this to me, baby please," she begged. Chasity was on her knees, holding his leg.

Grabbing her arm, he lifted her to her feet. "Don't do that."

"But I need you."

"And so does Bianca and my kids." Diesel shook his head. "I can't do this."

"Kids? What do you mean, kids? Y'all have one child."

"Bianca is pregnant."

"Really Diesel! You got her pregnant?" The switch in Chasity's mind clicked and now she was upset. "So, you just gone fuck me like that and leave me? That's so unfair."

"I know it is," he sighed. "I'm sorry. And that's why this can't happen again. We've taken this too far."

"Baby, please don't do this to me. I can't be without you." Chasity was crying and wiping away snot that dripped from her nose.

"I've done too much damage to my marriage. It's time for me to do the right thing for my family." Diesel's Nokia phone rang. When he looked at it, Bianca's name was flashing across the screen. He put the phone back in his pocket and walked off.

"Is that her?" Chasity screamed.

"Goodbye, Chasity." Diesel walked out the hotel room and allowed the door to slam behind him. He could hear Chasity screaming at the top of her lungs, but he ignored it. That was the day he promised to keep his word and do right by Bianca. He loved her too much and didn't want to lose her.

A few days had passed since the last time Diesel saw Chasity. She had been constantly calling until he finally decided to change his number. Bianca was becoming suspicious once again, so he ended the problem for good.

After leaving the jeweler, Diesel headed home to surprise his queens. When he walked into the house, Bianca and Tori were in the den watching a movie, *The Little Mermaid* to be exact. It was Tori's favorite.

"How are the most important women in my life doing?" Diesel kissed Tori on the cheek and Bianca on the lips.

Bianca rubbed her belly and smiled. "We're good, baby. Just waiting on you to join us."

"How is my prince doing?" Diesel kissed and rubbed her belly. "He's doing just fine."

"I have something for the both of you." Diesel produced the bag he was holding.

"Is it candy, Daddy?" Tori jumped up from the leather sofa.

"It's better than candy." Diesel opened a small box and handed it to his princess. "Open it."

Tori opened the box and took out the necklace. It held a mermaid pendant. "It's so pretty, Daddy. Thank you."

"Not prettier than you, baby." Diesel put the necklace around her neck. Then he took the tiny ring from the box and placed it on her ring finger. "This ring symbolizes all the love I have for you. No man will ever love you more than me and don't you forget that."

"I won't, Daddy." Tori hugged his neck.

"I need you to do something for me."

"Okay." Tori batted her long lashes. She had the biggest, brownest eyes to match.

Diesel and Tori turned their backs to Bianca. Then he whispered in her ear. Tori giggled. "Do you remember what to say?" She nodded her head yes. "Okay, let's do it."

Tori walked up to Bianca and held a ring in front of her face. "Will you marry my daddy again?"

Bianca was flattered, yet surprised. Things with Diesel weren't easy, but he was worth the fight. There wasn't another man she wanted to be with besides him. They had a baby on the way and things between them finally looked promising. Just like it was in the beginning. Bianca wiped her eyes.

"Of course, I'll marry him again."

Diesel was happy with her answer. They shared another kiss, but this time there was passion with it. "I love you, Bianca, and I'm sorry for everything I've done. You didn't deserve that, and I want to spend the rest of my life making it up to you."

"I love you too, baby, and I forgive you."

Later on that evening, Diesel took Tori and Bianca out to dinner to celebrate their engagement. Then they went to the beach and sat underneath the stars. As he reflected on his past mistakes, he realized it was time to be the perfect husband. For the first time in a long time he was doing the right thing and it felt good.

By the time they reached their house it was almost eleven o'clock at night. Tori had fallen asleep on the way home. Bianca relaxed in the front seat. As he got ready to pull into the driveway, he spotted a familiar car. It looked like Chasity's car, but he couldn't be too sure since it was dark.

Diesel picked Tori up from the backseat and closed the door. The lights towards the road caught his attention. There was no doubt in his mind it was Chasity riding past. Not wanting to ruin their night cap, he ignored it and went inside.

***

Chasity was furious as she drove past Diesel, living a happy life, while she suffered. Eazy wasn't trying to reconcile or let her back in the house for the sake of their children. Eazy barely answered the phone and when he did, he had Kilo to answer. The worst part about the entire situation was her children not wanting to come and visit at their Uncle Justin's house.

As she sat at the stop sign, Chasity screamed and banged on the steering wheel. Her life was unraveling, and she didn't know how to handle it. Drinking had become her coping mechanism and it worsened by the day. At the moment she was loaded and ready to hurt Diesel for discarding her like trash. The sudden blowing from a horn rattled her thoughts. Chasity yelled out the window.

"Go around." The car sat behind her and continued to blow the horn. Their actions made her furious.

Chasity put her car in park and opened the door. As she approached the vehicle, she spotted a woman sitting behind the wheel. "I said, take your ass around."

The woman cracked her window. "Get the fuck out the road. You in the fucking way."

"I'll show you who in the way." Chasity pulled the handle on the woman's door, but it was locked. Ready to fight, she kicked the door and banged on the window.

The woman behind the wheel grabbed her phone. "I'm calling the police on you, you psychotic bitch."

"Nah, get your ass out the car," she yelled.

Chasity kept kicking the door trying to get her to come out, but she wouldn't. When she saw the woman dial 911, she ran back to her car and pulled off.

The following day, Chasity woke up in Motel 6 with a hangover. She didn't go home out of fear the police would locate her car. Chasity saw she had a missed call from Eazy and a voicemail, she decided to listen to it. As suspected, the police had run her tag and showed up to Eazy's house. He told them she didn't live there anymore. Feeling a bit of relief that he hadn't snitched on her whereabouts, she decided to lay low until nightfall. In the meantime, Chasity picked up where she left off. Drinking and smoking.

After drinking and smoking for hours, Chasity decided it was time to make Diesel suffer. He hurt her to the core. Therefore, it was time for him to pay the piper and she knew just how to hit him where it hurt.

The sun had disappeared and darkness took over the skies. Chasity dressed in an all-black sweat suit and covered her hair with a hoodie. "You want to leave me, bitch? I'll show you that you can't."

Chasity got into her car and pulled out the parking lot. "All you had to do was choose me, Diesel. It was simple. You can't just fuck people mentally and physically. Who raised you?" She had a full conversation with herself, as she drove to her destination.

The shopping center was empty when Chasity drove by. Pulling over, she parallel parked her car and waited until she saw the lights go out. That was the moment she had been waiting on. Chasity grabbed the .380 handgun from the glovebox and put it in her pocket. Nervous was an understatement as she walked briskly on the concrete.

Chasity approached the pharmacy quickly. The woman locked the door and turned around to the barrel of her gun. Thinking it was an armed robbery, Bianca quickly raised one of her hands in the air and threw her purse with the other.

"You can have everything, just don't hurt me or my baby please," she begged. "I have a husband and a daughter at home waiting on me."

Something that was supposed to be a silent and quick movement, turned out to be the complete opposite. Bianca was really pregnant and it hurt Chasity to see her standing there, carrying the child for the man that she loved.

"Shut the fuck up, Bianca. You think you have the perfect marriage, but you don't. And when I kill you and that child, Diesel will belong to me."

Bianca looked closer and realized she knew the perpetrator. At first, she only saw the gun, but now she knew it was an old friend of hers. "Chasity, what are you doing?"

"What does it look like? Getting rid of my competition." Chasity rested her finger on the trigger. "Your husband thinks he can just fuck me and get rid of me like yesterday's trash. But I'm here to show him that he has another thing coming."

Bianca wanted to beat Chasity's ass for fucking her husband, but she had to remember she was carrying their son. And that the deranged bitch had a gun. "Chasity, think about what you're doing. If you kill me, you'll never have Diesel. You'll be in prison and he'll be with another woman."

Chasity was fuming and breathing like a raging bull. "All you had to do was stay with Eazy and none of this would be happening. Why did you take him back?"

Bianca tried her best to be rational under life or death circumstances. For the life of her, she couldn't understand how a single person never entered the damn plaza. "What happened between me and Eazy was a mistake. It should've never happened, but we were both hurt and drunk. One thing led to another and we slept together. It only happened once."

"I don't care." Chasity waved the gun. "Eazy didn't love me anyway. All I wanted was the perfect marriage like you and Diesel." Chasity wiped her tears away. "I'll get that now."

"That's not true, Chasity. Eazy cherished the ground you walked on. You just didn't have the patience to deal with him being in the dope game." All Bianca had to do was make it to her car and she could defend herself. Diesel bought her a gun since she got off late, working as a pharmacist.

"No, he didn't."

"You hurt him, and Diesel hurt me." Bianca shook her head and lowered her hands. "You know me and Diesel's marriage was never perfect. We just did a good job in public. Behind closed doors, there was a lot of turmoil, but we never exposed our daughter or friends to it. You have no idea what's it's like to be married to Torin Price. That's a hard job. It's damn near impossible."

"Well, I'll make him a better man and I'll be a good mother to Tori."

Those last words sent Bianca into a fit of rage. Forgetting about her belly, Bianca rushed Chasity and hit her in the face, causing her to stumble. The gun fell from her hand and hit the ground. Arms and fists were swinging, and Chasity was losing the fight. Somehow, she'd managed to push Bianca off of her and grab the gun. Chasity looked Bianca in the eyes and squeezed the trigger twice, hitting her in the stomach. Chasity took off running when Bianca's body hit the pavement. It took one week for the police to arrest her. She pleaded guilty to manslaughter, and aggravated assault with a deadly weapon, and was sentenced to fifteen years.

Destiny Skai

Chapter 14

Fresh sat in a chair in the corner of their bedroom watching his angel sleep peacefully. It was such a relief to have her back home and under his watchful eye. The time they spent apart damaged him. As her provider and protector, he felt like he failed her. Once Fresh paid the ransom to get her back, he vowed to never let anyone else hurt her and that was a promise. Thinking back on his journey to find her, Fresh was glad that he didn't overreact and kill Tron.

A soft moan followed by a low cry parted Dazzle's lips. Looking closer, he realized she was still asleep. She appeared to be uncomfortable by the way she moved around, trying to find her spot.

Fresh continued to watch Dazzle as her cries grew louder. Then she could be heard calling Terrell's name, begging him to stop. Fresh's heart broke listening. He couldn't watch her have the nightmare any longer, so he sat down beside Dazzle to bring the bad dream to an end by shaking her shoulder.

"Baby, wake up." He kept his voice low to keep from scaring her. "You're home, baby, wake up."

Dazzle snapped out of her dream and looked around the room. She was happy to see Fresh sitting there, instead of wicked ass Terrell. Fresh wrapped his arms around Dazzle and held her tight.

"You're safe now."

The room appeared to be spinning, making her dizzy. Dazzle pushed Fresh away. He was confused by her actions. Just as he was about to question it, Dazzle flipped the blanket back and moved to the edge of the bed. Before she could plant her feet on the floor, she leaned forward and threw up on the wood floor. Fresh moved his feet right on time.

Dazzle breathed heavily as she looked up at Fresh. "I'm sorry. Can you get me a towel please?"

"Don't apologize. I'll clean it up." Fresh went into the storage closet and returned quickly with the necessary supplies. He sat a bucket beside the bed. "Just in case you can't make it to the bathroom."

"Thanks, baby."

"Are you okay?" Fresh was genuinely concerned about her well-being. He could see her shoulders stiffen, as if she was afraid. "You were crying in your sleep. You called his name too." Fresh paused to get his next question together. He wanted the answer, but he was afraid to hear the truth. But he couldn't spend another day not knowing what happened. "Did he rape you?" Dazzle shook her head. "No."

Satisfied with the answer, he asked the most obvious question. "Are you pregnant?"

Dazzle nodded her head. "Yes," she sniffled.

"Is it my baby?" Fresh didn't believe she cheated. That was just another way to confirm his previous question for a second time.

Dazzle grew teary eyed. She wasn't sure. Especially since Tron had raped her. However, she didn't want to reveal that information for some apparent reason. Dazzle felt as if he probably wouldn't believe she was violated by the father of her child.

"Yes." She nodded.

Fresh had a feeling that she was and now she confirmed his very thoughts. Quietly, he sat on the bed. His mind was going a million miles a second. Dazzle felt like there was a sudden tension in the air. Maybe she should've kept quiet. *What if he didn't want a baby?* There were so many things going on in her own mind. Finally, she opened her mouth.

"Are you upset?"

Fresh grabbed her hand. "No. I'm just thinking, that's all."

"Do you want me to have an abortion?"

"Of course not. I want you to keep my baby. Our baby." Fresh wiped a fresh tear from her eye. "I'm happy. I'm just not kissing you cause our breath stink right now."

Dazzle laughed it off. "Be quiet. You can kiss me."

"Nah, I really can't." Fresh help her from the bed. "Go clean yourself up so I can mop this floor. Then I'll show you how happy I am."

While Dazzle showered, Fresh cleaned the floor. The room smelled like fresh lavender. Much better than the strong stench of old, spoiled food. His heart was filled with joy after finding out he was expecting a baby with his soulmate. Dazzle was his world. Forever was already in their future. The baby made it official.

Dazzle walked into the room smiling. Fresh flashed a seductive smile back at her. The shower gave her a burst of energy and she was ready to love on her man. They hadn't had sex since her return. Closing the door and locking it, Dazzle opened her robe and dropped it to the floor. Fresh took the hint very well and undressed immediately. As soon as he removed his boxers, his dick sprung upwards like a diving board. He'd held out long enough and was ready to spring into action.

Dazzle approached him as if she was about to ride the stripper pole. Standing in front of him, she placed her lips onto his and tongue kissed her man. The passion was hot and steamy off the rip. Fresh raised her leg and pulled her onto his lap. Dazzle eased down on his pipe slowly. In between their kissing, she released a heavy moan as he filled her up. Fresh placed both hands on her cheeks, while she rode him at a fast pace. It wasn't hard to tell they were anxious for their first encounter. Grunts and moans filled the room like a studio session.

Fresh stood on his feet with Dazzle in his arms. Gently, he placed her down on the edge of the bed, without losing his place inside the warmth of her walls. Slow thrusts were what he delivered. Dazzle planted her feet on his firm chest, giving him full access. Fresh placed both hands on her stomach and pumped harder. If she wasn't already pregnant, tonight would've been the night he knocked her up.

"Damn, I missed this," he grunted.

"Me too," she panted.

Dazzle could feel the pressure deep in her guts. It hurt, but the pain was good and definitely needed. All the built-up pressure she had inside, needed to be released. She desperately craved an orgasm from him. Placing two of her fingers on her clit, Dazzle gave him some assistance by stroking it. With Fresh beating her down, it was going to be harder to reach a climax.

Fresh watched his woman add to the pleasure he was giving her. Watching a woman play with herself was an absolute turn-on for him. Sweat trickled from his forehead. "Play with that pussy, baby. Give daddy that nut."

"I am. I am," she moaned. "Just keep going."

"I'm not stopping." Fresh moved his hands to her shoulders and went deeper. Dazzle instantly felt weak.

"Ooohh, shit!" The pain in her stomach hit hard, but she would never tell him to stop or slow down. All she could do was call his name repeatedly until she felt a heavy release.

Fresh knew it was his turn. Grabbing her leg, he propped it on his shoulder and put his knee on the bed. Fresh gripped her cheek with his right hand and plunged deep. Aggressively, he rammed his Mack truck inside her little garage. He was grunting hard. She was screaming.

"Shh." Fresh didn't want Jamir to hear them. Dazzle grabbed a pillow and covered her mouth, so she could scream in peace.

Suddenly, there was a knock on the door. "Mommy!" Jamir shouted.

Fresh laughed, as he slowed down. "I told yo' noisy ass to be quiet. Answer him."

Dazzle moved the pillow. "I'm coming, baby."

"You talking to me or him?" Fresh joked.

Dazzle smacked his arm. "Go back in the room and I'll be right there."

"Okay," Jamir replied.

Once he was gone, it was back to the regularly scheduled program. Fresh tried to kill something, until he felt that nut surface after minutes had passed. His body rocked like he was having convulsions. "Shit!" he grunted.

When Fresh was finished, he put his clothes back on. "Go see what my son want."

Dazzle put her robe on and smile. "Yeah, make me go out here."

"He was calling you. Not me." Fresh sat down on the bed, while Dazzle opened the door.

"Jamir? Come here, baby," she called out.

Jamir came running down the hallway. He walked into the room and looked around. "Mommy, you okay?"

"Yes, baby. Mommy is fine. What's wrong?"

Jamir looked at Fresh. "Did you hit Mommy?"

Dazzle wanted to laugh so bad, but she held it in. Fresh looked at the noise box and shook his head. "No. I would never hit Mommy."

Jamir cut his little brown eyes. He appeared to be confused. "I heard you."

"We were playing, that's all. Mommy just gets loud at times," Fresh assured him.

"I'm sorry I scared you, baby. We were just playing a game, that's all."

"Okay." Jamir left and went back to his bedroom.

Fresh was still shaking his head. "I told you to be quiet. You don't listen."

Dazzle sat down beside him and smacked his leg. "Well, if you wasn't trying to break my pelvis, I could've kept quiet," she joked.

"I tried not to, but I couldn't help myself. That pussy fie." Fresh placed his hand on her thigh. "Learn how to control your tone."

"I'll try. I can't make any promises."

Fresh looked at Dazzle and placed his hand on her stomach. "I want you to stop working for Tori. You need to keep my baby and yourself safe. I can't have you in the streets like that."

"Okay." Dazzle wasn't about to argue with the man of the house. He spoke and she was going to listen.

"That's it? Just like that."

"Yes. You want me to quit. I will."

"Damn, it's that easy?"

"You've taken care of me all this time. Why shouldn't I listen to you? I know you won't steer me wrong."

"As long as you know." Fresh kissed her. He was surprised she didn't put up a fight. Although, the kidnapping could've played a huge role in it. "I love you."

"I love you too." Fresh and Dazzle cuddled up for the rest of the evening, enjoying each other's company.

***

Eazy, Fabian, Honcho and Lala sat at the kitchen table playing spades. There was a lot of shit talking, smoking and drinking going on. "You a cheater like your man, huh?" Eazy joked.

"We are not cheating. Y'all just losing." Lala laughed.

"Pops can't take an ass whooping," Honcho added.

"Yeah, we gone see about that. It's my deal next. You or your cheating ass woman won't get another book at this table," Eazy threatened.

"We'll see. Come on, baby, and let's beat they ass again," Honcho chuckled.

A heavy knock on the door interrupted their card game. Fabian looked at Eazy. "You expecting company?"

"Hell nah," Eazy sat his cards down and pushed his chair back. "We about to find out though."

Fabian stood up and picked up his gun from the counter. "Let's go see."

Eazy stood at the door, with Fabian standing behind him. Looking through the peephole, he sighed. "I know damn well."

"What?" Fabian asked.

Eazy didn't reply. Instead, he opened the door with a scowl on his face. "What the hell are you doing here, Chasity?"

Chasity looked Eazy up and down with a smile on her face. "I see time has been good to you," she smirked.

Eazy ignored her comment. "What are you doing here?" He repeated his question.

"Relax." Chasity looked at Fabian. "I see some things never change. You still rocking with him, huh?"

Fabian mugged her. The sight of Chasity irritated his soul, and he didn't hide it. "Unlike most people, I believe in loyalty. Especially to those who have been good to my family."

Chasity giggled. "Touché. I get it, but that's a thing of the past. I forgot about it. You should too." Pushing past Eazy, she entered his home. "Where are my sons? I want to see them."

Eazy scratched his head. Aggravation wasn't the word for what he was feeling. "That's funny. You remember you have kids now?"

"How could I forget? I pushed them out my coochie." Chasity put her hand on her hip. "Unless you forgot that."

Eazy was frustrated with her appearance and he wanted her out of his house pronto. "Honcho is in the kitchen and you know Kilo is dead."

Chasity froze. "What? Kilo is dead?"

"That's what I said."

"No. No," Chasity shook her head. "What do you mean he's dead?"

"Just what I said. He's dead. I called the prison to arrange a compassion visit, but you weren't available. I don't know if you were in trouble or what. I even sent you a letter, but I didn't get a response. What the hell did you expect me to do? After you didn't reach out, I gave up."

Chasity felt the wind being knocked from her chest and leaned against the wall. "My baby. My baby is dead. I don't believe that. He's not dead."

All the commotion caused by Chasity finally brought Honcho and Lala into the living room. When he saw his mother's face, he froze in place and just stared at her.

Chasity's eyes met his and she was overjoyed. "Honcho? My baby. Is that you?"

"Yeah, it's me." Honcho recognized his mother immediately. All of the time apart didn't make him forget her face.

Chasity walked up to Honcho and gave him a hug. He hugged her back. Honcho couldn't believe his mother was finally out of prison. It was truly a surprise. He remembered seeing her when his grandmother, Chasity's mother took them to visitation. The visits stopped when she passed away from a massive heart attack and all communication stopped. Even when he got older, he didn't bother to reach out. That was a relationship he didn't care to mend. Honcho heard a piece of the story and he couldn't believe she could commit such a horrific crime. He didn't hate her, but he couldn't forgive her so easily. In his eyes, Chasity had abandoned her family behind dick.

"Wow." She stood back to get a good look at him. "You've gotten so big."

"Yeah. I'm a grown ass man now. Not the little kid you left behind all those years ago." The sarcasm dripped heavily from his tongue.

Chasity expected her homecoming to be a little more welcoming, but she was wrong. "Baby, it wasn't like that. People make mistakes. I made a mistake."

"I'm sure." Honcho pulled Lala in his direction and started to walk off. "We out, Pops. We'll be back."

"Where are you going?" Chasity asked. "I came over here to see you."

"I don't do to well with pop-up visits. Besides, me and my girl have a date." Honcho didn't give Chasity a chance to say another word. He exited the door, as quickly as she had arrived.

Chasity looked at Eazy. "I see you've been planting bad seeds in his head."

"Nope. That would be you. It's not my fault you put another nigga before your own family. You made your bed. Now lay in it. Like he said, he's a grown ass man. He has his own mind and voice. I don't need to tell him shit." Eazy walked to his front door and opened it. "You can leave now."

"Oh, it's like that now?" she hissed.

"It been like that. Now, bye."

"I'll be back."

"Do me a favor and don't." Eazy slammed the door once she crossed the threshold.

Chasity was bothered by the way things turned out. Especially with Honcho. Eazy was another story and she would handle him another day. In the meantime, she had something more important to address. Pulling out her cell phone, she autodialed a number.

"Agent Tillman speaking."

"What the fuck happened to my son?" Chasity screamed, while getting into the car and speeding off.

Chapter 15

Tori was stretched out in the passenger seat, as Jude drove them into Orlando for the weekend. Despite his many pleas about bringing Capone along for the ride, Tori stuck to her guns and left him with his grandfather. The quick trip out of town was exactly what she needed. It would also give her the time she needed to kick back, unwind and get closer to her man. Since their relationship developed so quickly, Tori didn't get a chance to learn him fully.

The night Jude met Tori was by a stroke of luck. Her reputation was stellar. No one in the hood could get any play from her. However, when he came along, Tori was still grieving and lonely. If Tori was in her right state of mind, she would've never given up the goods so early. In the end, he proved he deserved the goodies. So that was a thing of the past and it was time to give him a real chance at making her happy or fucking up royally. The choice was up to him.

Jude stole a quick look at her. "You good over there, baby?"

"Yeah. I'm good."

"This weekend I want you to relax and enjoy yourself. Don't think about business or anything of that nature. It's all about us for the next few days. I'm going to make this the most memorable weekend. One you will never forget."

Tori shifted in her seat. "I'm looking forward to whatever you have on the menu."

Jude licked his full, luscious lips. "Well, I do have something in mind for my dessert tray."

That comment alone made Tori blush. The thought of his thick tongue caressing her womanly parts made her clit thump. When it came down to his head game, the man was a ferocious beast.

"You are so nasty." Tori acted as if she wasn't fazed by it.

"You love that shit."

"That's what your mind is telling you."

"That's what your actions show me." Jude was confident in his sex game. No one could tell him otherwise. Not even his woman. He studied women and knew what to do to their bodies. Two things for certain and one thing for sure, he paid close attention. Therefore, he had something to prove since Tori wasn't aware of it.

"Whenever I caress your body, you get the shivers. When I kiss between your thighs, your body squirms. I can make you cum just like that," he boasted. "And when I tongue kiss that pearl, you lose your marbles. You get wet just by looking at me. Just like you are doing right now."

"Whatever." Tori crossed her legs. He was telling the truth.

Jude laughed out loud. "One time I thought you were having a seizure when I hit that spot."

Tori tooted her nose up. "Ha-ha very funny."

"And we not talking about those fuck faces. Lawd have mercy," he shouted.

"Or your moaning," she giggled.

"I don't moan."

"Yes, you do. I know you heard it."

"Nope. I don't know what you talking about."

"Yeah. Okay."

The car was silent as they pulled into the Star Island Resort and Club. Tori looked at Jude and smiled when she saw the immaculate property and waterfall. "Nice choice."

"I knew you would love it."

"The verdict is still out on that. Looks can be deceiving."

"You'll change your mind once you get inside." He winked at her before shutting off the car. "I guarantee you that."

Tori stood beside Jude as he checked into the resort. Once he was finished, they took the elevator upstairs. Tori walked in and was amazed with the suite. Apparently, he proved her wrong. The king-sized bed, Jacuzzi tub and mirrors beside them is what drew her in automatically. Tori pictured herself showing out and doing tricks in front of the mirror.

"I must say you proved me wrong, sir," she smirked.

"I knew I would." Jude stood behind Tori, while holding her waist. Sweetly, he kissed her neck. "Where do you want to start, in the Jacuzzi or the bed?"

Tori placed her hands over his. "The Jacuzzi, of course."

"When you gone be ready?"

"How soon can you get us a bottle of champagne?"

"Let me call for room service right now." Jude released her and went to the phone to make the call.

Twenty minutes later, there was a knock on the door. Jude took the bottle and tipped the worker before returning to Tori. She was laid across the bed anxiously waiting. Jude held the bottle in the air. "It's time to get wasted, baby." It was about to be a long, eventful night and she was ready for it.

***

Lance sat off in the corner at a bar on the beach, sipping on his drink and watching the crowd. It was full of unfamiliar faces. All walks of life occupied the building. Since he touched back down to the states Lance remained held up in a private condominium close to the beach. Agent Smith had been leaving voicemail messages, trying to find him. That wasn't going too easy, since he disabled the phone. Eventually, he would resurface and pop up at the office. But it wouldn't be for a few more days.

A group of loud women distracted him. When he looked towards the crowd, Lance could see all of them taking shots and dancing. It was obvious they were having a good time. Lance laughed at their wild ways. It actually reminded him of his younger days of partying and hanging with his friends. Most importantly, his girl. Lance shook his head and took another sip of his liquor. It was crazy how life could be perfect at one moment and change for the worst in the matter of seconds.

Lance needed to get his mind right, but the bar wasn't going to help him with that. Opening up his wallet, he removed a fifty-dollar bill and left it on the table. Lance walked through the crowd and exited the bar.

The bright light from the moon glistened against the waves in the ocean. A cool breeze rubbed his face, as he took a nice stroll down A1A, a strip on the beach. The view was beautiful. All he needed was a woman hanging on his arm to make the night complete. Right now, that wasn't an option, but time was winding down slowly but surely. There were a group of loud-talking guys walking towards him. That quickly grabbed his attention. Lance was strapped so he wasn't worried about shit.

The rowdy group of fellas were drunk and shouting loud obscenities to half-dressed females on the opposite side of the street. One dude was so wasted he was stumbling. His friend grabbed his arm and pulled him away from the road.

"Nigga, keep on stumbling yo' ass towards the road and you gone be road kill," one of the men chuckled.

Lance kept it pushing, ignoring the outside distractions. In passing, he bumped shoulders with one of the tipsy fellas.

"Damn, bro, watch where the fuck you going," the dude snapped.

Lance didn't reply, but the mean mug he gave tipsy dude silenced him for several seconds. Lance put his hand behind his back just in case he had to blast on the fools. Tipsy dude finally blinked.

"My bad, fam. I didn't recognize you."

Lance was puzzled. "Nah. You don't know me homie."

"My bad," he apologized again.

Lance nodded his head and turned around. The sudden chatter decreased his pace. He could hear them cackling about their homeboy apologizing. "Nigga, you soft like Charmin."

"Shidd, I thought that was Kilo," Tipsy dude's voice was slurring.

"That nigga been dead. You trippin', bro. Don't give this nigga another pill either." Another dude from the crew spoke up. "If that nigga was alive, Jude wouldn't be banging the shit out of Tori and you can bet that." Lance shook his head and continued on his journey.

***

For the past eighteen hours, Jude fucked Tori in every position throughout the entire suite. There was no stone left unturned. The only time they came up for air was to eat, drink and use the bathroom. It was a wonder she could walk when they took their final break.

Tori moved at a snail's pace as she made her way into the bathroom. Her legs were stiff from being on Jude's shoulders for a long period of time. Tori sat down on the toilet to pee and closed her eyes from the relief her bladder felt. Sleep was out of the question ever since they popped the top on the first bottle of champagne. Three bottles later, she was extremely tired and worn the fuck out. Jude had officially knocked her pussy out of commission. The kitty needed a break. Tori had so many orgasms that she didn't believe another one could surface.

Tori cleaned herself up and washed her hands before making her way back to the bed. Jude was lying on his back with his phone in his hand. Joining him, she laid back and covered her torso with the comforter. Jude sat his phone face down on the nightstand. Then he turned to face her with a beaming smile.

"You ready for round twelve?" he joked.

"Absolutely not," she hissed. "I don't know about you, but we need a break over here. My legs, thighs and pussy sore." Tori laid on her side. "I don't even think I could cum anymore after this."

"Negative," he grinned. "I can definitely make her cum for daddy again." Jude moved closer to her just as his phone vibrated.

Tori looked at him and frowned. "Yeah, if that phone don't keep you busy for the remainder of our trip."

Jude smiled at the little trace of jealousy she displayed. Something she had never done before. But after the way he handed her sexually, it was liable to surface. "Aww! That's cute. My baby jealous. I didn't think you cared."

Tori slapped his arm playfully. "Oh, my gosh. Why would you say that? You know I care about you."

"I know, baby. I'm just joking." Jude picked up his phone and typed another message. "This the last one. I promise."

"It better be."

Jude hit send after the last message was complete and powered off his phone. Turning the screen in Tori's direction, he smiled.

"That's it. I turned it off. Everyone else has to wait until we get back. Now you have me all to yourself."

"That's how it's supposed to be."

"I got you, baby."

Tori pulled him close to her and slipped him some tongue. Attention, love and affection was what she craved, and Jude had no problem providing them all. Round twelve was definitely in the works. Her body still craved his touch.

After one hour of recuperating, the happy couple finally left the room and went downstairs to receive a spa treatment. They both slipped into a robe to enjoy their Swedish massage, as well as a cucumber facial for her. Tori was happy that she agreed to a slight vacation. She was skeptical about going away on such short notice, but the exclusive treatment was worth the disappearance.

The masseuse had hands like an angel. It was relaxing and sensational. Every now and again, a slight moan slipped between Tori's lips. Jude found himself rubber necking to see what was happening on her end. He was enjoying his massage, but it seemed as if too much satisfaction was going on at Tori's table. The male masseuse was so deep into the massage, it seemed like he was enjoying himself a little too much.

"You enjoying my lady over there?" Jude chuckled to keep from coming off so rude.

The guy looked at Jude, but he continued to caress Tori's skin passionately. "No, sir." He nodded. "Just doing my job, that's all."

Tori laid still, but she was able to speak through the face opening on the table. "Ignore him. Baby, enjoy your massage and leave him alone."

"I got my eyes on you." Jude put his head back down and closed his eyes.

After dinner and a long night on the town, the two retired to their room to relax, just after two in the morning. Tori took off her heels and dress, and tossed them onto the chair. "I am tired," she huffed, while flopping down on the bed.

"Lay down and relax. I'll find us something to watch on the television." Jude took off his shoes, dress shirt and pants, before sitting down on the edge of the bed.

Tori's head hit the pillow and she knew it wouldn't be long before she was knocked out. The king-sized bed was so comfortable and soft. The cold air didn't make it any better. Sleep was certainly on the way without a doubt.

With her eyes halfway open, she struggled to watch the movie in front of her. That was when her cellphone rang out disturbing her groove. The set ringtone let her know that it was one of her workers. Which one, she didn't know. It was hard to move, so she just laid there and let it go to the voicemail. That didn't last long because it started ringing again. For someone to be calling that late, it had to be an emergency. Tori sat up and answered the phone.

"What's going on?" she asked.

"Aye, Tori, I know it's late, but I had to call you and let you know what happened."

Tori was wide awake at that point. "What happened?"

"Somebody hit the spot. When I got here, the shit was ransacked. It wasn't too much left in here, but they took what was left."

"And how much was that?"

"Eight of 'em. I was about to get rid of 'em right now. They fucked up the door and shit. It's trashed in here."

"Ain't that a bitch!" she snapped. "If it ain't one thing it's another. I swear." Jude watched Tori in an effort to see what was being said.

"We gone find out who did this shit. When you getting back? I'm going to need your help."

"I can leave now," she blurted out.

"Is everything okay, baby?" Jude asked.

Tori shook her head no. "I need to get back to Lauderdale, like now. It's an emergency at my duplex."

"Baby, do you see what time it is? It's late. We can head out in the morning."

Tori looked down at her screen to check the time. That wasn't what she wanted to do, but she decided to go with what he said. "I'll be there in the morning. In the meantime, just be careful."

"Fa' sho."

"I'll call you as soon as I make it back."

"A'ight." Tori ended the call and rubbed her hand over her face.

"What happened?"

Tori looked up at him and shook her head. "Somebody broke into my duplex and stole some keys from me. I don't know who's behind this, but I'm about to put an end to it."

"How many was taken?" he quizzed.

"Eight."

"I know you mad, baby, but that's not too much of a big loss. It could've been worse." Jude tried to grab her hand, but she moved it.

"Not a big loss? Anything I lose is a loss. I don't care how small it is. That's like throwing one hundred and sixty thousand dollars out the window. I'm in this game to win, not take losses behind some bullshit. I don't fuck with nobody, but shit keep happening."

"You right. I'm sorry. That came out wrong. I'm just saying, it could've been much more than that. Think about it, you just received product. Imagine losing a whole shipment. That's the worst that could've happened."

"Then, on top of that they fucked up my apartment. There's no door on it, so I stand to lose a lot if they really fucked it up."

"Damn." Jude shook his head. "Whatever you wanna do, I'm 'bout that. Who you been beefing with?"

"Nobody. That's the thing that's fucking with me. But I'm thinking that whoever is behind this, is probably behind shooting up my father's funeral."

"I hate to say this, but do you trust the nigga that just called you?" Jude was serious about the question. The vein in his forehead told it all.

"Yeah, I trust him, and I know he had nothing to do with this." Tori was immediately on the defense.

"Are you sure about that?"

"Yes, I'm sure. Why do keep asking me that?" Tori was growing slightly agitated with him within a matter of seconds.

"I'm just asking, baby. This is the dope game. You can't trust everyone and that's a well-known fact."

"Don't you think I know that? I'm not new to this game, Jude. I've been in and around it all my life. I know the risks. It doesn't mean I'm not allowed to be upset."

"You right. I'm sorry."

Tori didn't reply. She just sat there in deep thought.

"Don't you worry, I'm putting an end to all this shit when we get back. I won't sleep until I bury every nigga involved." Jude kissed Tori's forehead. "We can head out early in the morning."

"Thanks." Tori laid back and contemplated on what was happening right before her eyes.

***

The following morning, Jude had Tori back in Lauderdale before noon, as promised. As she walked up to the entrance of the duplex, she spotted the first set of damages. The walk-through of the apartment was even worse. Tori shook her head.

"This the type of shit that pisses me the fuck off." Ace stood at her side listening. "I already know this the work of a fuck nigga. I don't fuck with females like that, so I don't beef with them either."

Jude stood in silence with a mean mug on his face.

"I feel you on that, Boss Lady. You know niggas hate to see a queen in the position you in. They get envious. Greed takes over and that loyalty shit goes out the window." Ace leaned against the counter and studied Jude on a sly tip. "Me and the crew ready for whatever and whoever. These niggas about to feel my wrath, on God."

"I'm ready too," Tori added.

"Nah. Keep those pretty ass hands clean and let us handle your dirty work. You just keep doing you and make these weak ass niggas bow down to the throne."

Tori nodded in agreeance. "I'm about to head out and check on my little one and send someone over to fix this door. Keep me posted."

"Will do boss lady."

Jude walked out the door. Tori exited behind him but was stopped when Ace reached for her arm. "I need to holla at you real quick, in private."

Tori was curious about what he wanted to say. "Jude," she called out. "I'll be right there. I need to use the bathroom first."

Ace pulled out a piece of paper as soon as the door was closed and passed it to her. "What's this?" A funky look crossed her face.

"When I got here, I found that on the floor. Whoever was in here was sent by someone. This wasn't random, Tori. Someone close to you is trying to take you down."

Tori stared at the piece of paper aimlessly, as if the answer to her questions were about to appear.

"You need to think about every person that knows about this spot. Once you figure that out, you'll get your answer." Ace had so much to say, but he wanted to choose his words wisely. Then again, he had never been the type to hold his tongue or sugarcoat the way he felt.

"Aye, Tori."

"Yeah."

"You not gone like what I'm about to say, but you need to hear me out." Ace had her full attention.

"I'm listening."

"That nigga, Jude, I don't trust him. That's why I didn't bring up the note in front of him. He gives me a bad vibe. I know I'm young and everything, but I'm a good judge of character and something ain't right. Keep your eyes open." Tori's silence let him know he had her wheels turning in her head, and that was all a part of the plan.

128

Chapter 16

One week later

Parkland, FL

Tori unlocked the door to her home and stepped back so Capone, Lala and Honcho could enter. Once inside, she locked the door and stood in the middle of the floor. "This is it. My new house," she smiled.

"Damn, sis, this bitch is lit." Honcho had his fist up to his mouth in shock.

Lala looked around the living room with a huge smile on her face. "Sooo, when you throwing a party, girl? You know we have to break this bitch in."

"The verdict is still out on that one. I'll keep you posted."

"I can't believe you bought a damn house and didn't tell nobody." Honcho stated.

"Why not?" Lala laughed. "This the same girl that hid a whole damn child for four years. You know she can keep a two-month secret."

Honcho laughed. "You right about that."

"Y'all gone get off of me," Tori giggled.

"Yoo, I love this fuckin' picture of you and bro." Honcho walked closer to the painting of her and Kilo.

"Damn, I didn't even see that." Lala stood beside her man, checking it out as well. "I know Jude haven't been here."

It was more like a question versus a statement. Lala needed an answer. From what she knew, Jude was too jealous to be constantly reminded of Tori's one true love, who was no longer with her in the physical form. It was bad enough he had to see his face tattooed on her body, a son out the blue, and now a big ass portrait that displayed the love they shared.

"Nope," she popped her lips. "He doesn't know I bought a house. He thinks I live at my daddy's house and that's the way I plan on keeping it."

"For real?" Lala put her hand on her hip. "But isn't he your man? I'm just a little confused," she admitted.

"Fuck that nigga. She ain't gotta tell him shit." Honcho refused to be cordial with Jude. That wasn't happening at all.

Tori thought back to the conversation she had with Ace. His comments had been playing in her head since he spoke his truth. "The verdict is still out on him too. I just don't know what I'm doing right now. It's—" Tori paused when she felt Capone tap her on the leg.

"Mommy, can you give me some juice?"

She looked down at her handsome baby and smiled. "Of course, I can. Come on."

Capone led the way into the kitchen. Tori turned on the light and opened the fridge for him. He reached inside, took out a juice box and handed it to his mother. Tori removed the plastic from the straw, punched a hole in it and handed it back to him.

Tori watched as he sipped away. Every time she looked at him, it was like staring at Kilo. He was certainly his mini-me. Kilo was a huge fan of Jordan and that's the way she dressed him. From the shirt, shorts, socks and shoes. Capone rocked a fat Cuban link chain with a medallion and the letter C, encrusted in diamonds. If he wasn't wearing that necklace, he was wearing a white gold chain with a diamond-cut pendant with a picture of Kilo in it. His father was his guardian angel, so it was only right that he wore him around his neck.

"Do y'all want a drink?" Tori asked.

"We surely do," Lala replied.

Tori took three glasses from the cabinet and sat them down on the table. One by one, she poured Grey Goose into them, followed by a few cubes of ice and some cranberry juice. They all sat down and engaged in small talk. Capone was in his own world. He sat his book bag on the table, took out his coloring book and crayons.

"My lil' nigga serious over there." Honcho chuckled and took a sip from his glass. "Nephew, what you doing down there?"

Capone glanced up briefly from his book. "Coloring."

"Man, he is bruh reincarnated, I swear." Honcho kept his eyes on his nephew. "He left-handed, just like him."

Tori rubbed the waves on the top of his head. "You just realizing he's left-handed?"

"Hell yeah," Honcho exclaimed. "It's different 'cause I'm watching him color. When he was at the house, I peeped how he did a lot of shit with his left hand. I ain't think nothing of it though."

"Who knows?" Tori shrugged. "Maybe he'll use both when he gets older."

The sound of Tori's phone cut their conversation short. She leaned back and grabbed her handbag from the counter. Rummaging through her things, she finally pulled it out. It was Jude.

"Hello."

"What's up, baby? What you doing?" Jude rubbed the top of his head.

"Just sitting here at my father-in-law's house. What's up?" Tori cut her eyes at Lala, as the lie rolled off her tongue.

"I handled that business we discussed last week. How fast can you get to my spot?"

Right away Tori knew exactly what he was talking about. "I'm on my way right now."

"Okay."

Tori ended the call and stood up. "I need y'all to stay here until I come back."

Honcho's brow creased. "What's going on?"

"Jude tracked down the person that hit the duplex. I'm about to go over there and see who it is. It's time to get to the bottom of this. He might be the one who shot up my daddy funeral too." Tori grabbed her bag and threw it on her shoulder.

"Sis, how much does this nigga know? Did you tell him you killed Diesel?" Honcho didn't trust Jude for shit, so he was hoping she wasn't pillow talking with the dude.

"Hell no. Jude doesn't know any of my personal business."

"Does he know about the drug business?" Honcho was ready to twenty-one question her ass to death.

"No. He doesn't." Tori was thrown off by his line of questioning. "What are you getting at?"

"Nothing. I'm just trying to figure out what's up with dude. It's my job to look out for you."

Tori toned down the irritation. "I know. I'm good. He doesn't know a lot. I kept it that way for a reason." Tori placed her hand on his shoulder. "Trust me, I'm good and I'm paying attention to everything."

"My brother would flip if I let something happen to you. You're my sister and I love you."

"I love you too." Tori rushed out the house and jumped en route. She was anxious to see who was behind the hit. Most importantly she was curious to know how Jude found him before her crew did.

Tori arrived at Jude's trap house in under thirty minutes, thanks to the turnpike. During the ride over, she tossed around one hundred possibilities and came up with nothing. Jude was standing on the porch when she arrived. Quickly, she hopped from her vehicle and stood in front of him.

"What happened?" Tori asked.

"My boys were conducting some business with one of my buyers. It was time for a re-up, but he kept saying one of his homies hit for a few keys and he was straight on copping from me."

Jude stuck his hands in his pockets and looked blankly towards the road. "They had the work on the table. My lil dawg saw it and recognized your packaging. He didn't say shit. He just left and hit me up. I caught the nigga slipping and snatched his ass up."

"Where is he now?"

Jude nodded towards the house. "He in here. Come on."

Tori followed Jude inside. Sitting in the living room was a dude tied up to a chair. His shirt was covered in blood. "Is he dead?"

"Nah. Not yet. I wanted you to see him first." Jude walked over and pulled the pistol from his waist. Using his left hand, he smacked the dude across his face. "Getcho bitch ass up!"

Tori studied his face to see if she knew him. He looked familiar, but she couldn't place him anywhere near her. Being that she didn't know him personally, it meant someone sent him at her. But *who,* was the question. Tori approached him and stopped directly in front of him. "Who sent you?" The guy shook his head and grunted, but he didn't open his mouth. "Who sent you to rob my spot? I suggest you answer, because it only gets worse from here."

Jude stepped up beside her. "He can't talk."

Tori was caught off guard. "What do you mean he can't talk?"

Jude grabbed his jaw and shook it. "I cut that bitch tongue out. See, he can't talk. When I questioned him, he wouldn't answer me. I had to show him I was serious, so I cut it off and put it in his pocket."

Tori was furious. "Why though? How am I supposed to find out who behind this shit if this muthafucka can't talk?"

"Baby, the most important thing is, he can nod. So, ask him yes or no questions. Come on now, you not new to this." The dude was going in and out of consciousness, so Jude smacked him awake.

"Aye, Mike. Open your eyes," he shouted. Mike's eyes fluttered open. "Did you rob my lady's spot? Nod your head for yes. Shake it for no."

Mike nodded his head.

"Did someone hire you?" Jude questioned him again.

Mike nodded once more.

"Did you shoot up Diesel's funeral?"

Mike shook his head no.

"Do you have any more questions, baby?"

Tori shook her head no. It was pointless to speak with someone who didn't have a tongue to speak. Without warning, Jude raised his gun and pulled the trigger. Mike's brain matter flew midair, as his body went limp.

"Oh yeah, I took your work back too." Jude's smile was devious. "I told you I would handle that for you. It's in that duffle bag on the sofa. Grab that and get out of here, so I can get this mess cleaned up. Tori picked up the bag and left. His actions left her with mixed emotions. Jude made her a promise and he executed it. *How could I not trust a man that would kill for me?* That ran through her mind as she drove back home.

Chapter 17

Two months later

What was supposed to be the honeymoon stage of their relationship after being separated for so long, turned out to be nothing but a nightmare on Elm Street. Day in and day out, all Tron and Tweety did was argue, fight and fuck. The fucking only came after Tron beat her ass and left her battered and bruised. Quite frankly, Tweety was tired of being in World War III. She was finally having regrets about being with Tron in the first place.

Tweety desperately wanted to call it quits but couldn't find it in her heart to do so. The walking away would be easy, especially after the way he'd been mistreating her over and over again. It was the *"I told you so,"* part that she didn't want to hear. She would rather front in public and cry in private.

From day one, Tweety had been told that she wanted what Dazzle had. Lala for that matter, too. Her eyes been on Honcho, but he didn't want her. Rejection was what she couldn't deal with. It really fucked with her self-esteem.

In her twisted mind, Tweety was certain she could make an honest man out of Tron, to turn him into the man that she wanted him to be. There wasn't a shred of doubt that Tron would treat her the way he did Dazzle. After being out for a short period time, Tweety was hit with a rude awakening. Tron treated her ten times worse than he did Dazzle. That's what happened when karma showed up and out.

Instead of putting him out like her mind kept telling her, Tweety followed her misleading heart and ignored her brain. Not to mention, the obvious signs. Deep down inside that dark, treacherous heart, she felt defeated, used and abused. That part of her life was classified information and she refused to share that with anyone. To everyone else's knowledge, they were a happy couple on the outside. The inside was a different story.

Tweety had mixed feelings. She wanted the relationship to work because if it didn't, that meant she lost her best friends for nothing. Tweety was losing her sanity behind a man that didn't give two fucks about the way she felt. She hadn't smiled in months, trying to prove to another woman that she wasn't going anywhere. The sad part about it was, Dazzle had a real man that provided for her and her child. That was something Tron didn't do.

Tweety sat on the sofa, flipping through a magazine, wondering how and why everything went sideways. She waited on Tron to come home for three years and once he got comfortable, he gave her his ass to kiss. Just then Tron walked out the room dressed in a pair of sweatpants and no shirt. Fresh scratches covered the upper part of his body, but Tweety couldn't decipher if it was from their fight or another woman. His actions proved he was sleeping with someone else, but she ignored all the signs. Tweety had a feeling it was Mya, due to the distance Mya placed between them since his release.

Tron had tunnel vision when he walked through the living room and into the kitchen. He acted as if he didn't see her sitting there. Tweety sat the magazine down on the coffee table and took a deep breath, as she waited on him to return. Tweety could feel the argument before it started.

"Tron, we need to talk."

"For what?"

"Is that a real question?" She exhaled deeply.

Tron was instantly irritated, and the conversation hadn't started yet. "What do you want to talk about?" he asked, with his back turned towards her.

"Us. What are we doing?"

"I don't know."

"Tron, can you at least look at me?"

"For what? Just talk."

"See, this is exactly what I'm talking about. You don't respect me. Whenever I try to have a conversation with you, you act like I'm getting on your nerves."

Tron turned full circle to face her. "You do get on my nerves. Now what? What do you plan on doing about that?"

Tweety shook her head. "I can't believe you."

"Believe what? You wanted to talk, so talk without doing all that damn crying. A nigga don't wanna hear that shit all the time. Damn!"

Tweety felt daggers pierce her heart. That was not the man she fell in love with. Prison certainly changed him and not for the better. "You treat me like a bitch off the street. Like I didn't sit around and ride a three-year bid with you when no one else was there for you."

Tron grabbed the bridge of his nose. "See that's where you wrong at. But let me make this crystal clear," he pointed his finger in her direction. "You were NOT the only person there for me. Every time I turn around, you bringing up what you did for a nigga. Like damn, what the fuck you want in return?"

"You always blowing shit out of proportion."

"And you always throwing what you did back in my face. Last time I checked, I've been helping you since I got back on my feet. I'm not sitting around living off of you. I pay all the bills in this bitch."

Tweety rolled her eyes. "I never said you didn't. All I'm saying is that I've been there and look at how you treat me. I wonder how you would treat me if I let you sit in there by yourself."

"The same way I do now." Tron moved closer to her. "You so stuck on yourself that you don't realize I act like this because of you. From the day I got home, you've been stressing me the fuck out and I'm sick of it. Yeah, you rode with a nigga, but I would've survived without you too. So, don't get it twisted."

"That's easy to say when you free, but you were singing a different tune when you were behind that wall. All you did was sell me a fake ass dream. You probably sold the same dreams to other bitches too."

"What, you want your money back?" Tron dug inside his pants pocket and pulled out a wad of money. Removing the rubber band, he peeled off several hundreds and threw them at her. A few bills hit her in the face and the others hit the floor. "There's some of it. I hope that makes you feel better. I can't wait to get up out this bitch."

Tron went into the room and put on a shirt. Kicking off his slides, he laced up a pair of Air Max's and snatched his wallet from the dresser. His cellphone was next to his car keys. He grabbed them both and headed out. Tweety stood up. "Where are you going?"

"Don't worry about it." Tron grabbed the doorknob, but before he could open it, Tweety grabbed his arm.

"You not going anywhere," she screamed, while forcing a space between Tron and the door.

"You wanna bet?"

"That's all you do when we argue. You won't even try to communicate with me." At that point, Tweety's eyes were wet from the tears. "I'm going through something and you haven't noticed. I've been losing weight and you haven't asked why. That shows me how much you really care about me."

"I can't do this with you. It's too much. You too much for me and I'm tired." Tron pushed Tweety to the side and opened the door. "I'm gone, man."

Tweety fell to the floor and cried hard and loud. She was in pain. The world around her fell and exploded. There was a secret she had been keeping from Tron, and it was killing her on the inside. The worse part of it all was that he didn't even notice.

Tron blew off steam as he took the stairs to the lower level. Once in the parking lot, he popped the locks on his Impala and climbed inside. He was able to push the work fast and snatch up some wheels. The dope game was sweet. Too bad his relationship wasn't. But that was about to change quick, fast and in a goddamn hurry. He was at his wit's end with Tweety, and he wanted out of the dysfunctional ass relationship. Before pulling out the parking lot, he hit up Mya.

"Hey baby," she squealed into the phone.

"What you doing?"

"At the playground pushing AJ on the swings."

"Did y'all eat yet?"

"Earlier. Why?"

"I'm on my way over there. What do you want to eat?"

"Umm, I don't know. Just get anything."

"Alright now, I asked you first. Don't complain when I get there." Tron's line beeped in his ear. "Hold up. Let me see who calling." It was the one person he didn't want to talk to. "Here she go with the bullshit." Tron rejected the call.

"Who was that?" Mya asked, already knowing the answer.

"You already know. I'm so sick of this bitch."

"Yeah right." Mya rolled her eyes.

"Dead ass. It's a wrap, so I hope you ready for me to move in."

"I been ready. I'm waiting on you, remember?" Mya stood behind AJ while he climbed up the slide. "But you have your many reasons why you have to stay."

"That's over with. Before my homie Mike got killed, he introduced me to his partner, Jude. I'll be copping work from him, so I don't need her ass no more."

Mya's smile was bright as the afternoon sun. "So, when you leaving?"

"In a few days. I have to go back and get my shit. We was arguing before I left, so I didn't get a chance to grab nothing."

"I told you to leave some stuff over here, but you don't listen to me. Just stop at Walmart on your way here and grab some stuff."

"You good for something besides running that mouth of yours," Tron chuckled.

"Whatever," she smacked her lips.

"Do you need anything for the house since I'm going?"

"Pick up some wipes, and pull-ups for AJ to sleep in."

"A'ight. I'm pulling in. I'll see you in a little bit."

"Okay."

Tron ended the call and turned off the car. Just as he was about to get out, a familiar face walked past. He was taken aback by her appearance. Quickly getting out the car, he followed the woman. By the time she climbed inside, he was standing at her door.

"What's up baby mama?"

Dazzle's heart skipped a beat when she saw his face. She hadn't seen Tron since the day he raped her. "What do you want, Tron?"

"Damn, I can't speak to you and see how you doing?"

"I'm fine. You should be asking about your son and not me." Dazzle started her car, but Tron stepped closer. "Can you move so I can leave?"

"I heard you were missing, what happened?"

"None of your business."

"It's definitely my business, since your nigga hid in my car and pistol whipped me, because he thought I did something to you." Fresh never disclosed that information to her, so she didn't know if she should believe him or not. "I don't know what you talking about."

"He knows. Ask him."

"I will."

Tron reached into Dazzle's car and touched her stomach. His touch made her cringe. Swatting his hand away, she tried to close the door. "Don't touch me."

"So, you pregnant, huh?"

"Why is that your business?"

"I need to know if that's my baby." Tron rested his foot on the car frame.

"I don't know why you think that?"

"We had sex three months ago, girl. Did you forget that?"

Dazzle looked Tron directly in the face for the first time. "No, we didn't. You raped me. Did you forget that?"

"We had consensual sex and I nutted in that pussy. Besides, we both know if it was rape, you would've called the police on me." Tron was so delusional that he believed his own lies.

"Something is really wrong if you think I volunteered to have sex with you, after you been fucking Tweety."

"I'm not with her anymore."

"Good for you. I don't give a fuck," she spat coldly.

"You better tell me what I wanna know before I show my ass out here and I'm not playing with you." Tron threatened.

"And you better back away from my car before I start screaming out here." Dazzle looked around the parking lot to see if anybody was nearby, just in case something happened.

"Just answer my question. Is that my baby?" Dazzle kept her mouth shut. "If you don't tell me, I'll just ask yo nigga."

"Tron, this is not your baby. Just leave me alone and move on with your life."

"How can I just move on like that? How could you move on like that? You know how much I love you."

"Tron, please. You do not love me."

Tron smirked, "Do you still love me?"

"No, I don't. Now, go play with Tweety. I'm finally happy and you not about to ruin that." Dazzle's phone rang, but she didn't bother to look at it. She already knew it was Fresh calling to check on her. When she decided to go to the store alone, he contested it. Fresh didn't want her anywhere alone. Tron was the prime example of why.

"That's yo' nigga? Let me talk to him." Tron was determined to harass her at any cost.

"Tron, move out the way. I need to get home."

"Why, that nigga gone beat yo' ass or some shit?"

Dazzle shook her head. It was best that she said nothing at all. But when she saw a patrol car on the next aisle, it made her bold. "First of all, my man is nothing like you. He has never and I mean never, put his hands on me, unlike you. I have a real man in my life for my kids. He took care of your son, when you wasn't helping me do shit. When I almost lost my apartment because of you, he paid my rent and said you had to go. That's why I put your sorry ass out. Now go play in five o'clock traffic on I-95."

Tron's clenched down on his teeth. Rage was starting to take over his body and he wanted to beat her ass. Tron balled up his fist, preparing to knock her lights out. Dazzle peeped the sudden change in his demeanor. Before he could do anything, the patrol car creeped in front of them. That was her chance to get away. Dazzle laid on the horn. The patrol car stopped abruptly. Tron knew it was time to go. Before he walked off, he shot Dazzle an evil glare.

"Listen here, bitch, you gone pay for what you did. I promise you won't get comfortable. I'm going to make your life a living hell until I find out the paternity of that child. And bitch, you better pray it ain't mine." Tron stepped away and walked towards the store's entrance, plotting on ways to ruin Dazzle's life.

Chapter 18

Valentine's Day

Jude opened the passenger door to the brand-new Mercedes Benz ML350 he purchased for Tori. "I can't believe you bought me a truck, and it's the one I wanted at that." She couldn't hide the excitement in her voice even if she tried. Tori sat down on the soft leather seat and placed her bag between her feet.

Happy he was able to put a smile on her face, he kissed her cheek. "I'll buy you whatever you want, as long as I can see that beautiful smile forever."

Tori sat back and got comfortable for the surprise. For years, she despised Cupid's Day. They held such bittersweet moments. That was the day she married her one true love and was just about to reveal her pregnancy, before he was taken away from her and their child forever. Once that happened, she vowed never to celebrate that day again and for years she kept that promise. Today, all of that changed.

For weeks, Jude had been begging Tori to celebrate Lover's Day with him. Each time he asked, she declined. Jude was persistent. On the twentieth day of him begging, she agreed. But only after hearing him preach a sermon about moving on and creating new memories with him. Jude expressed the hurt and pain he felt of not being able to celebrate one of his favorite holidays with her.

Of course, it made her feel bad. Especially after he exacted a deadly revenge against Mike. The man that broke into her duplex and stole her work. Ever since Jude sent a message all of Tori's beef died down, allowing her to run a smooth operation with him at her side. Since then they'd been rocking hard and getting money like it was going out of style. So, going out with him and making her man happy was only fair.

Jude drove them out to a country club in Boca Raton. It wasn't the surprise Tori was expecting, but she was grateful for his effort, nonetheless. Who knew, maybe the night would turn out to be a magical one. Tori stepped from the truck dressed in a black slim-fit, lace Chanel dress, looking like a runway model. Jude complimented her style with a black and white Tom Ford suit. As they approached the venue it made sense as to why they were all dressed up. The crowd of men and women on the inside were dressed to the nines as well.

The setup was nice and it looked like a fancy dinner party was going on. Tori brushed it off and decided that since she was in attendance, she might as well enjoy the night. For the next two hours, they enjoyed a delicious steak dinner, dessert and champagne. To her surprise, the occupants of the party were Jude's family members on his father's side. The DJ was spinning hit after hit and everyone was on the dance floor. There wasn't a stiff body in the room.

Tired and sweaty, Tori excused herself and went to the bathroom to freshen up. The air conditioning had to be on full blast because it was cold, but it felt good. Once she was dry and refreshed, Tori made her way back to Jude. Upon her arrival, the ballroom was quiet and everyone was seated. Mr. Simmons, Jude's father was up on stage giving a speech about family, love and growth. It was touching.

"At this time, I would like to call up my beautiful wife of forty years to the stage and our one and only son."

Tori watched as Jude escorted his mother to the stage. It was crazy how his persona was completely different in the presence of his family. True enough, he was sweet, but Tori knew a killer lived underneath the mask he was wearing. Once they were up on stage, Mr. Simmons was back on the mic.

"I remember when I met this woman many years ago at a party. The moment I laid eyes on her I knew I wanted to spend the rest of my life with her. We dated for four months before I asked her to marry me. My friends and family thought I was crazy because we weren't together that long. They said we wouldn't make it six months but look at us, forty years later."

Mr. Simmons looked at his wife with so much love in his eyes. They were like teenagers all over again. Tori could see they had a genuine love for one another. It made her wonder if that was the way she and Kilo would've turned out. Tori could feel the tears gracing her pupils, but she quickly wiped them away.

"We received a lot of doubt throughout the course of our marriage. We were even given the most devastating news about being unable to conceive children. At first, we gave up all hope, but after my wife's forty-second birthday and twenty years of marriage, our great God from up above blessed us with our son Jude. We named him Jadiah, which means 'Messenger of God's will.' That was the happiest day of our lives."

The crowd looked on and shed tears.

"Before I talk y'all to death, let me get to the purpose of this special dinner." Jude reached into his pocket and handed his father a box. "Janet, my love, I planned this evening just for you. I want to know if you would take my hand in marriage one more time."

Janet smiled and said yes. Jude took the mic so his father could place the ring on his mother's finger. Tori was elated that Jude included her in such a special event. Their future was looking brighter by the day.

A loud sound came from the mic before Jude started to speak to the crowd. "I would like to thank everyone for coming out and sharing this special moment with my parents. We really appreciate it. However, this concludes the dinner. But, before you go, I would like to introduce a special lady in my life. Come up here, baby."

Tori wasn't shy by nature, but to be put on the spot wasn't what she was expecting. Sucking it up, Tori rose to her feet and joined Jude on stage. Facing the crowd, she smiled as he continued to speak. "Family, I would like you all to meet my lady, Tori."

The crowd started to shout and clap. When Tori turned to face Jude, he was down on one knee with a diamond ring in his hand. At that moment she completely froze. Tori could see his mouth moving, but she couldn't hear a single word. When she finally came to, she could hear his voice.

"Tori, I love you. Would you be my wife?"

Tori stood there a few seconds longer before bursting into tears and running off the stage. She didn't know where she was headed. Tori just wanted out of the awkward situation. That had to be the most embarrassing moment of her life. Finding her truck, she stood beside it and cried.

In between the crying she could hear Jude's voice getting closer and closer. Jude unlocked the truck door and helped her climb inside. The stunt she pulled had him stunned. "Tori, what's wrong?" he asked.

Tori shook her head. "Take me home."

"Tell me what's wrong. Why did you run out of there?"

"If you have to ask, then you don't know me at all." Tori sniffled and wiped her face with a napkin.

"Baby, I'm asking you." Jude grabbed her hand. "Just tell me, what's wrong?"

Tori turned to face him. "Why would you propose to me like that?"

"What do you mean?"

"Valentine's Day. You know how I feel about today. I stressed that to you repeatedly. We've gone through this and you would propose to me on this particular day." Tori was fuming. The night didn't turn out to be magical at all.

"So, let me get this straight. This is about Kilo?" Jude gnashed his teeth when she nodded her head with a boatload of tears drowning her face. The woman that he loved was in love with another man. A man she could no longer have. Not only did that fuck with his heart, it dismantled his pride. Kilo was dead and gone and he still held the torch that lit her heart.

"Wow." He nodded. "You're upset with me because I proposed to you on the day your ex-husband died? What kind of shit is that, Tori?" Jude was yelling at this point. When he looked to the right, he could see his family walking out. Not in the mood to explain what just occurred, Jude left the golf course in a hurry. Once they were off the property, he repeated his questions again.

Tori's eyes stayed on the road. She couldn't stand to look at him. Not even for a second. "When I met you, I told you what I was going through. You know his death was hard on me. Four years after his death I was still wearing that ring. I asked you was that a problem and you said no."

"How long have we been together? I've shown you love repeatedly. I was there for you when your father was killed, when your friend was kidnapped, and I rode hard for you when that nigga robbed you. That's a murder charge. If I would've got caught, I would've been locked up for life, trying to prove my love to you. And for you to downplay my feelings like they don't matter is fucked up."

Tori leaned back further into the seat with her lips locked.

"It's like I'm competing with a fuckin' ghost. A nigga that ain't never coming back. You can't get close to me, because you still holding on to him."

The remainder of the car ride was silent until Tori's phone rang. The number wasn't programmed in her phone, so she ignored it. That didn't help because it rang again. Tori answered just in case it was one of her workers.

"Who is this?" she answered snappily.

"Ms. Price or should I say Mrs. Kingsley, how is the world treating you?" the man asked.

"Who is this?" she repeated.

"Don't you recognize my voice?"

Tori's pressure was already through the roof. Therefore, she didn't have time for prank calls. "Listen, if you don't tell me who this is, I'm hanging up."

"It's Detective Andrews. Now, before you hang up, tell me this. How much is your freedom worth?"

"My freedom? What are you talking about?" Tori questioned.

Her comment definitely caught his attention. Jude looked at her, but she shook her head no, as if trying to keep him quiet. Tori put the phone on speaker, so he could hear.

"If you want to stay out of prison, you need to get me fifty thousand dollars in the next few hours," Terrell demanded.

"That's short notice. I need more time than that." Tori was trying to stall him out. Being extorted wasn't in her bible to the dope game.

"I need fifty thousand dollars within the next few hours. If you can't make that happen, then you'll be hearing the metal door close behind you, while you await trial in a maximum federal prison."

Jude shook his head and mouthed the words, *do it.*

"Okay. Okay. I can get it. Just give me a location."

"Just get the money and I'll be in touch in a few hours. And remember, your freedom is riding on this."

Tori sat the phone on her lap after Terrell disconnected the call. In deep thought, she folded her arms and took a deep breath. If it wasn't one thing, it was another. First that whack ass proposal and now this. Jude powered on the stereo and turned the volume up loud to make sure she heard the lyrics to "Comfortable," by Lil Wayne.

"I'm not saying this to shake you up. I'm just saying this to wake you up. It's all good when we making love. All I ask is don't take our love for granted, cause granted, my love for you is real. Baby, if you don't love me somebody else will, so baby girl, don't you ever get too comfortable."

When they arrived at Jude's apartment, he parked the truck in front of his building and left it running. Turning off the stereo, he looked at Tori. "When you get the address to the location, send it to me. Take one of your hittas with you when you meet up with that slimy ass detective."

Tori was lost. Although he was upset, she figured he would accompany her to do the drop off. Instead of questioning him, she nodded her head.

"I'm going to get the money back from him and that's it. You won't see me. I'm going to take some time for myself. You do the same, because we're not on the same page about our feelings."

"How are you planning to get it back?"

"Don't worry about it. I'm going to handle it." Jude grabbed his phone from the cup holder, his gun from underneath the seat and opened the door. "I'll let you know when it's done, so I can tell you where to get the money from."

"Aren't you going to have it?"

"Nah. I'll have one of my boys meet you. Be careful." Jude stepped out the car and left Tori in her thoughts.

Detective Andrews sent Tori to a location at ten o'clock that morning. He wanted to make sure she had enough time to get his money together. The one hundred thousand dollars he received previously was for bringing Dazzle back in one piece. The fifty grand was to keep him from locking her ass up.

Detective Andrews had Tori meet him at a local gas station. His instructions were precise, *park next to the air pump and wait.* For the exchange, Tori recruited Ace to join her, just in case it was a set-up. Backed in at the pump, they sat quietly. Jude was parked at the gas pump waiting. They hadn't spoken since last night, but he was present.

For the next few minutes, they watched every car, truck and van that entered the gas station come and go. Just as she was getting antsy, the familiar black car pulled in and parked beside them. Ace had the choppa on his lap, just in case some shit popped off.

Terrell got out of the unmarked car and climbed into the backseat. "Good morning, Mrs. Kingsley," he smirked deviously.

Tori rolled her eyes. She hated law enforcement with a passion, but what she hated most was an Uncle Tom ass nigga. That shit made her skin crawl. Therefore, she was in no mood for pleasantries.

"All of it is in the bag. I hope that meets your demands."

Detective Andrews took a stack of bills out the bag and sniffed it hard. "Most definitely. Until the next time," he chuckled. "I'm glad to see you take your freedom seriously. I would hate to send your pretty ass to prison."

Ace raised his choppa in the air so he could see it. "Aye, we ain't doing no disrespecting up in here. Grab your money and bounce, fuck nigga."

Tori turned her body towards the backseat so he could see her face and the darkness in her eyes. "I don't know what your game plan is, but after today, don't call me again. You've received more than enough money from me and I'm not doing this again."

Detective Andrews stuck the money back in the bag and stared up at Tori. "If you want to run a smooth operation, you'll continue to make me happy."

Tori raised her phone and pressed play. "If you don't want this recording leaked to the media, you'll leave me the fuck alone. So again, make this your last time hitting my phone."

Ace lowered his gun when Detective Andrews stepped out the vehicle and got into his car. Tori watched as Jude trailed Detective Andrews from the gas station.

Chapter 19

For the past few days Jude had his work cut out for him. Aside from hustling, he had been watching Detective Andrews' every move. Jude knew where he worked, lived, who he was cheating with and the days he cheated. For him to be on the force, the detective wasn't too sharp if he could be easily followed. Jude sat in his car patiently until the coast was clear. Once all the neighbors disappeared into their homes, Jude exited his car and walked into the backyard. It didn't take long for him to break into the home after smashing the glass with a gloved hand.

Jude walked through the house with his gun clutched in his hand and finger on the trigger. As he tiptoed throughout the dwelling, he moved quickly and quietly. The sound of the shower running sent him into the master bedroom. Jude observed the silhouette and slid the door open.

Marsha released a high-pitched scream, while holding her perky breasts with the palms of both hands. "What the fuck are you doing in here?"

Jude smirked while tapping his finger on the gun that rested in his right hand. "Just checking out the merchandise."

Marsha's eyes zeroed in on the weapon clutched in his hand. From her years of experience with the force, he wasn't a burglar. That crime didn't fit his appearance. "Please don't rape me. I'll give you whatever you want."

Jude chuckled and stroked the hair on his chin. "You think that's what I want? Bitch, don't flatter yourself."

"Well, what do you want?" she asked again.

"Get out the shower and I'll tell you."

Marsha leaned forward and turned off the water. Jude leaned forward to get a peek from the back. The drops of water sliding down her ass cheeks had his attention for a moment. When Marsha turned around, she noticed Jude licking his lips. He was definitely intrigued.

"See something you like?" Marsha moved her hands slowly, revealing her bare breasts, in hopes to keep him distracted and turn the tables on his ass.

"Not really," he grinned.

Marsha stepped from the tub, grabbed a towel and wrapped it around her body. "Your eyes tell a different story."

Jude waved his gun at her. "Get in the room." He then followed Marsha into her bedroom. "Grab your cellphone."

Marsha picked up her phone from the dresser. "What do you want me to do?"

"Call that nigga, Terrell." Jude pointed his gun at her.

Marsha shook her head. Something told her that Terrell's ass was the reason for the surprise visit. Highly irritated, she dialed his number and waited for him to pick up.

"Hello."

"There's a—" Jude snatched the phone away from her.

"Detective Andrews," Jude snickered.

"Who is this?" Terrell asked.

"No, no. You don't get to ask questions." Jude let it be known that he was not in control.

"Well, how can I help you?"

"I'ma need you to get over here before I hurt your bitch." He kept his eyes on Marsha.

"That's not necessary. I'll be right there." Terrell busted a U-turn at the light.

"Oh, and bring that fifty thousand dollars you took from my bitch the other day."

"What?" Terrell wasn't sure if he heard him correctly.

"You heard me right. Bring that money you took from Tori and I'm not fuckin' around with you. Yo' ass have thirty minutes to get here with that cash or I'm blasting this bitch."

"O-kay, o-kay. I'm on my way," Terrell stuttered.

"If you call anybody, I swear, your wife and kids are dead too. All I have to do is send the word."

"I won't call anyone. I promise." Terrell made his way back to the stash house to get the money he got from Tori. "Just don't hurt her please."

"Oh, I'm not gone hurt her. I might fuck her though," Jude chuckled, as he ended the call.

That comment made Marsha nervous. She sat down on the bed and put her back against the wall. Jude could see the fear in her eyes and in her fidgety behavior.

"Chill out. I'm not gone touch you." Jude put her cellphone inside of his back pocket. "I just need his cooperation."

Marsha heard his reasoning, but she wasn't completely sold on the matter. Whatever would save her life, she was with it. Marsha rubbed her arms rapidly. The cold air from the A/C unit produced chill bumps on her skin.

"May I put on some clothes please? I'm freezing."

"Go ahead." Jude watched closely as she opened the drawer and pulled out a sweater.

Marsha's eyes were on the small caliber handgun tucked off to the side, next to her panties. The move was far too risky being that he was standing right there with his gun locked, loaded and aimed in her direction. Out of fear of him catching her, Marsha pulled out a pair of sweatpants and closed the drawer. Her assailant's eyes were glued to her body. It was an uncomfortable feeling for her. Removing the towel, she quickly slipped into her garments.

"Come on." Jude nodded his head towards the door. "Let's wait for him downstairs."

"Okay," she agreed and led the way.

Marsha's heart was beating hard against her chest. It felt as if it would explode at any given moment. Silently, she prayed the ordeal would be over as soon as Terrell arrived.

"Have a seat over there." Jude pointed to the sofa that sat against the window. Once she was seated, her captor sat in the loveseat on the opposite side of the room.

Jude kept an intimidating, evil scowl on his face to keep her in line. Marsha did her best not to stare. Periodically, he checked the time on his watch. Twenty minutes had passed and the shady detective still hadn't arrived. Pulling out her cell, Jude called Terrell back. As expected, he picked up on the first ring.

"Hello."

"What's taking so long? I'm running out of patience." Jude's tone of voice was low, but hard.

"I'm driving as fast as I can," Terrell replied in a panic. "I'll be there in less than five minutes."

"When you get inside, have your gun in your hand so I can see it. I don't have to tell you what will happen because I already did that."

"I got it, man. I swear."

"You better."

Two minutes later, Detective Andrews pulled up in the driveway. Jude spotted him immediately. "Come here."

Marsha inched towards him like she was about to get an ass whooping from her father. Jude wrapped his forearm around her neck and placed the barrel of the gun against her temple. "You better hope your little boyfriend doesn't try no slick shit. 'Cause if he does," Jude licked the side of her face. "I'll kill yo' thick ass."

Marsha took a deep breath and did her best to remain calm. "I've done everything you asked me to do. Don't kill me on the account of him. Kill him instead." Her focus was on saving her own skin.

"I'll keep that in mind." The locks could be heard disengaging. Jude bit down on his bottom lip and waited on the detective to hit the corner. He didn't know what to expect, but he was prepared to bust his gun.

***

Ever since Dazzle ran into Tron, she had been unable to shake the words thrown at her. In the back of her mind, Dazzle knew that wouldn't be the last conversation she had with him about her pregnancy. Nothing would make him happier than to ruin the best relationship she'd ever had.

154

Tender aches pattered in Dazzle's heart, as she thought of a million ways to tell Fresh the truth. Tears dropped from her eyes like raindrops onto the pillow. Of course, Dazzle didn't want to come clean, but if Fresh didn't hear it from her, that would ruin their relationship without a shadow of a doubt. It would also destroy the trust they established from day one. A lifetime with Fresh was what she aimed for and Tron was not about to ruin that. Dazzle's body trembled when she heard the bathroom door open.

Fresh walked out wearing only a towel. For the past few days, Dazzle had been in bed with morning sickness. So, he made it his business to make her as comfortable as possible. "Baby, are you awake?" he asked while applying lotion to his body.

"Yeah," she spoke softly with a slight sniffle.

Automatically, that caught his attention. Fresh put on his boxers and wife beater before walking to her side of the bed. Sitting down he observed a face full of fresh tears. Off the bat, he assumed it was the pregnancy. "Damn, bae, the baby putting a whooping on you already. Do you need something?"

Dazzle rocked back and forth. "No."

Fresh placed his hand on her belly. "Take it easy on Mommy 'cause you killing her right now." He then rubbed her forehead gently. "Were you like this with Jamir?"

"No."

"Let me find out you having a girl," he sighed. "I need another son. My daughter already a handful and she in another state."

The guilt was eating away at Dazzle. There was no way she could go another day lying to him. It just didn't feel right. Taking a deep breath, she exhaled slowly. "I'm sorry."

Fresh was confused by the apology. "What are you sorry for?"

"I need to tell you something and you're going to be so mad at me." Dazzle blinked several times before grabbing his hand. "Please don't leave me," she begged. "I love you so much."

Fresh didn't know what she was about to reveal. All he knew was that cheating better not had been involved. If that was the case, it was a wrap for them. Infidelity wasn't something he tolerated, especially since he wasn't doing it. From day one, he showed Dazzle and Jamir, nothing but love. When Fresh decided to be in a committed relationship with Dazzle, he took Jamir in as a son.

Fresh said the first thing that came to mind. "What did you do?"

The slick tone in his voice frightened her. Dazzle knew for a fact her confession was about to cause problems in her happy home. She just hoped it wasn't something they couldn't get past as a loving couple.

"Promise me you won't leave me."

"I can't promise you that without knowing what you talking about." He exhaled and rubbed his temple. "Dazzle, just please tell me what's going on."

It was too late to turn back. Dazzle put her fear to the side. Regardless of how he reacted, she wasn't going to let him go. She was prepared to fight for the love of her life.

"Do you remember when Tron came home a few months back?"

Fresh lowered his gaze, so he could look her in the eyes. Just the sound of Tron's name angered him. Immediately he thought the worst and snatched his hand away. "Don't tell me you fucked that nigga. 'Cause if you did, it's over. I swear to God."

"Just listen to me," she pleaded before continuing the story.

Fresh sat in silence, as he listened to the full account of what happened between Tron and his girl. The attack was vicious. His trigger finger started to itch. Fresh wanted to run down on Tron at that very moment, but then an important factor came to mind. He looked at her with uncertainty in his eyes.

"Is the baby mine?"

Dazzle lost her breath for several seconds. That was the one question she hoped to avoid. The fury in his eyes made her rethink the response. He didn't have to say it, but she felt it in her heart that if she wasn't certain, he was going to leave her.

"Yes," she stated through tears.

"How can you be so certain?"

"Baby," she whined. "I know my body. This baby is yours. I swear it is."

Fresh was beyond furious. His nostrils flared like a bull. In his vision all he could see is red. Fresh flew into a fit of rage and knocked multiple items from the dresser onto the floor. "Fuck!" he shouted in agony.

Dazzle damn near jumped out of her skin. "Baby, stop please," she cried. "I'm sorry."

"I can't believe you."

"Me?" Dazzle sat up with her hand on her chest.

"Yeah, you." Fresh was so close to her, she felt his breath on her face. "I told you to stay away from that nigga. You probably fucked him willingly."

Dazzle was hurt by his reaction. Not once had she cheated on Fresh. That was never a thought. And for him to think that she would stoop so low was like a slap in the face. Dazzle hauled off and smacked Fresh in the face for the first time.

"Fuck you," she screamed. "I never cheated on you."

Since they became a couple, domestic violence was never an issue. Therefore, she didn't know how he would react to the slap. Dazzle stood there nervously. But was quickly surprised when Fresh threw on a pair of basketball shorts and left the room. To hear the love of her life accuse her of cheating, and not taking her side, made Dazzle feel lower than the day she was raped. The morning sickness had her weak. Dazzle laid back down and wrapped herself in the blanket.

***

Detective Andrews stopped in place, dropped the duffle bag on the floor and put his hands in the air. The sight of Marsha being held at gunpoint put knots in his stomach. Droplets of sweat on her forehead showcased her fear.

"My weapon is in the holster on my hip," Terrell informed him.

Jude put a round in the chamber. Marsha closed her eyes when she heard the click. "I see you don't follow directions."

"I know. I know, but I couldn't get out with my gun in my hand while the neighbor was outside. That looks suspicious. But I can reach down slowly and give it to you."

"Slowly," Jude stated through clenched teeth.

Detective Andrews eased his right hand down and retrieved the pistol. With the barrel pointed towards the floor, Terrell sat the gun on the glass end table. Satisfied, Jude nodded his head. "Have a seat on the sofa."

Once Terrell was seated, Jude grabbed the bag of money and escorted his victim towards the living room, and pushed her towards the sofa. "Sit on the other chair."

Jude picked up Terrell's gun and sat in the reclining sofa. Picking up the bag of money, he unzipped it. All of the bills seemed to be there, but he needed to be certain. Jude threw the bag of money at Terrell. "Dump it out on the floor."

Terrell held the bag up and dumped all of the wrapped bills onto the floor. "I never touched it."

"I'll be the judge of that. Now count it."

The only sound that could be heard for the next twenty minutes was Terrell's voice. "Fifty thousand," he sighed after laying down the last bill. Quickly, he tossed the bills back into the bag and zipped it up. "Here's your girl's money back."

Jude tapped the gun against his leg and grinned.

Terrell looked Jude square in the eyes. "I did what you said. You can leave now."

"I will." Jude raised the pistol that he took from Terrell and aimed it at Marsha. With one pull of the trigger, Jude split her wig with a single bullet to the forehead.

Terrell watched helplessly as Marsha's body slumped over and covered the sofa with her blood. A gut-wrenching scream escaped his lungs and echoed throughout the room. Terrell ran over to Marsha and held her lifeless body. "What did you do? Why did you do that?" Terrell turned to look at the gunman briefly. "I did what you asked of me." Then he held on to Marsha's body and rocked while crying.

Jude eased up from the sofa without making a sound. His movements were so quiet, Terrell didn't hear him approaching until the cold piece of steel was against his temple. By then it was too late.

Boc!

Terrell's body fell sideways and hit the floor. Jude placed the gun on the floor, next to the recliner. With little effort, Jude used his one-hundred-eighty-pound frame to lift Terrell's dead body and sit it upright in the reclining sofa. When he finished staging the crime scene, Jude grabbed the duffle bag and headed out the front door.

***

Fresh sat on the porch long enough to smoke a blunt. During that time, he managed to do some heavy thinking. The battle between his heart and mind led him to the conclusion that he needed to be on Dazzle's side. It wasn't that he didn't trust her. The problem was her waiting so long to disclose that information to him in the first place. On another note, he felt like Tron tried him on a disrespectful ass level and he needed to be dealt with.

Fresh went back inside with a clearer mind. Dazzle was still lying in bed, but their eyes met. She parted her lips slowly. "If you don't believe me, you can check my phone." Dazzle passed him the phone. The messages he sent would surely back up her story.

As Fresh read the harassing messages, the angrier he became. She had only responded to a handful before she blocked his number. Removing the restriction, Fresh called the number and waited on the slimeball to pick up.

"Well, if it isn't my estranged baby mama," he grinned. "I see you finally unblocked me. What, you trying to see me?"

Fresh could no longer hold his tongue. "Nah, fuck nigga. I wanna see you though."

Tron froze for a few seconds when he heard Fresh instead of Dazzle. "Fuck you wanna see me for?"

"Oh nigga, you know exactly why I wanna see you. My girl told me what happened. So now, this shit is personal."

"It been personal since the day you pistol whipped me, nigga. Or did you forget about that?"

"I ain't forget shit. But let me give you a fair warning. When I catch you, you better be prepared for a gun battle and that's on everything I love."

"It's whatever, nigga. I ain't running or hiding." Tron didn't really want no smoke, but he knew it would eventually come to gun-play.

"This is your one and only warning. I want you to know I'm coming for yo' azz." Fresh hung up the phone and tossed it on the bed. "I'm killing that nigga."

That wasn't what Dazzle was expecting him to say. It caught her completely off guard. "Baby, I know you're upset, but that's not the answer. He's still Jamir's father."

"You think I give a fuck? No. Look at what he did to you. He wasn't worried about you, so don't worry about him. Fuck that nigga. Jamir barely know his ass now." Fresh stormed out the room.

Dazzle didn't know how to feel in that moment. True indeed she hated Tron, but she didn't want him to die.

Chapter 20

Capone sat in front of the big screen television, snuggled underneath a fluffy blanket, enjoying quality time with his mother. Their favorite movie, *The Lion King*, played. Tori smiled. Those were the moments she cherished the most.

"Mommy, turn it up," Capone screeched with excitement. Tori grabbed the remote and increased the volume. When the music started, Capone started to rock back and forth, as they sang along with the music.

"I'm gonna be a mighty king, so enemies beware. Well, I've never seen a king or beast with quite so little hair. I'm gonna be the main event, like no king was before. I'm brushing up on looking down. I'm working on my roar."

Capone tossed the blanket to the side and stood up. From there, he bounced around while continuing to sing. Tori's laughter was loud and hearty. His hyper behavior came from the ice cream and cookies they consumed less than an hour ago.

Tori's phone vibrated hard against the table. Leaning over she picked it up and checked the notification. It was a message from Jude.

Jude: I handled that for you. I can drop it off if you like.
Tori: I'm not home right now
Jude: Cool. Let me know when you ready to pick it up, so my partner can meet you.

A simple thank you was what he received before she went back to enjoying her mother-son date for the night. The pickup from Jude would have to be later. There was no way Tori was going to let him come to her.

When the movie was over, Capone was knocked out completely. Tori picked up her little man and took him into his bedroom. The light from the hallway was bright enough to where she didn't need to turn on his room light. Gently, she laid her baby boy down and covered him up with his race car blanket.

For a few minutes, Tori just sat there and watched him sleep. If only Kilo had pulled through, they would be one big happy family.

Instead, she was forced to be a single parent, with no luck in finding a man that could brighten her life the way he did. It wasn't about the money. She had her own. Kilo was one of a kind. He had principles and morals. Kilo was faithful. There weren't too many alive that possessed those same qualities.

Before leaving his room, Tori took one last look at him, turned on his night light and left. Sleep was nowhere in sight. Tori decided to return to the living room area and enjoy a night cap in hopes that she would fall asleep soon. Grabbing the baby monitor, she turned it on and sat it beside her. Eventually, sleep came after she finished her second cup of wine.

The house was pretty silent besides the sound of the TV and a ringing cellphone. In a matter of minutes, all of that changed. "Mommy, Mommy, Mommy," Capone screamed.

Tori was a light sleeper. So, the sudden, chilling screams caused her to spring from the sofa and run up the steps. It was natural that he had nightmares, but it only happened from time to time. Running down the hallway, Tori ran into his room. Capone was sitting up, hugging his pillow tight.

"What's wrong, baby?"

"There was a scary man in my room," he pointed towards the window. "He ran away."

"A scary man?" Tori repeated, knowing it wasn't possible. The alarm system would've definitely gone off had someone entered their home. "Mommy will look, okay?"

"Okay." He nodded.

Tori walked towards the window and to her surprise, it was unlocked. Staring towards the window, Tori could see a man dressed in dark clothing, walking past her neighbor's house. That really threw her for a loop, but it could've been a coincidence, being that he was casually walking and not running. Tori locked the window and walked over to Capone.

"Mommy's here. There's no need to be afraid." Hugging him tight, she kissed his forehead. "I'll never let anything happen to you, okay?"

Capone nodded his head. "Can I sleep with you?"

"Of course you can."

Tori tucked Capone into her bed and checked her Desert Eagle to make sure one was in the chamber. Then she double-checked the locks and alarm system. Tori decided first thing in the morning, she would be calling to have cameras and motion detectors installed, just in case.

***

Lance made his way to Agent Smith's apartment complex and knocked on the door. Looking around he checked his surroundings once more. He didn't visit his colleague often, but that night he didn't have a choice. No one came to the door, so he knocked again. That time, he could hear talking.

"Who is it?"

Lance remained silent and stepped in front of the peephole, to make sure he could be seen and not heard. Smith opened the door and stepped to the side to let him in. "It took you long enough to get here."

"I was busy checking into some details on a classified case and you almost blew my damn cover calling my damn phone." Lance's identity was almost revealed less than thirty minutes ago.

"My bad," Smith chuckled. "Is that why you're dressed in all black?"

Lance removed his hoodie from his head. "What's so urgent that you needed me to come over this late?"

Agent Smith sighed and sat down on the bar stool. "The trial with Charro should be underway soon and it will finally be over."

"I know that, but that's not the reason you called me here."

"You're right." Agent Smith brought his hand over his freshly shaven face. "We need you to testify."

Multiple lines crossed Lance's forehead. "Hell no! That wasn't the agreement. I provided all of the evidence needed to convict this muthafucka without a testimony. This is bullshit."

"I know that, but with your testimony, we can throw the book at him." Agent Smith was doing his best to convince him otherwise.

"No!" Lance stood firm on his answer. "I did my part. Case closed. I'm not taking no fucking stand. The fuck you trying to do, get me killed? This man has a very extended reach and an army of soldiers that are not in custody or facing charges."

"We can protect you and you know that."

"Fuck that!" Lance spat viciously. "I'm not about to be walking around with a fucking price tag on my head."

"Dammit Lance," he sighed.

"Y'all better use the guns and drugs you found in his home. Better yet, offer one of his men a deal to flip. That's your only option."

"Fine. Who do you think will be easier to crack, Emilio?" Agent Andrews asked, while looking at his laptop.

"Hell no! Emilio is a certified soldier. He ain't snitching. You need to grab one of his bottom boys. One of them is guaranteed to snitch with no hesitation." Lance walked over to get a closer look at his screen. "Let me take a look."

Agent Smith got up so Lance could sit down. "I'll be right back."

"What, you got company or some shit?"

"Nah."

Lance tapped away at the images on the screen. There were tons of photos of him and every member of Charro's organization on there. As Lance continued to click on photo after photo, he stopped on one in particular. His heart began to race. Staring back at him were a pair of innocent, baby brown eyes. He couldn't believe what he was seeing. Lance left the image up and rose to his feet when he saw Agent Smith walking towards him.

"Did you find one?"

"Yeah."

"Who is it?"

"Talk to Pablo. He should be easy to crack." Lance insisted.

"Good. Let me take a look." Agent Smith sat down and looked at the screen. "Why is this photo up?"

"That's funny," he stroked his beard. "I was about to ask you the same thing."

"Well, since you must know, I've been trying to find Charro's connections in the states. I'm not sure if she's a part of it, but I have a strong feeling she is."

"How so?"

"This is Tori Price-Kingsley. The daughter of Torin Price. He went by the street name, Diesel. He was the biggest kingpin in South Florida, next to Domino." Agent Smith rubbed his hands together. "If I can prove this theory, this will be the biggest bust in my career." He tapped Lance's shoulder. "Yours too if you can help me."

Lance scratched his head and placed his hand behind his back. Swiftly he pulled out a Berretta M-9 and aimed it at Smith. "I'm sorry, partner, but I can't do that."

Agent Smith's eyes expanded wide in the sockets as he looked into the barrel of the gun. "Lance, what are you doing?"

"That's my wife and I can't let you do that."

"Your wife?" Smith was puzzled. "Lance, how is she your wife? I'm confused."

"I can help you with that," he smirked. "First and foremost, my name ain't no goddamn Lance, it's Kilo. Secondly, I've been with this fuckin' bullshit ass department for five years, trying to save my father Eric 'Eazy' Kingsley and my wife Tori Kingsley. I've missed out on my son's life and hers just so they could stay out of prison."

Agent Smith was sweating bullets. "How-how is that possible?" he stuttered. "I looked you up."

Kilo laughed. "I'm sure you did but let me give you a little intel. My god-daddy, better known as Donovan Hampton, Director of the Federal Bureau of Investigation is responsible for my new identity. As well as this bullshit ass job."

Agent Smith couldn't believe what he was hearing. He slumped down in his seat and shook his head. "So, I guess because you told me all of this, that means you're going to kill me."

"You would be correct. Now get up and go into the bedroom."

Agent Smith rose to his feet and headed to the room. The life he knew to be great was about to come to a tragic end. From the time they met, he knew it was something off about his partner, but he couldn't put his finger on it. When he did conduct a private search, he couldn't locate anything on him. Now, he knew why.

Kilo took Agent Smith by surprise when he put his forearm around his neck and squeezed it. With a quick move Kilo snapped his neck. Agent Smith's body went limp instantly. He then tossed his body onto the bed and left the room. On his way out, he put his hoodie back on and snatched up the laptop.

***

The Hampton Estate

Kilo walked through the oversized mansion until he reached the private study. Opening his phone, he hit record on the screen and slid it back into his pocket. Kilo tapped on the door twice before entering the room and closing the door. Donovan was sitting at the desk with a slight grin on his face.

"Is it handled?" he asked.

"Yeah. I just left his apartment."

"Did anyone see you?"

"No," Kilo replied as he sat down in a chair and sat the laptop down.

Donovan was proud to hear the good news. For weeks, he had eyes on Smith and realized that he was getting too close for comfort. Therefore, he had to be handled. "Is it messy?"

"No. I broke his neck," he confessed.

"Hmm, I see those MMA classes paid off nicely."

"Absolutely." Kilo pulled a USB drive from his pocket and passed it over. "I was able to recover one hundred million of Charro's money," he lied.

"You keep that and wire me fifty million into my offshore Baker's Transporting account. You earned that."

"So, what's next?" Kilo asked, while leaning back in the chair.

"For now, nothing. I'm working on getting you a new identity so you can get out of here."

"I can't leave without my family." Kilo sighed.

The thought of being away from Capone and Tori another moment was killing him on the inside. He was willing to risk it all for them, just as he did a few hours ago when he snuck into her house once again. That had become a part of his normal routine whenever he was in town.

"I've been gone for far too long as it is. My son is getting big and I'm missing out on everything."

Donovan knew his absence took a toll on Kilo's family, but it had to be done in order to save them. "You're right. It's time." Donovan held his finger up. "But you need to be careful. And what I mean by that is not being out in the open, like we didn't have a funeral for you."

"I've been undetected for years. I know what to do."

"I hope so." Donovan stood up and walked around to face Kilo. "I truly appreciate everything you've done. I know it wasn't easy to leave your family and allow them to think that you've been dead all these years. But, nonetheless, they'll be happy to have you back."

"I'm just glad this shit is over."

"Hopefully. We just have to wrap this case up and it will be." Donovan hugged his godson tight. "I had a change of heart. Keep the money. You're going to need it more than me and besides, you earned it."

"Thanks." Kilo left the house feeling like the weight of the universe had been taken off of his shoulders and put down at his feet. The easy part was over. The hardest part was about to go down.

Destiny Skai

Chapter 21

For months, Tron had been grinding his ass off and it finally paid off. He was out from underneath Tweety's locks and chains and on his own. That moment was better than walking out those prison gates. Tron pulled up in front of the trap house and got out. There were two dudes standing on the porch, side-eyeing him.

"I'm here to see Jude."

"You packing?" the taller one asked.

"Nah."

"I'll be the judge of that. Hold your hands up." Tron held both of his arms up while Jude's guard dogs patted him down for a weapon. He knew better, so he left it in the car. "Let me see that backpack."

Once he was cleared, Tron walked inside and Jude was seated on the sofa, playing the video game. When Jude looked up, he sat the controller down. "Wassup, lil homie?"

Jude and Tron slapped hands. "Shit, coolin.' Ready to get to this paper."

"That's what I like to hear. Follow me." Jude stood up and went into the kitchen. Reaching inside the cabinet, he pulled out a black plastic bag and sat it on the counter. "That's a half-brick."

Tron opened the bag and tested the product quickly.

Jude laughed. "Damn, lil nigga, you don't trust me?"

"It ain't like that, homie. It's just business." Tron pulled his money out and sat it on the counter. "Just like you about to count my money," he chuckled.

"Damn right," Jude laughed, while thumbing through the bills. "It's all good."

"Thanks, man. I appreciate that shit."

"It's cool. Any friend of Mike is a friend of mine."

Tron was about to head out, but he suddenly hesitated. "Hey, quick question."

"What's good?"

"Have you heard anything about the nigga that killed Mike? That shit been fuckin' with me heavy. Me and dude go way back, so I'm trying to see what's up."

Jude raised his brow. "Not yet. Why, you heard something?"

Tron suddenly felt strange when he noticed the shift in his mood. It seemed off-key, but Tron brushed it off as if the question caught him off guard. "Nah. That's why I was asking."

"It sounds like you want in."

"I'm trying to stay free for my kids. I can't afford to go back to prison."

"I feel you, homie." Jude slapped his shoulder. "I'll let you know what I find out."

"Thanks. I appreciate that."

"No problem."

Tron made his way home. Their first face-to-face transaction was smooth as silk and he was looking forward to coming up in the game. His next move was the one he had been waiting on for weeks and it was finally about happen.

Upon entering his residence, he encountered Tweety. For the first time in weeks, her face was clear of bruises. Tron had been doing his best to keep the peace. Their relationship had run its course and it was time to move on. Piece by piece, he'd managed to ease some of his belongings out of the house.

"Wassup?"

"Nothing," she smiled. "Just finishing up the laundry." Tweety finally felt like their rough patch was being ironed out at a slow, but steady pace. "You are missing some clothes and shoes."

"Yeah, I know. I left them at my old girl house when we was doing all that fighting," he lied smoothly.

Tweety went into the kitchen to get a bottle of water. Once she made it back into the bedroom, Tron was lying in bed with his eyes glued to his phone. He was so into whatever he was doing that he never noticed Tweety standing there. She made a mental note to remember his passcode for future reference. For once, things were going good and she didn't want to ruin it by asking who he was texting.

The couple laid in bed quietly. There were no words being exchanged, except for the folks in the movie. A mild sex scene played and Tweety's lady parts were dying to be touched. Easing closer to Tron, she placed her leg onto his and her hand on his rod.

"What you doing?" Tron asked as if he didn't know.

"What do you think?" Tweety stroked his dick with ease and kissed his neck.

Tron wasn't in the mood to have sex, but he didn't want to start a pointless argument. "Turn on your side."

Tweety was wet, willing and ready. She pulled off her shorts and panties and tossed them onto the floor. Tron did the same. Raising her leg, Tron rubbed his dick against her wet pussy before dipping inside. Tweety closed her eyes and held the pillow. Side booty wasn't what her appetite desired, but it would suffice for the moment.

Tron held her waist and pumped feverishly. His mind was on catching a quick nut and going to sleep. The constant vibrating of his cellphone could be heard. Tron knew it was Mya. He was supposed to stop by earlier, but he didn't. All she had to do was wait one more day before he moved in for good.

Tweety moaned seductively while throwing her ass back on him. It was as if she knew that would be the last time and had to drain him for all he had. Her movements were definitely throwing off his rhythm. Tron took control by putting her on her stomach. Without a doubt, he knew she couldn't interfere with his nut.

Tron held Tweety down against the mattress and beat her backside in. Her girly soft moans turned into the heavy winded moans that he was used to hearing. The headboard knocked on beat. Tron was giving her one last good performance. And just as all good things come to an end, so was their session. Tron gripped down on her waist as he exploded for the last time. After he was done, Tron pulled out and laid on his side of the bed. Tweety was all smiles when it was all over, even though she didn't reach an orgasm. It was okay for the moment. Tweety had plans to ride him once he caught his wind.

One hour later, Tron still hadn't caught his wind. Instead, he was on his back fast asleep. Tweety just laid in bed staring at the ceiling. She tried her best to join him, but that thing called *a woman's intuition* was beating her ass. Every thought in her mind pointed to Tron's involvement with another woman. That was the one thing that tore her ass up more than his fists on a daily basis.

Unable to keep her jealousy under wraps, Tweety decided it was time to dig for answers. Tiptoeing to the opposite side of the bed, Tweety checked to make sure Tron was still asleep. Raising her right hand, she waved it in his face. When he didn't move, she proceeded with her sneaky tactics.

Tweety moved slowly and carefully to pick up Tron's phone without making a sound. With his phone in hand, Tweety backed up smoothly. As she turned around and headed towards the door, Tron spoke up.

"After you finish reading those messages, go in the bathroom and cry. I don't want to hear all that noise while I'm trying to sleep." Tron rolled onto his stomach and got comfortable.

Tweety's heart felt like it dropped into the seat of her panties when she heard his voice. His words came as a shock, but she knew they held meaning and confirmation of her thoughts. Tweety's hand trembled as she clutched the phone with a tight grip. Sitting down on the sofa, she put in the code to unlock the phone. Knots formed in the pit of her stomach. Mixed feelings surfaced. She was afraid of the truth, but it was too late to turn back. It was time to face her fears.

With her hands still trembling and heart thumping fast, Tweety scrolled through the messages between him and Mya. Every message between the parents were heartbreaking for her. There were countless discussions about how much he loved Mya, them becoming a family and the worst, him leaving Tweety to be with the mother of his child. The nude photos and sex videos of Tron and Mya in bed made her sick to her stomach.

Tweety doubled over at the waist in pain. Her forehead rested against the floor, as she cried. It hurt because Tron acted like he had an issue with Mya. When in fact, he loved her more than he loved

172

Tweety. According to the messages, Tron was using her at that point. Remembering what he said about the noise, Tweety put her hand over her mouth and let out a gut-wrenching scream.

Minutes passed, but in Tweety's brain, it felt like hours. Her eye sockets were sore. Every limb on her body felt weak. Somehow, she managed to pull herself from the floor. The weight of her body felt light as a feather. Tweety took small baby steps towards the kitchen. Not once did she blink. It was like she had totally spaced out. Standing at the counter, Tweety pulled the biggest knife from the red block set and proceeded to the bedroom.

Tron snored loudly, as he slept peacefully. Tweety stood over him with both hands in the air covering the sharp knife. Swiftly, she brought the blade down and slammed the blade into his back.

"You son of a bitch!" she screamed. Tron's eyes opened, as he let out a painful scream. He didn't have a clue about what was happening. "You been fucking Mya and plotting on leaving me all this time?"

Tweety yanked the blade from his skin and slammed it into his back once more. Tron managed to roll over onto his back once she pulled it out again. His eyes widened in surprise when he saw Tweety standing over him with a huge knife.

"Tweety," he gasped. "What the fuck are doing?"

"You gone pay for what you did to me, you bitch." Tweety slammed the knife into his stomach. That time she held it in place and looked into his eyes. "You played me, and I let you."

Tweety blacked out for a few moments. When she came to, Tron was hanging over the side of the bed. In shock, Tweety dropped the bloody knife onto the floor after realizing what she had done. Dropping down to her knees, she grabbed the side of his face and moved it.

"Tron! Tron!" she called out.

Tweety went back into the living room and picked up his cellphone off the floor. Opening up his recent call log, she saw Mya's number, clicked send and hit call.

"Boy, you lucky you called me back," she giggled. "You better be on your way. I've waited long enough."

"Well, I hate to be the bearer of bad news," Tweety stated nonchalantly.

"Who is this?" Mya frowned and looked at her phone screen to make sure she saw Tron's name.

"Oh, you don't know my voice by now?"

"Who the fuck playing on my man phone?" Mya shouted.

"The woman that helped your trifling ass when your mama put you and your son out," Tweety spat.

Mya was taken by surprise when she finally realized it was Tweety calling her.

"I just called to tell you Tron is dead."

Mya's whole world crashed when those words planted themselves inside her ears. "What? What happened to him?"

"I killed his no-good ass." Mya let out a horrific scream just as Tweety hung up on her. Satisfied that she was able to hurt Mya in return, Tweety dialed 911.

"911, what's your emergency?"

"Yes. Umm. I would like to report a stabbing," Tweety stated calmly.

"Who's been stabbed, ma'am?"

"My boyfriend."

"Do you know who's responsible?"

"Yes," Tweety replied.

"Is the assailant still there?" the operator asked.

"I'm the assailant. So, get someone here fast."

Tweety hung up and unlocked the front door. Then she went into the kitchen and grabbed the bottle of Amsterdam that was sitting on the counter. Back in the living room, she smoked a blunt and drank the liquor out of the bottle.

It took responders fifteen minutes to reach her residence. Heavy pounding could be heard. Tweety didn't say a word. Instead, she waited for them to enter on their own. Two police officers walked into the apartment, wielding their guns.

"Ma'am, where is the victim?" Tweety pointed towards the bedroom and watched as they rushed to Tron's aid.

One officer kept his gun pointed at Tweety, while the other one supplied her with a pair of silver bracelets, and escorted her out of the apartment. Tweety smiled as they put her in the back seat of the patrol car. All of the commotion had the neighbors standing outside, trying to figure out what was going on.

A truck pulled in front of the patrol car. The light shined brightly in Tweety's face. Squinting, she could see a small figure appear from the passenger side. Mya ran towards the building, but an officer grabbed her by the arm. Tweety couldn't make out what was being said. Mya then swiveled her head towards the car. The sight of Tweety caused her to run towards the car.

Mya snatched the door open and started to punch Tweety repeatedly in the face. "What the fuck did you do to him?"

The officer grabbed Mya by the shirt and slammed the door. Mya was a mess. She was kicking and screaming, while the officer tried his best to restrain her. Things got worse when Mya spotted the coroner's van arrive on the scene.

Destiny Skai

Chapter 22

"One more big push, Mommy. The umbilical cord is wrapped around the baby's head," the nurse shouted in a panic.

"I can't. I can't," Lisa screamed.

"Come on, baby. You have to do this." Jarvis held Lisa's hand, trying to comfort the mother of his child. "Push baby, please," he begged.

One nurse held one of Lisa's legs open to keep her from closing it, while the head nurse coached her through another painful contraction. "Push, Mommy. The shoulders are coming through."

After six repetitious sets of pushes, the baby made his entrance into the world. The head nurse put the baby on Lisa's chest. Jarvis panicked when he observed a faint color of blue on his son's face. His son wasn't moving or crying.

"Why isn't he crying? What's wrong?" Jarvis released Lisa's hand, so he could cut the cord. Right after, the nurse grabbed the baby and took him to the incubator. Jarvis followed her.

Jarvis was numb as he watched the nurse smack his son's butt and pat him on the back. Using a suction, she removed some fluid from his mouth and nose. The nurse laid him down and shook him roughly a few times, while patting him in the back over and over again. Jarvis bit his nails while waiting on his son to cry out.

"Come on, daddy man, scream for me please." Jarvis rocked anxiously on his heels. Seconds felt like minutes. Then suddenly a faint cry could be heard. Jarvis was relieved. "Whew," he sighed.

The nurse cleaned Lisa up and allowed her to hold their son. She smiled and kissed his forehead. "I'm so happy to finally meet you."

Jarvis had his chance to cradle his son before the nurse took him for a few tests and observations. A few hours later baby Jarvis was fast asleep in the bassinet on the side of the bed.

Labor was tiring for Lisa. She was dozing off and on for the past hour. Jarvis dozed off as well, but the sound of his cellphone woke him up. "Hello."

"Aye nigga, where you at?" Jude asked.

"I'm at the hospital. My girl just had the baby."

"Oh, that's what's up. Congrats."

"Thanks, fam."

"Aye, remember that job I had for you?" Jude sat in his car drinking.

"Yeah." Jarvis thought back to the conversation they had.

"Well, tonight is the night. I need you to come through like right now."

"I can't right now. My girl need me." Jarvis wasn't ready to leave his family's side at that moment.

"For what? Didn't she have the baby already?" Jude was starting to get aggravated.

"Yeah."

"Nigga, she don't need you then. I do." Jude gnashed his teeth. "I need you at the location in thirty minutes real shit."

Jarvis watched Lisa toss and turn and shook his head. "A'ight, man. I'm coming."

"Don't make me come find you," Jude threatened.

"I'm coming, man. Chill out."

"Yeah."

Jarvis stood and put his phone in his pocket. Then he walked over to the bed and put his hand on Lisa's side. "You okay?"

"No. I'm still in pain."

"I'm about to get the nurse to bring you something for the pain."

"Okay."

Jarvis went out to report Lisa's pain to the nurse. Upon their return, the nurse gave her some morphine in her IV. Jarvis kissed her head. "I love you and I'll be back."

"I love you too," she whispered. It took no time for Lisa to pass out from the administered drug.

***

"Uncle Honcho is going to watch you until I come back, okay baby?" Tori knelt down and kissed Capone on the cheek.

"Okay."

"I still don't know why you won't let me go with you." Honcho placed her hand on Capone's shoulder. "I don't want you going anywhere alone."

"I'm just going to meet Jude to pick up the money that Terrell took from me. And I have something to discuss with him, so I need some privacy. It won't take long. I promise." Tori kissed Honcho on the cheek as well. "I'll be in like an hour."

"One hour. That's it. Anything longer than that, I'm coming for you. Something not sitting right with me."

"I'll call you."

"You better." He nodded.

***

Tori drove away in deep thought. When Jude hit her up about picking up the money, she agreed to meet him at her hair store. For days, Tori had been contemplating on reaching out to him, but she wasn't sure about her final decision. The relationship with Jude had been put on ice since the proposal. However, a shocking revelation made her reconsider her thoughts and feelings about him. Hopefully, by the time they hashed things out, she could come to a conclusion.

The plaza where the shop was located was dimly lit, with the exception of the bright lights on the main road. Jude wasn't there yet, so she decided to call him.

"Hello," he picked up.

"I'm here. Where are you?"

"I'm up the street. Go inside and I'll be there in two minutes."

"Okay."

Tori got out the car and stood in front of the door. Her mind was all over the place. Unlocking the door, she pushed the door in and walked inside. Just as she was about to close the door, a figure appeared out of nowhere and pushed their way inside.

"Getcho ass inside and turn on the light," the man barked.

Tori was completely taken off guard. Had she not been so wrapped up in her confession to Jude, she would've been on high alert. Tori hit the switch to brighten the store. When she turned around, she couldn't believe her eyes. "Jarvis, what the fuck are you doing?" she snapped.

"You'll find out shortly." Jarvis pointed his gun at Tori. "Back up and sit down."

There was a chair next to the wig station, so Tori sat down like she was told. One thing she was aware of was that a scary person would kill out of fear. To make sure she made it out alive, she complied with her old soft ass worker.

"My boyfriend is on his way." Tori hoped that would make him leave.

"Good. That means I get two for the price of one," he chuckled.

"Why are you doing this?" Tori needed answers before she killed him. Allowing him to live after the current stunt wasn't acceptable.

"You know, Tori, it's funny you asked me that." Jarvis leaned against the glass case. "Ever since that day you embarrassed me on the block, I vowed to pay you back."

"Jarvis, that was years ago. Are you fuckin' serious right now?"

"You goddamn right." Jarvis tapped the glass lightly with his nails. "Yo' ass walked around this bitch untouchable for so long and now my chance for revenge has finally surfaced. I got rid of Kilo, but what I have questions about is, who got rid of Diesel? He was your last piece of protection."

"What the fuck do you mean by you got rid of Kilo?" Everything else he spoke about was irrelevant.

Jarvis had a sinister look on his face when he leaned forward and looked deep into Tori's eyes. "I killed Kilo, not Sherrod."

That unknown information knocked the wind out of Tori. He had to be lying. "What?"

"You heard me. I. Killed. Kilo," he reiterated. "That's the lie I told Eazy. That's why he tried to kill your father."

The thought of Kilo dying at Jarvis' hands hit her the same way it did years ago. Tori rocked in her seat as tears began to well up in her eyes. "Did my father tell you to kill him?"

"Honestly?" he smirked.

"Yes."

"No. He wanted us to kidnap him, but that shit went left. Kilo shot Sherrod, so I killed him. That rowdy nigga left me no choice."

Tori was burning up on the inside. Killing Jarvis was certainly mandatory. He was the reason for her heartache. Before she could reply the bell from the door sounded off. Tori was relieved to see Jude appear with a strap in his hand.

"Baby, shoot him," she screamed.

Jude looked at Tori, then at Jarvis. "What the fuck you doing, nigga?"

"Exactly what you told me to do."

"I didn't tell you to pull a gun out on her, stupid."

Jarvis sat his gun down on the glass case. "You must've forgot who this crazy bitch is."

Jude pointed his gun at Jarvis. "Aye, watch yo' mouth."

Tori was confused as hell. "Jude, what's going on? You know him?"

Jude had an evil smile on his face. "Sorry, baby. Where are my manners? Um, this is my cousin, Jarvis. Jarvis, this is the woman who turned down my proposal."

"Your cousin?" she blurted out.

"I'm sorry. I've been meaning to tell you, but it slipped my mind. We ain't that close." Jude shrugged his shoulders. "What can I say? It's a small world."

Tori didn't know where to start. "You had him to come here?"

"I did."

"Why?" Tori frowned. "Have you been plotting on me this whole time?"

"No." Jude stood in front of Tori and stroked her cheek. She quickly moved her head to keep him from touching her. "I loved you, Tori, but it's obvious you didn't feel the same way about me. I've done everything in my power to prove that. I introduced you to my family and proposed to you. But what did you do? Turn me down."

"That's not true, Jude. You know how I feel about you, so stop it. All I wanted was for you to understand the reason I didn't feel the proposal was appropriate at that time."

Jude grinned and shook his finger in her direction. "Oh yeah, I remember now. You still in love with a dead muthafucka and you refuse to give me your heart."

"That's not fair. I have a son with him. You knew from the beginning what my struggle was."

"You right, I guess." Jude stood in the middle of the floor and looked back and forth between Jarvis and Tori. "That shit hurt my feelings. You made me look stupid. The same way you looking now. You have no idea of the things I did just to prove my love to you." Jude rubbed his eyes. "I killed one of my friends for you, but did you appreciate that? No!"

"What friend? I didn't ask you to kill anyone."

"Mike."

"He stole from me and you killed him." Tori stopped and thought for a moment. "Did you set me up?"

Jude nodded his head. "I did."

"Why?"

"To prove to you that I would do anything to keep you. Niggas come a dime a dozen and they can't be trusted."

Tori heard all she needed to hear. "What are you going to do to me?" She wasn't afraid of Jude, but right then and there, he had the upper hand. Now she wished she had listened to Honcho and let him come along.

Jude leaned his head to the side and gritted his teeth. "It's simple. If I can't have you, no one can."

Tori had to think fast. Her life was on the line and she couldn't allow Capone to be alone in the world. "You already have me."

Jarvis yawned loudly. "Cuz, can we get this shit over with? I need to get back to the hospital to my girl and baby. This bitch does not want you."

Jude cut his eyes at Jarvis. "Call her another bitch."

Jarvis held his hands up. "My bad, fam, but she ain't worth the trouble."

"You mean like you?" Tori spat.

"Fuck you talking about?" Jarvis asked.

Tori needed her captors distracted, so she had to be quick on her feet and be smart at the same time. Based on their pillow talk, that wouldn't be hard to do. "You're the reason your family is dead. That was all your fault. Did you tell him that?"

Jude's eyes turned into tiny, dark slits as he eyed Jarvis. "What the fuck is she talking about?"

"I don't know, fam," Jarvis lied.

"Yes, you do," Tori yelled. "Tell him why y'all grandmother, uncle and auntie is dead."

Jude pointed his gun at Jarvis. "Say it."

Jarvis' heart raced and his palms became sweaty. If he didn't come clean, he knew Jude would kill him. He had to save himself without taking the blame.

"I was given an order by Diesel to kidnap Kilo. He made that difficult when he shot Sherrod. So, I shot and killed him. His father Eazy found out about it and I told him it was Sherrod that shot Kilo." Jarvis stopped talking and looked at Tori.

Jude lowered his gun. "Keep talking."

"I told Eazy Diesel ordered the hit. Diesel found out it was me who told. And since I was on the run," Jarvis stopped and took a deep breath. "He killed Grandma them, and that was why I shot up his funeral."

"It was you?" Tori couldn't believe what she was hearing. She knew for a fact it was Eazy who killed his family.

Jude hadn't cried since the funeral, but he missed his family. Especially, his grandmother. Without blinking, Jude raised his gun and shot Jarvis in the stomach. *Pew!* The silencer suppressed the sound.

Jarvis' body hit the floor. Using both hands, he placed them over the fresh, bloody wound he'd just sustained. "Come on, Jude. I have a family. My girl needs me. I can't leave my son out here alone."

Tori took that as her chance to get away. Easing out her gun, she pointed it at Jude. It was like he felt it because he turned around quickly and met a bullet to the chest. Jude stumbled forward, but there wasn't any blood. By the time Tori realized he was wearing a bulletproof vest, it was too late. Jude tackled her to the ground and pummeled her with his fists.

"Bitch, you just tried to kill me," he shouted, while slapping the woman he claimed to love.

Tori fought back, but she was no match for Jude. In between breaths, she clawed at his face and screamed, "Jude stop! Please." Her pleas and cries fell on deaf ears, but she didn't give up. Not even when he wrapped his hands around her throat. "Jude, please stop. I'm pregnant," she cried.

Jude loosened his grip, but he kept his hand on the base of her neck. "What the fuck you just said?"

"I'm pregnant with your baby."

"You're lying."

"I'm not," she gasped. Tori needed his trust for a few seconds. After that, she was taking him down with a headshot. "I took a test. That's why I've been distant."

"You was gone kill my baby?" Jude was surprised by the news, but he wasn't happy. Tori didn't love him. Therefore, he knew she would have an abortion.

"That's what I wanted to talk to you about."

"It's too late for that. We were supposed to be engaged and running this empire together, but you want someone you can't have." Tears finally escaped his eyes. "I loved you, Tori, but I have to kill you."

Jude gripped her neck tighter. Tori screamed, as she laid under the frame of the most vicious killer she'd come across. He then banged her head against the tiled floor, knocking her unconscious. The sound of the bell went unnoticed by Jude. When the door slammed, Jude turned around to see a familiar face. It was like he seen a ghost.

"What the fuck?" he uttered.

"Yeah, nigga, I'm back from the dead." Kilo pointed the gun in Jude's face and pulled the trigger. Blood and brain matter splattered against the glass case.

Kilo kicked Jude's body over and knelt down to check on Tori. Her face was slightly bruised and blood seeped from her mouth. "Damn, baby, I'm so sorry. This is all my fault. I should've never let this go so far."

"Help me," a faint voice called out.

Kilo stood up and walked over to the other body on the floor. Once he was close enough to see who it was, he put another bullet in the chamber and knelt down.

Jarvis looked Kilo in the eyes. "Kilo?" he whispered.

"Yeah, it's me, fuck nigga."

"Is this a dream? Am I dead?"

"You ain't dead yet, but you about to be." Kilo had been waiting on his day to get revenge.

"Call for help, please." Jarvis was losing blood profusely.

Kilo laughed. "Yeah. I'll call for help, just like you did when you shot me, pussy."

"Please," Jarvis begged. "My son was just born."

"Well, he gone be a lucky ass kid to grow up without a fuck nigga for a father. I'll catch you on the other side."

Kilo put the barrel of the gun against Jarvis' temple and pulled the trigger. Walking back over to Tori, he cradled her in his arms and carried her out to his car.

Chapter 23

The next morning

Kilo stood on the patio inhaling the fresh scent of salt water in the air. The sound of the ocean waves were soothing to the soul. After rescuing Tori the night before, he hadn't been able to sleep. The guilt he felt for leaving her behind for all those years weighed him down like a three-hundred-pound dumbbell. Then, to see her being beaten by the man she was dating, ripped his heart to shreds. He'd never understand how a man could put their hands on a woman.

The sound of the glass door sliding made him turn around. "Hey," she smiled. "Are you okay?"

"Not really," he sighed and ran his hand over his face. "How is she doing?"

Before answering his question, she stepped out onto the balcony and slid the door closed. "She's going to be okay. There are quite a few bruises on her body that will heal over time, and she has a slight concussion."

"Any broken bones?"

"No. But there is some spotting."

"What do you mean?" Kilo asked with a raised brow.

"What I mean is," Nurse Shelly hesitated for a few seconds before explaining, "she's having a miscarriage."

"What? A miscarriage," he repeated. That wasn't the answer he was expecting.

"Yes. We'll wait it out a few days and see what happens."

Kilo sat down and rubbed his face. For obvious reasons, he felt like Tori cheated on him. He knew it wasn't right to be upset, but it was hard to accept that his wife was pregnant by another man. A nigga that wanted to walk in his very own shoes at that.

Nurse Shelly observed the sudden shift in his mood and sat down beside him. "Are you sure you're okay? You seem pretty hurt by the news."

"I am."

"I'm sorry about your friend, but she's strong." Nurse Shelly looked him in the eyes. "Everything will be okay. She's a fighter."

Kilo had the saddest look in his glassy eyes. "She's not my friend. That's my wife."

"Oh Kilo, I'm so sorry," she said sincerely.

Kilo cleared his throat and stood up. "It's cool. I'm good."

Now feeling bad, Nurse Shelly rose to her feet and headed for the door. "I'm going to go back inside and check on her."

"Thanks. How much do I owe you?"

"Nothing. Your godfather took care of the bill." Nurse Shelly smiled once more and went to check on her patient.

Once he was alone, Kilo pulled out Tori's cellphone and powered it back on. Since the rescue, her phone had been blowing up for hours on end, particularly by his baby brother, Honcho. Many times, he wanted to answer the call, but he needed to see his family in person to the break the news to them.

Eventually, Nurse Shelly was gone, and Kilo found himself sitting beside the bed Tori slept in. All he wanted was for her to wake up. There was so much he needed to say. Until then, he would watch her sleep.

After a while, Kilo could no longer just sit in place. Moving closer, he reached out and grabbed her hand. Gently, he kissed it and placed her hand on the side of his face. "Tori, I love you so much. These last few years have been nothing but pure heartache. I'm sorry I had to leave you alone to raise our son."

The sunlight began to fade away, leaving beautiful traces of pink and purple across the sky. It was so peaceful on the balcony and that's where he was able to tap into his thoughts, deepest feelings and hopes for the future. All of a sudden, a piercing scream shrilled through the air. Knowing exactly where it came from, Kilo ran back into the bedroom.

Tori was sitting upright in the bed with a frightening look on her face. The sight of Kilo was scarier. She was speechless. Kilo proceeded towards her. Tori's breathing grew heavier by the second, as she continued to scream. "Don't come near me." She looked down at the IV in her arm. The drugs had to be affecting her vision.

"Tori, relax. It's me, baby," Kilo pleaded.

"No. You're dead." Tori inched backwards until her back was against the wall.

"I didn't die that day."

"Kilo," she whispered, while wiping her eyes. "Is that really you?

"Yes, baby. It's me." Kilo eased down onto the bed and sat beside her.

Tori raised her hand slowly and stroked the side of his face gently to see if it was a warm body or just his spirit. "Is this really you?"

"Yes. It's a long story."

Tori lifted her hand an inch away from face and slapped him. *Whap!* Kilo shook his head and smiled. "I deserve that."

"How do I know it's really you?" Tori was in utter shock. She didn't know what the hell was going on, but she was about to find out. "Am I dreaming? What am I doing here?"

"No. You're not dreaming. The last time I saw you was when you were holding me after I was shot. I told you to name our son Capone."

Tori felt like she was going crazy.

Kilo exhaled. "Last night I saved you from your boyfriend Jude and Jarvis, the nigga that used to work for you. Do you remember any of that?"

The mention of their names took her back to the hair shop less than twenty-four hours ago. Tori shook her head. "I do, but this isn't making any sense to me. You died. How is this happening?" Tori started to panic. Raising her arm, she pinched her skin as hard as she could.

Kilo grabbed her arm to keep her from ripping the needle from her arm. "Tori, you're not dreaming. It's really me."

"But how? I don't understand," she whined.

"I'll explain everything to you." Kilo prepared for the moment he had been waiting on for the past five years.

***

Flashback February 14, 2011

Kilo whipped his brand-new silver BMW in the driveway and put the car in park. The buzzing of his cellphone caught his attention, so he dropped his head and grabbed it from the cup holder. It was Tori.

"Yeah, baby."

"Do you want me to grab us some food before I come home?"

"Nah. We going out to dinner with the family, so we can celebrate our marriage."

"Okay. I'll be home in a few minutes."

Kilo froze when he spotted two men approaching his vehicle dressed in all black. "What the fuck?"

"What's wrong, baby?"

Kilo dropped the phone and grabbed the gun that rested on his lap. Sherrod snatched the door open and attempted to unarm his subject. Both men tussled with the weapon. Kilo knew he was outnumbered and there was only one way out. Squeezing the trigger, he let off one round.

Boc!

The bullet struck Sherrod in the shoulder, causing him to stumble backwards.

"Kilo!" Tori screamed through the phone, while mashing hard on the gas pedal.

Jarvis stepped in and let off two shots, hitting Kilo once in the chest and in the stomach. "Bro, let's clear it." Jarvis and Sherrod ran back to the truck and fled the scene.

Kilo felt light-headed when he leaned up. Blood coated his fingers when he placed his hand on his chest. "Fuck!"

Sweat protruded from his forehead and he was losing his breath. Using the little bit of strength he had left, he pushed his body forward. On the ground, a wounded Kilo fought for his life, as he struggled to breathe. Images of Tori being pregnant filled his brain. Tears began to roll, as his eyes grew heavier by the second.

"Come on, Tori. Please, baby," he mumbled.

God had to be listening because seconds later, he heard screeching tires, followed by loud screams. Tori had already called the police the second she heard the first shot. Dropping down to her knees, she cradled his head in her lap.

"Help is on the way, baby. Just stay strong. We need you." As she rocked back and forth, she kissed his forehead. "You have to fight, baby. I can't. I can't live without you." Her own tears soaked her face.

"I love you, Tori."

"I love you too." Kilo was fading in and out of consciousness, so she shook him. "No! Don't close your eyes. Don't go to sleep. Please. Stay with me."

"I feel cold, baby." His bottom lip trembled.

"Baby, please don't go. I'm pregnant. I'm having your baby."

A faint smile spread across his lips. "I know. I found your test underneath the sink."

"That means you have to fight."

Kilo was trying his best to stay strong, but the grim reaper was calling his name. "If it's a boy, name him Capone." Just as he uttered his last sentence, they heard sirens.

"Help is on the way." Tori gripped his hand. "You're going to pull through this, and we can name him together."

"Keep me close to your heart and take care of our son."

The paramedics rushed towards Tori at a high rate of speed. "I need you to step aside, ma'am. We got it from here." Tori stood up and watched closely as they made every attempt to save his life.

The medics rushed Kilo through the hospital doors and directly into the hands of the best surgeon in Florida. It was his first gunshot victim for the day, and he was prepared to perform a miracle. Kilo was placed on the operating table and his shirt was cut off. He lost a significant amount of blood, but the bullet missed his major organs.

Surgery lasted four hours, but it was successful to say the least. Kilo's vitals were stable, and he was doing great. The doctor cleaned himself up so he could go and deliver the good news to his family. On his way out of the room, he was greeted by two well-dressed men.

"Excuse me, we're looking for gunshot victim, Kilo Kingsley," one of the men spoke up.

"I'm sorry, but I can't help you with that," the surgeon stated.

"I'm sorry. Let's try this again." Agent Tillman pulled out his badge and flashed it. "I'm Federal Agent Tillman and this is Federal Agent Ross. We are looking for our fellow team member, Kilo Kingsley. He was brought in for a gunshot wound and we need to know the status of his health."

"Well, the surgery went well and he's in stable condition."

Agent Tillman looked at his partner, then back to the doctor. "So, he's expected to make a full recovery?"

"Yes."

"Can we see him?" they asked.

"Not yet. I'm about to go down and provide his family with an update."

Agent Ross stepped in. "Not so fast. We can't have you do that."

"Why not?" The surgeon was confused.

"That's classified information, but what I will say is speak to your boss. He knows all about it," Agent Ross replied.

Agent Tillman put his hand on the surgeon's shoulder. "This is what we need you to do. Go downstairs and let his family know that he has passed away."

The surgeon shook his head. "I can't do that. It's not right."

Agent Tillman gave him a menacing stare. "If you want to continue to practice medicine in the United States, you'll do exactly what we tell you."

After being persuaded to lie by the feds and his boss, the surgeon went downstairs and delivered the most devastating news to the Kingsley family. A few days later, Kilo was taken to a safe house, where he received private medical attention by the government.

"Wait," Tori interrupted his story. "So, you mean to tell me that the feds took you into custody and you've been off the grid for all these years?"

"Yes."

"Why?"

"A few weeks before we got married, I was stopped by these two officers. They snatched me out the car and put me inside this truck. That's when I found out they were the feds. They had been investigating my father, but they couldn't catch him doing anything. Apparently, they had been watching us for a while because when I denied knowing anything, those muthafuckas brought your name into it. They claimed to have info about you running dope for Diesel."

Tori sat in disbelief about the chain of events, but she didn't interrupt because she needed to know the absolute truth.

"They kept popping up on me, asking me for information, but I wouldn't say shit. That's when they told me I had two choices, turn y'all in, or come work for them and take down the supplier. I denied that too. So, when I was shot, they used that to their advantage and made me disappear. I couldn't let them take you or my father to prison. So, I had to help take down the connect in Mexico." Kilo gazed into her eyes. "I did this for you."

Tori's stare was vacant. The man that she mourned for years was alive and well all that time. "I don't know what to say."

"You don't believe me?"

"That's not what I'm saying. All of this is just crazy and it's hard for me to comprehend what the hell has been going on all this time."

"Hold on." Kilo went into his bedroom and returned with a thick brown folder. "Here's the proof."

Kilo pulled out an FBI badge with his alias and photo, multiple passports and assignments. There were even documents and photos of her, Diesel and Eazy. Tori looked through the items with a puzzling stare.

"I need a drink. This too much for me." Tori looked down at her arm. "Can you take this out please?"

"You need to be hydrated."

"I'm fine." Tori held out her arm. "If you don't take it out, then I will."

Kilo chuckled. "Still stubborn, I see."

"I am."

Kilo removed the tape that held the IV in place. Using gauze, he placed it on top of the needle and slid it out gently. Tori rubbed the crease of her arm. "Thank you."

Kilo couldn't keep his eyes off her. "I've missed you so much. This has been so hard for me, but I'm not getting the same feeling from you."

"I'm still in shock. I've mourned you for so long and to see you in front of me feels like a dream I can't wake up from."

"Do you still love me?" he asked.

"I never stopped."

Tori grabbed his arm and pulled him close enough for her to cover his lips with hers. It felt good to have him back in her arms. The evidence he showed made sense, but they were a long way from her developing a solid understanding. Tori needed to know *why* he never showed any sign of life. For now, she would let it go.

"My heart feels whole again," she confessed, while playing with his fingers. "I thought I was going to die without you."

"I'm glad you were strong enough to endure that pain. I don't know what I would've done if I returned to some news like that."

"So, when are you going to see your father?"

"I wanted you to see me first. Now I can go see him."

"I need to ask you a question." Tori eased from the bed and planted her feet on the floor. "How did you find me last night?"

"I've been following you for months now, but I couldn't let you see me." Kilo was ready to tell it all.

"Well, you did a good job living off the radar." A light bulb went off in Tori's head. "You've been in my house, haven't you?"

"I have. We had sex too," Kilo grinned.

"Wait! What?"

"Yeah. I put something in your Patrón so you wouldn't wake up. You were crying. I had to leave before I blew my cover. That shit was hard as fuck, because I wanted to tell you then, but I couldn't."

"Hell no!" she screeched.

"It's true." Kilo had to take her back down memory lane so she could remember.

Tori slept peacefully with a light snore. Darkness crept throughout the room and coldness caressed her spirit. The home was completely silently until heard a soft noise. Her eyes struggled to open, but the sleepiness was winning. "Mrs. Kingsley."

The sound of his voice rattled her spirit. When she rolled over, she saw him. "Baby, is that you?"

"Yes. It's me and I need to talk to you."

"About what?"

"I miss you so much and I never pictured life without you. But life happened. Diesel didn't want us together."

"Kilo, I love you so much. Why did you leave me here?" Fresh tears flowed from her eyes like a waterfall in Jamaica.

"I didn't have a choice, baby. But later for that. Listen to me carefully. I know all about Jude and no, I'm not mad with you for moving on. You've waited four years and you deserve to be happy. He's not a man of my caliber and you deserve better than that. Just keep your eyes on him. Also, what I need for you to do is to be careful, my love. Watch your surroundings and the ones closest to you. They don't mean you well. I'm sorry I'm not here for you and Capone, but not a day goes by that I don't think about the two of you. And believe me, I over-stand your reasoning for doing what you did."

"Kilo, I'm so sorry. I didn't want to do it, but I had no choice. Please don't be upset about that or Jude. He's just here to fill the equator-sized hole you left in my heart. I swear, I'll never love another man the way I love you."

"I know, baby. I've been watching you daily."

"Just come back to me. I'm going to die without you," she cried.

"You have to continue to live, Tori. Our love is eternal, and I'll be here with you forever. I promise."

"You promise?"

"I do. That's why I married you. I love you so much, Tori, and don't you ever forget that. Someday, we'll meet again." Kilo stood

up to leave, revealing his all-black attire. "Be safe and make sure *you reign supreme. You are the true Queen of the Trap.*"

"*Kilo, please don't leave me.*"

"*I love you, Tori.*"

"*I love you too, baby.*" *She could feel his lips on hers, his hands on her body and slow strokes of passionate love. It was a feeling she never wanted to let go.*

Tori remembered that night clear as day. It was one of those dreams she never wanted to wake up from. "No wonder it felt so real when I woke up. This is crazy as hell."

"After I saw Capone the other night, I knew it was time for me to return. That was my last night of active duty. I'm waiting on some documents so I can be released, but no one can know about me being alive, except the family."

"I'm not going to say anything. I promise."

"Good. Now let's go, because I'm ready to see my son. This has been a long time coming."

"I need to take a shower first."

"Come on." Kilo helped her from the bed and walked her to the bathroom.

Chapter 24

Broward County Courthouse

"Number thirteen, Davina Ingram," Judge Collins spoke loudly in the courtroom. Tweety approached the podium dressed in an orange jail uniform and stood beside the female counselor.

"State your name for the record, please."

"Davina Ingram."

"Ms. Ingram, you've been charged with one count of attempted murder with a deadly weapon, the bond for that is zero. Do you have legal counsel?"

"No, ma'am."

"Okay, well a public defender will be appointed. You may have a seat. Thank you."

"Thank you, Your Honor."

After being dismissed by the judge, Tweety returned to her seat on the bench and waited for everyone's name to be called. Zoned out, she thought back to the events that led her to be thrown in jail. She was certain she had killed him. In her mind, Tron didn't deserve to live for the way he abused and treated her like a common-day street walker. Tweety put her entire life on pause for him. She took care of his son, and helped his thot ass baby mama, and he had the audacity to be sleeping with Mya. Tweety didn't care what happened with her life at that point. She had no one on the outside and nothing to go home to. Tweety had come to terms that she would die in prison anyway.

When court was over, Tweety and the rest of the detainees were placed in the holding cell, until they were taken back to their dorm. For minutes she stared at the free phone, before deciding to make a call. The phone rang four times before she got an answer.

"Hello."

"Tori, it's me, Tweety."

"Oh, what's up? You have a new number?"

"You can say that." Tweety stopped talking when she heard a voice come over the intercom.

"What's that noise?" Tori quizzed.

"I'm in jail."

Tori's heart instantly skipped a beat. Her first thought was that she was caught with the dope. "For what?"

"I stabbed Tron."

"What?"

"I stabbed him."

"Is he dead?" Tori thought about Dazzle and AJ.

"I thought he was. I just left first appearance court and they're charging me with attempted murder."

"Damn, Tweety." Although they weren't close, Tori didn't want to see her go down bad like that.

"I just wanted to call and let you know before you saw it on the news. Also, can you come down here and pick up my property, so you can get inside my apartment and get your clothes?"

"Yeah. I can do that." Tori knew exactly what she meant. "Do you have an attorney?"

"I have a public defender, but I'm good. I'm going to plead guilty anyway."

"You sure you want to do that?"

Tweety wiped the water from her eyes. "Yeah. I am. I'm guilty. There's no changing that. I'm prepared for whatever they give me."

"I'm going to put some money on my phone so you can call me. I won't leave you in there alone."

"I don't deserve that. I've caused so much pain to other people and now it's my turn to suffer. That's karma."

"We're human. We make mistakes."

The doors unlocked and the C.O. shouted it was time to go back to the dorm. "Thanks, Tori. I have to go back to my dorm now." Tweety hung the phone back on the wall and left out the holding cell.

***

Mya stood at Tron's bedside with AJ on her hip. Ever since his arrival, she hadn't left the hospital. "See, Daddy?"

AJ shook his head. "He sleepy."

Tron's mother, Sheila, was present as well. She stood on the opposite side of the bed and rubbed her son's head. "I told you to leave that no-good bitch alone. She lucky she in jail 'cause I'll beat her ass my goddamn self." Tron was her only child, and she didn't play that shit when it came down to her baby.

Mya cried so much the night before, her eyes were still red. "I told him don't go there last night, but he didn't listen to me. I knew something was going to happen."

"I told him to leave her alone when he came home. His ass so damn hardheaded."

The door opened and the nurse walked in the room, with a man on her heels. "Sorry to interrupt you, but this is Dr. Levi and he needs to talk to the both of you."

Dr. Levi walked up with his hands inside his jacket pocket. He was a very attractive middle-aged black man. "Are you his mother?"

"Yes, I am."

"Okay, I'm the one that conducted your son's procedure upon his arrival. He has sustained major injury to his spine and a punctured lung."

Mya freaked out instantly. "A punctured lung. Oh God, is he going to die?"

"Mya hush that noise and listen," Sheila snapped.

"Now, I did repair the lung tissue. That takes about six to eight weeks to heal."

"Tron, why!" Mya damn near fainted from the news.

"Excuse me for one second." Sheila stormed over to Mya and took AJ from her arms. "Go outside and get some air, 'cause you making my damn nerves bad."

Mya went inside the bathroom and closed the door.

"I'm sorry. That's his girlfriend and she is worrisome."

Dr. Levi chuckled with a slight smile. "Trust me, I get it. I've seen worse."

"I can only imagine," Sheila agreed.

"Now, back to your son. It will take six to eight weeks for his lungs to heal. That's just the beginning. The damage with his spine has him paralyzed." Dr. Levi saw the worry in her eyes and placed his hand on her shoulder. "Before you panic, it could be temporary, or it could be permanent. It's too early to say. He will need rehab. That means once he leaves here, he needs to start physical therapy right away."

Sheila's heart sank. He had just got home and was finally getting his life on track. "And how long is that?"

"Right now, I'm not sure. He's going to be here for a while, so be prepared."

"Thanks, Dr. Levi."

"You are more than welcome. If there is anything that I can assist you with, please don't hesitate to reach out to me."

Dr. Levi left the room and Mya exited the bathroom. "You so damn dramatic," Sheila huffed.

"Sorry, but your son is the love of my life. He's my everything." Mya stood over Tron and kissed his lips. "Wake up, baby."

Sheila rocked AJ in her lap, while reaching for her cell. "Your mama is something special." Scrolling through her contacts, she found Dazzle's number and pressed send.

"Hey Ms. Sheila."

"Hey honey. How you doing?"

"I'm fine and you?"

"I haven't heard from you or my grandson. How is he doing?"

"He's fine. I've just been busy, that's all." Dazzle didn't want to tell her the real reason she hadn't seen her grandson was because of her nasty ass son.

"Well, I called to give you some bad news."

"What? Your son is back in jail?" Dazzle tooted up her nose. She was halfway hoping it was true.

"No, Dazzle. He was stabbed last night and he's in the hospital." Sheila didn't appreciate the slick remark.

"Oh, I'm sorry to hear that. What happened?" Dazzle needed to know who was responsible for his bad karma.

"Unh-huh. Well, that thang he was with, Tweety, stabbed him last night. She punctured his lung, and he might be paralyzed. It's too early to say right now, but we'll see in another month or two."

"Damn, Tweety stabbed him," she repeated in disbelief.

"Yes. She lucky I didn't catch her ass." Sheila exhaled heavily into the phone. "He's going to want to see his son when he wakes up, so can you make that happen, please?"

"Yes. I can drop him off to you. Just let me know when you want him."

"I would appreciate that."

"It's no problem."

"Okay. I'll talk to you soon."

"Bye-bye."

Sheila observed Mya watching her closely and rolling her eyes in the process. "Don't start no shit."

Mya giggled. "What? I didn't say anything."

"You didn't have to. Your facial expression said it all."

"I'm about to take a nap." Mya climbed into the bed with Tron.

"Girl, get off my baby. What is wrong with you?"

"This is my baby now." Mya kissed him again and turned sideways to keep from lying directly on his frame.

***

Tori climbed into the front seat of Kilo's car and put on her seatbelt. Tori's body was sore and her stomach ached. It wasn't too bad, considering everything that happened. The pain meds she received helped tremendously. Kilo closed the driver's door and fired up the engine.

"Can you believe Tweety almost killed Tron? That's crazy." Tori was still in shock. So much had occurred in twenty-four hours. It was unbelievable. Especially the return of her husband.

"Yeah, it is. I'm just tripping on how Tweety thought she would get better results from that nigga. She saw how he was doing your other patient."

Tori laughed when she took a ride down memory lane. "Yeah, you always called Dazzle my patient."

"Shit, she was your patient."

"You right, was. That's past tense. Your boy taking good care of her now."

"Who?" Kilo glanced in her direction.

"Fresh."

"Ahh, hell nah. They together now?"

Kilo thought back to when he always tried to keep Fresh away from her. It wasn't because she wasn't good enough for him. Kilo couldn't take the chance that if something went wrong, he would be the blame for setting them up.

"Yep. They been together for like three years now."

"That's what's up." He nodded. "She still stripping?"

"She quit when they got together."

"Damn, just like that?"

"Yep!"

Kilo maneuvered through the streets without a problem. It was like he never left and in no time, he was pulling up to the place he used to call home. Killing the engine, he sat back in the seat, took a deep breath and exhaled.

Tori placed her hand on his lap. "You nervous?"

"It's a feeling I can't explain. My biggest fear was returning and you were too upset to talk to me."

"You sure that was your only fear and not me moving on?" Tori wanted to know how he truly felt.

"I wasn't worried about that."

"Why not?"

"Well, you saw what I did to that nigga, Jude. And besides, I saw your house. That let me know you hadn't fully moved on." Kilo kissed her ring finger. "By the way, I love that painting. That shit dope as fuck."

Tori teared up when she thought back to the pictures Kilo took of their dead bodies. "You saved my life. I would be dead if it wasn't for you."

"Don't you worry, I'm back now. I got your back and your front." Tori nodded her head. Kilo opened his door. "Come on, so I can face the music."

With her keys in her hand, Tori unlocked the door and they entered. Judging by the loud talking, Tori knew they were in the living room. Kilo walked behind Tori, but he stopped and let her enter first.

"Yo, where the fuck you been?" Honcho shouted. "I've been blowing your shit up all night and today. You had me riding around looking for that nigga, 'cause I thought he did something to you."

"This nigga wouldn't go to bed. We been up all day looking for you too," Eazy added.

"I'm sorry. Something did happen to me. That's why I couldn't answer my phone."

Eazy jumped up from his loveseat when he spotted the bruises on her face. "What happened to you? And who the fuck do I need to kill?"

Kilo was happy to know they took care of Tori in his absence.

"Nobody now. He's dead."

"Tori, who?" Honcho was getting irate. "And who the fuck were you with?"

Tori looked over shoulder. "Him."

"Who?" Honcho shouted again. Kilo stepped from the shadow and stood beside Tori. "What the fuck?" he uttered.

Eazy stood up. He couldn't believe he was looking in the face of his firstborn.

"What, you resurrected this nigga like Pac or some shit?" Honcho remained seated.

"It's a long story," Kilo replied.

"Well, we ain't got shit, but time." Honcho snapped.

Eazy walked up to Kilo and hugged him tight. He wasn't worried about the details. He was just happy to see his son again and not some damn ashes in an urn. Eazy held onto Kilo for dear life. When he finally released him, Eazy's face was soaked with tears.

"I'm back, Pops, and there's so much that I need to tell you." Kilo walked up to his baby brother. Honcho stood up and hugged his brother. "I missed you, man."

"I missed you too, bro, but I'm mad as fuck." Honcho wiped his tears away fast before they released each other.

"Where's my son?" Kilo noticed he wasn't present.

"He's upstairs," Honcho replied. "You have to sit down and tell us what the hell happened, and where the fuck you been all these damn years. You had my sister around here about to lose it. This girl wouldn't eat, sleep or go to school."

"I can only imagine." Kilo sat down and pulled Tori down onto his lap. "I'm sorry for that. You know all of that was beyond my control."

"We listening, bro." Honcho sat back and folded his arms.

Kilo got comfortable and repeated the same story he revealed to Tori. But this time around, Kilo revealed some important details that he hadn't told Tori. He wanted to tell that particular part when they were all together, so he wouldn't have to repeat himself. One hour later, Eazy had the full details that caused his son to disappear and he was livid.

"I'ma kill that bitch when I catch her," Eazy spat with pure hatred lacing his tongue.

"Pops, no. You can't do that. The feds gone be all over her, and you for that matter," Kilo pleaded with his father.

"Your mother is the reason all of this shit happened. I can't let her get away with this."

"You have to. Just let it go," Kilo warned. He patted Tori's leg. "I need to see my son."

"Come on." Tori stood up. "Let me talk to him first."

"Hold up." Eazy stopped them in their tracks.

"Wassup, Pops?"

"You standing in my goddamn living room." Eazy got up from his chair.

"In the flesh," Kilo smiled.

"Well, who the fuck is that in that urn?"

The entire room busted out laughing. Kilo shook his head. Out of everything he was expecting to hear, that wasn't it. "Shit, some John Doe from the morgue," he laughed heartily.

Tori walked into Capone's room. Eazy turned one of the spare rooms into a personal room for his grandson. He was lying across the bed watching television. As soon as he saw Tori, he jumped up with a huge smile on his face. "Mommy!" he jumped into her arms.

"Hey, baby. Mommy missed you."

"I missed you too."

"Come on. Mommy needs to talk to you." Tori sat him on her lap and grabbed the pendant around his neck. "Do you know who this is?"

"That's Daddy." Kilo smiled, as he eavesdropped from the hallway. He was happy Tori didn't allow him to forget who he was.

"Remember when I told you Daddy went to a special place and he was watching over us?"

"Yes."

"Well, Daddy is back from that special place. Do you want to see him?"

Capone nodded his head. "Yes."

"I want you to give him a big hug when you see him, okay?" she whispered in his ear.

"Okay."

"Bae, come in," Tori shouted.

Kilo walked into the bedroom and his heart melted when Capone jumped down from Tori's lap and ran in his direction. Kilo bent down and picked him up. That was the one embrace he waited on for so long. It hurt his heart that he missed out on everything, but going forward, they would be making plenty of memories together as a family. Tori wiped the tears from Kilo's eyes and hugged the both of them.

"I'll never leave y'all again. I promise." That was one promise Kilo intended on keeping.

"Can we go home now?" Capone whispered.

"Yes. We can go home," Tori kissed his cheek. "I thought you liked staying with Grandpa and Uncle Honcho."

"Uncle Honcho aggravating," Capone said innocently.

Tori and Kilo laughed. "This definitely my child."

"Don't I know it," Tori giggled, as they left the room.

Chapter 25

One month later

Kilo woke up early in the morning and took a brief stroll through the house. His first stop was Capone's room. He was knocked out for the count. They didn't go to bed until two in the morning. Friday nights had become a movie night for them. They ordered takeout and ate junk food while watching kiddie movies.

He was able to get Tori to take a much-needed break from the dope game to focus on what was important and that was *family*. Since Kilo's return, they had a lot of catching up to do and she was enjoying every second of it. Honcho and Lala relocated temporarily to Georgia to handle the drug business. Things were a little crazy, so Tori had to send some reinforcement, Tank, to get things back in order. Even if that meant a bloodbath. Fresh and Ace handled the local business.

Kilo moved his things out of the apartment on the beach and into the home Tori purchased. On his second night, Tori had a miscarriage just as the nurse said she would. Kilo drove her to the hospital even though he wasn't supposed to be out in public like that. However, he didn't care because his wife needed him. It was a relief to know she was no longer carrying another man's child.

His relationship with Capone was great. There wasn't a single strain. It was like he hadn't missed a beat of his life. Every day he thanked Tori for constantly reminding him about his father. If it wasn't for her keeping Kilo's memory alive, he would've been a stranger to Capone. His age played a huge role in it too. Smaller kids could adjust to almost anything.

Once his security stroll was over, Kilo headed back to their bedroom. Tori was stretched out in the middle of the bed. When he raised the comforter, her legs were open and the nightgown she wore was up to her waist. That gave Kilo a clear shot of her waxed pussy. There was no way he could lie in bed beside his wife and not touch her.

Kilo closed the door and locked it. On his way to the bed, he removed his pajama pants and boxers before climbing in. Spreading her legs apart, Kilo used his fingers to separate her plump lips. Slowly, he licked her clit up and down before sucking on it. Tori's juices started to flow. He coated his finger before inserting it into her ass. It had been years since he had meaningful sex and there were no limitations. Moving his finger in and out, Kilo sucked and slurped on the juice box. It was so wet and juicy that he could've used a straw.

Tori's body was starting to respond to the pleasure she was feeling. Her hips moved back and forth. Kilo pulled his finger out grabbed her at the waist and pulled her close to his face. Tori struggled to open her sleepy eyes, but her moans released with no hesitation. When she finally got them open, Tori placed her hands on top of Kilo's head, and thrusted her hips forward. She wanted to feel every inch of his tongue. He needed to write his name on her ovaries and stake his claim all over again.

"I'm cumming," Tori moaned softly.

Kilo couldn't have her tapping out early, so he stopped abruptly and swapped out his mouth for his dick. Turning Tori on her side, he straddled one leg and held the other one on his shoulder. Completely penetrating the nookie, he stroked it with ease, while squeezing her cotton soft cheeks. His nut was coming too damn fast, so he pulled out and shook the rod.

"Damn, slow down, bruh. We got plenty of time." He gave himself a pep talk.

"Put it back in," Tori begged.

"I got you, baby. Just like old times."

"Yes. Please," she moaned.

Kilo kept one hand on her ass and one gripping her breast. Dipping in his wife once again was like heaven on earth. He hated the thought of slimy ass Jude fucking Tori. That really fucked with his manhood. He would've preferred she fuck with a square ass nigga that worked a nine to five. That was water under the bridge since he buried that nigga deep in the dirt. No one was going to find him. Kilo shook those thoughts from his head and focused on Tori.

Kilo grunted with every stroke. "Fuuuuck!" He could feel his nut surfacing again. Tori's moans were another turn on. "We about to make another baby."

"Not yet," Tori panted. "Pull out."

"You crazy. When have you ever known me to pull out?" Kilo wasn't about to stop for shit. He beat the pussy until he came hard and heavy. When he pulled put, he laid down to cuddle with his wife, but she wasn't finished. Tori sucked and slobbered on his dick until he was hard again. Once his soldier was at attention, Tori mounted up and rode him until they both came.

Tori snuggled up under Kilo and he held her in his arms. "I love you, Tori. My feelings for you never stopped, even in my absence."

"Mine didn't either and that's why I couldn't get close to anyone." Tori rubbed his bare chest with her acrylic nails. It was her chance to be honest. "My pregnancy was a mistake. I didn't love him. And to be honest, we weren't together when I found out about the baby. That's why Honcho was so upset. I never had any intentions on keeping it. Jude was jealous of you."

"Honcho made that very clear, but why was he jealous of me? As far as he knew, I was dead." Kilo wanted to understand what she was going though.

Tori turned his face towards hers. "I have been grieving you for five long years. I still wore my ring and this tattoo of you didn't make it better. He told me he felt like he was competing with a ghost. In reality, he was. Kilo," Tori's voice cracked. "I never let you go. Jude was something to pass the time and he couldn't accept that." Tori decided to keep the proposal to herself.

"Thank you."

"For what?"

"For keeping my son."

"I couldn't get rid of my only connection to you. I'm not going to sit here and lie to you. I went to the clinic to get an abortion, but I couldn't go through with it. I'm glad I didn't because he's the one who helped me through all of this heartache. I had to live for him."

"I'm glad you changed your mind, because I would've never forgave you for killing my child. You had a support system, so there was no reason to do that."

Tori rolled her eyes. "Tuh! Not my father."

"He would've came around eventually." Kilo peeped her reaction and that made him curious. "What happened to him? I heard he was killed, but no one was arrested. Do you know who did it?"

Tori stared at the ceiling with tears in her eyes. "Yes." Tori broke down and cried.

"Who, baby? I'll handle that for you," he promised. Tori rolled over to her side. Kilo wiped the tears away. "Who, baby?"

"Me," she confessed.

"What do you mean, you?" Kilo was puzzled by her response.

"I killed him."

"Tori." He grabbed her face. "Why would you kill your father?"

Tori didn't blink not once. She kept the remainder of her tears at bay. "He killed my mother and I thought he had you killed."

"What? I thought she overdosed on some bad dope."

"He put battery acid in it."

"Damn." He sighed, feeling her pain.

Kilo held Tori in his arms and held her tight. What she needed was comfort and not a damn jury. It didn't matter what crimes she committed. Tori killed on behalf of the people she loved. Nothing more, nothing less. He would love her until his time on earth truly expired, and even in the afterlife.

Kilo pondered on their future on a daily basis and it was time he shared that information with her. "How do you feel about moving away and starting fresh someplace else?"

Tori raised her head slightly. "That will be hard to do with everything I have going on. I can't leave the business unattended for too long."

Kilo rubbed the top of her head. "That's precisely my point. You don't think it's time to leave the dope game behind? You can't do this forever."

"I'm finally where I want to be. I can't just quit like that."

"Yes, you can." Kilo turned on his side. "I have eight hundred and fifty million dollars stashed in a few offshore accounts. We'll be set for life. We can go anywhere we want to go."

Tori sat quietly to process his request. It sounded good, but she was finally running the dope game like a certified queen. That was a hard decision to make on such short notice.

Kilo peeped her hesitation and called her out. "The dope game has done nothing but make you a target. Look at everything you've been through. Look at why I had to leave you and Capone behind. The streets don't love us, Tori, and the feds will never stop locking muthafuckas up. I can guarantee that I'll die protecting you, but why wait until it gets to that? Who's going to raise Capone if we die, or go to prison for life? Come on, baby, think for a second."

A gentle knock on the door could be heard. Kilo stood up and put his pajamas back on before going to the door. Tori did the same. Capone walked in, hopped onto the middle of the bed and laid down. They had gotten used to him wanting to lay between them. Capone put his arm around Tori and closed his eyes. Apparently, he was still tired. Tori kissed his forehead and rubbed his small back.

"You really want to risk this for the dope game?" Kilo was doing his best to convince her to bow out while she was on top.

"I don't," she finally responded.

"Are you going to quit?"

"Yes." Tori didn't want to risk losing her family all together.

"So, the dope game is dead?" he reiterated.

"Yes. But you know I have to fly out to Atlanta and tie up some loose ends."

Tori's phone rang, interrupting their conversation. Grabbing the phone, she stared at the restricted number. At first, she wasn't going to answer, but she quickly changed her mind and picked up.

"Who is this? I don't like private numbers, so please speak quick."

"I know this may be a bad time, and I'm not properly addressing you. The name is Tipton. You may not remember me, but we have mutual connections. I'm in bad need of your assistance."

"Tipton?" Tori repeated through the phone. "I do remember, but how in the fuck did you get my number?" She questioned suspiciously.

"Maybe I can explain to you better face-to-face. I'm sure you know what I'm capable of. I promise to make it worth your while. Please," he begged waiting for her response.

"I'll get back with you in twenty-four hours. Please don't miss the call, because I don't like sloppy business, Tipton." She hung up the line in his face.

As expected, Kilo was right there waiting on her to hang up the phone. His brow creased and he had wrinkles in his forehead. "Who was that, Tori?"

"This guy from Atlanta named Tipton."

"What does he want?"

Tori shrugged her shoulders. "Apparently, he needs my help."

Kilo remained calm because not even five minutes ago, she promised to quit the drug game. "Are you going to tell me why or do I have to pull teeth to get the full answer out of you?"

"No. You don't have to pull my teeth." Tori sat the phone down on the nightstand and turned her attention back to him. "He said he needed my help and if I do it, he'll make it worth my while. He wants to have a sit-down with me and discuss the details further."

Kilo grunted and rubbed the top of his head. One thing about his woman that irritated him was her being so damn hardheaded, spoiled and stubborn. Things always had to go her way. Kilo knew he was to blame for her behavior and so was Diesel.

Tori knew him like a book, despite their time apart. Therefore, she knew he was pissed off. Getting up from the bed, she walked over to him and put her arms around his neck. "Baby, listen to me. Let me go and hear him out, okay? This could be a really good proposal."

"Do you even know this nigga enough to trust him like that?" For certain he was worried.

"He's like the king of the whip game. A certified paper chaser. I know of him from me living in Atlanta for so long. Just like I've heard of him, he's definitely heard of me. That's why he reached out to me."

Kilo shook his head. "I don't like this, period. What if shit goes left?"

"What if this is my way out the game for good? This proposal could be just what I need."

"No!" Kilo decided it was time to put his foot down once and for all. "Hear me and hear me well. If you want to run this dope game, you gone have to do it without me. I've spent five years living off the grid, away from you and my son, to make sure you stayed out of prison." Kilo wiped Tori's tears away. "Those were the worst years of my life, but now we are free from the restraints of the feds and that's the way I want to keep it. Don't make my absence go in vain."

Tori nodded her head in agreement. "Okay, I won't go."

"Are you stepping down?"

"Yes."

"Yes what? I need to hear you say it."

"My days as the queen of the trap are over. I promise." Tori sat down beside Kilo and held his hand. "I don't want to risk losing you again or our son. I love you too much to risk it all."

"Thank you. That's all I wanted to hear. We have enough money to last us for the rest of our lives."

"I'll let them know tomorrow that I'm out."

"We will let them know it's over." Kilo kissed Tori to seal the deal.

The ringing of Tori's phone interrupted their lip lock. "Let me see who is calling." When Tori reached her phone, she didn't recognize the number, but she answered it anyway. "Hello."

"You have a collect call from, Tweety."

"It's Tweety calling from jail." Tori accepted the call. "Hello."

"Hey, Tori, thanks for putting money on the phone."

"No problem. What's going on? Did you speak to the attorney I sent to meet with you?"

"Yes. That's why I'm calling."

"What happened?"

"I fired him."

"Why would you do that? You can't fight an attempted murder charge with a public defender."

"I don't want to fight it," Tweety rebutted. "I'm taking a plea deal."

Tori was confused. "Why? And what are they offering?"

"Five years under the Crime of Passion law."

"You can beat that with an attorney."

"Just listen to me for a second." Tweety took a deep breath and closed her eyes. "I declined his help because I was diagnosed with stage-three ovarian cancer. I'm going to die. So, don't waste your money."

Tori's eyes widened in surprise and she couldn't believe the words that came through the phone. "What?"

"Yes. I found out a few months ago. There's nothing they can do for me at this point. It's over, Tori. I just wanted to call you and tell you thank you for continuing to be my friend, even when I didn't deserve it. Tell Dazzle I'm sorry for the pain I caused her, and that karma has had her day. I love you, Tori. This will be the last time you hear from me."

"I love you too." Tori stood there trying to digest everything Tweety said to her. Then it all made sense as to why Tweety declined Tori's help while she was locked up.

Kilo noticed the sadness in her face. "What's wrong, baby?"

Tori sat the phone down and stared him in the eyes. "Tweety is going to die. She has stage-three ovarian cancer." Kilo consoled Tori for what seemed like forever.

"I need a few minutes alone. I'll be back."

"Okay."

Tori left the room and went into her office. Sitting down at her desk, she pulled out a picture of Diesel. One lonely tear crept from her eye and slid down her cheek. "See Daddy, I told you I could run an empire just as good as a man. I'm killing the dope game right now. Perhaps even better than you did. Not only am I the queen of the trap, but my reach has now extended to Georgia. I'm doing everything you said I couldn't do. I proved you wrong. Things could've been different if you only accepted me for who I am, what I am and who I loved. But, I'm finally stepping down. My dope girl ambitions are finally over. I love you, Daddy."

Tori stared at his face a little bit longer before kissing his face and placing the photo back inside the drawer. Interlocking her fingers behind her head, she leaned back in the leather chair and closed her eyes. Kilo was right. The dope game took away the ones she loved the most and put her in harm's way.

Looking at the picture of her, Kilo and Capone, a bright smile spread across her lips as she thought about the brand-new possibilities that lie ahead. Now that her enemies were out of the way and her husband had returned, it was only the start of a new beginning.

Chapter 26

Tori and Kilo pulled up at the duplex where she conducted all of the drug business. One hour prior to their arrival, Kilo received a call from his godfather. The news of him being clear to resume his life was music to Tori's ears. The last thing she wanted to do was hide out in another country for the rest of her life.

In attendance were Tori's closest associates. The confused looks on their faces when they saw Kilo alive and in the flesh was priceless. Fresh still couldn't believe his boy had risen from the dead, so to speak. They G-hugged before Fresh sat down with the crew. Tori started the meeting immediately.

"As you all can see my husband, Kilo, is back and there are about to be some changes." Tori had the saddest look all over. It seemed like she was giving the commendation at a burial service. "Starting today, I will be stepping down from my position in the organization. I'm officially out of the dope game. I will be handing the business over to Lala and Honcho."

There were multiple sighs and grunts throughout the room. Lala and Honcho both smiled and nodded their heads to acknowledge their new positions.

Tori continued with her speech. "They will be the new bosses. I know this comes as a surprise, but it's time for me to move on and take care of my family."

Ace and his boys stood up and hugged her one by one. "We gone miss you, Boss Lady!"

"I'm going to miss y'all too. Treat my sister and brother with the same respect y'all showed me."

Ace nodded his head. "We got them. No worries."

Tori and Kilo left the apartment and made their way back to Eazy's house. The two pulled up in the driveway and from the looks of things, Eazy was outside arguing with a woman.

"Who the fuck is that?" Tori mumbled.

Kilo took one look at the woman and knew exactly who was outside doing all the shouting. "My mother."

"Your mother?" Tori was floored.

"Yep. That's her," he nonchalantly stated.

Kilo climbed from the car and walked towards the house. Chasity took one look at her firstborn son and ran into his arms. Kilo reciprocated and hugged her back.

"They said you were dead." Chasity grabbed both of his arms and looked him up and down.

"I'm in one piece, Ma."

"What happened?" Chasity asked Kilo.

"You know what the fuck happened," Eazy shouted, while walking towards them. "All this shit is your fault. Now get yo' snitching ass off my property."

Tori leaned against the car to see what was about to unfold. The last time she saw Eazy that mad, someone was killed.

Kilo stepped directly in front of his father and placed a gentle, yet firm hand on his chest. "I'll handle it, Pops. Just chill."

"I want that bitch off my property," he spat.

"Relax, please." Eazy immediately stood down and allowed his son to take control.

Animosity was lingering heavy in the air. Kilo was well aware of Chasity's wrongdoings, but he couldn't blatantly disrespect the woman that gave him life. Instead, he broke it down as nice as possible. "I've been living off the grid because of the feds, but I'm quite sure you knew that already."

"It wasn't like that. I was trying to protect you." Chasity grabbed ahold of Kilo's shoulder and pleaded her case through tears. "They were going to send you to prison and I couldn't let that happen. It was either give you up or turn in Eazy. I couldn't let them take you."

Tori had enough of the fake tears. "I'm going inside to check on the baby." When she walked away Eazy followed her into the house.

Kilo turned his attention back to his mother. "You really put me in the crossfire of a major drug bust. They threatened to lock up me, Tori and my pops, if I didn't work for them. How could you snitch on Pops like that?" He frowned, with wrinkles now appearing on his forehead.

"I'm sorry. That's not what I meant to do."

"Sorry is not gone cut it. My wife had to grieve my loss because of you. I missed the birth of my son. I missed his early stages in life, and I can't get that back."

Chasity felt bad for the damage she caused her son, but the mention of Tori's name piqued her interest. The woman beside him did look familiar, but now she was certain of her identity. "Tori," she repeated with a raised brow. "As in Diesel's daughter, Tori?"

"Yeah, why?" Kilo was curious to know where that question was about to lead their conversation.

"So, you two got married and had a baby?"

"Yeah."

"Umm…I…" she stammered.

"What?"

"Did your father tell you the full story as to why I was in prison?"

"Just that you attacked a woman, and she lost her baby."

Chasity sighed and rubbed her arms. "I might as well tell you now since you're old enough to know."

"Know what?" he asked.

"The woman I shot all those years ago was Tori's mother, Bianca." Chasity knew a follow-up question was coming, so she cut him off. "I was having an affair with Diesel. He broke up with me and I wasn't happy about it. So, to hurt him in return, I shot her."

Kilo's mind was blown. Stroking his temple with his fingers, he shook his head. "So that's the reason Pops put you out."

"Yeah. I'm not proud of what I did, but I've learned from my mistakes."

Kilo was at a loss for words. Then just like that, it made sense as to why Diesel was adamant about him and Tori not dating. Nodding his head, he stroked his chin. "For years, I wondered why Pops and Diesel were beefing. The reason me and Tori had to be on some Romeo and Juliet type shit. It was all because of you."

"Baby, I'm sorry." Chasity tried to reach for him, but Kilo took a step back. In that moment, she wanted to mention Eazy's infidelity, but Kilo was already pissed and on his father's side. Therefore, deflecting the situation was pointless in her eyes. It was time she owned up to her mistakes. "I know you're upset, but I think we should sit down and hash things out."

"I'm sorry, Ma, but I don't think that's a good idea. I need time to discuss this with Tori before we can do that."

"Wait, you're going to tell her?"

"I am. All our lives we've been lied to. Pops lied to me to protect you I guess, and Diesel lied to Tori. We've been through enough and I refuse to keep this information from her. Tori deserves the truth."

"If you tell her, I'll never get a chance to establish a relationship with my grandson."

"Then I guess we'll see what happens, but I'm not lying to my wife. I can't do that again."

"Well, I'll be here for another two weeks. After that, I'm going to Alabama to live with my sister for a while. Take my number. Call me when you ready."

Kilo took his mother's number, gave her a brief hug and went to join his family inside. The night was about to be long one, but he was prepared for anything that came his way.

Tori and Kilo made it home after cutting their evening with Eazy short. After they put Capone to bed, the couple sat downstairs for a nightcap.

"Babe," Kilo sat his glass down on the table. "I need to tell you something."

The seriousness in his voice and vacant stare in his eyes let Tori know it was a serious matter. "What is it, baby?"

"After everything we've been through, I never want to keep another secret from you."

"I know, baby. What's wrong?" Tori prayed silently that she wasn't about to lose her husband again.

Kilo picked his glass up and took another sip to prepare himself for her reaction. "Tonight, while I was talking to my mother, she made a shocking confession. But I swear, I didn't know." Kilo reached out and grabbed Tori's hand. "My mother is the one that shot your mother and killed your brother. Please don't be mad at me. I don't want to ruin our marriage or family because of this. We've already been through enough."

Tori held her stare into the love of her life's eyes and nodded her head. There was one thing she could bank on when it came to Kilo and that was pure honesty. From the time they began dating, he never lied to her. Calmly, Tori parted her lips to respond. "I know."

Kilo was surprised to say the least. "What do you mean, you know?"

"My father gave me my mom's diary. In one of her passages during counseling, she revealed it was your mother that shot her because of an affair she was having with my dad. She even revealed she slept with Eazy, because they were hurt by what your mother and my father did to them."

Kilo's soft side disappeared instantly. "What? My daddy and yo' mama fucked?" he blurted out.

Tori laughed at his response. "Yes."

"And you're not upset?"

"No," she shook her head. "This happened a long time ago and it has nothing to do with us. But that does explain why my daddy fought hard to keep us apart."

"This is some crazy shit," he chuckled. "I'm glad we can laugh at the fact that we were almost stepsister and brother."

"Yeah. Despite the fact that we've been lied to all our lives."

"I just want to put all of this behind us and move on with our lives." Kilo kissed her knuckles.

"I couldn't agree with you more," Tori added with a smile.

"So, my next question is, how do you feel about Canada? I get the sense that we need to get away and start over. The business has been handed over to Lala and Honcho. Jenna and Torin are stable. What's holding us back?"

Tori thought long and hard before responding to his questions. A fresh start could be a good thing, especially after she gave up the business and put Jenna in charge of the property. All she had to do was find a manager for the beauty supply store and manage the money made from each business. Life got not no sweeter than that.

"That sounds like a great idea. I could come back and forth to check on the businesses and I could bring Torin back with me for the summer. I have to make sure he's good at all times." Tori looked around at her immaculate kitchen. "I love my house though."

"That's cool. You should do that." Kilo flashed a wide smile. "We can keep the house and travel back and forth."

Tori walked over to Kilo and straddled his lap. "This is like a dream come true. I never thought I would see your face in this life again, except when I look at Capone and our pictures. The day I saw your face, I just knew that I would be admitted to the looney bin."

Kilo laughed and caressed her backside. "I'm not gone lie. I wasn't expecting you to take me back so soon."

"Well what can I say, you're my soulmate and we mesh well together." Tori placed her hands on the back of his head and licked the side of his neck. "I can think of someone that's missed you an awful lot."

"Who is that?" Kilo grinned.

"Let's go in the bedroom and I'll show you. You owe me five years of make-up sex."

"I'm with that." Kilo scooped Tori up and moved swiftly into their bedroom.

***

One year later

Toronto, Canada

Kilo sat on the patio smoking a Cuban cigar, while Capone and Torin rode their four wheelers in the spacious yard. The past year had been the happiest he'd been in a long time. It was a lot of work, but worth it in the end. He purchased a new home for their family and matching BMW trucks. One day prior, they renewed their vows with their closest family members and friends. In two days, they were set to go to Paris for their honeymoon. Kilo couldn't wait to have his wife all to himself. No kids, no family, just the two of them. The door slid open and Tori appeared with a puzzling look on her face, holding their newborn baby girl, Capri, in her arms. In zombie mode, she sat down in front of him with a blank stare. That quickly put him on high alert. "Baby, what's wrong?"

Tori rocked Capri in her arms and bit down on her bottom lip. "I just received a phone call that Tweety died this morning. She lost her battle with cancer."

Kilo rose from his seat, took Capri from her arms and hugged Tori tight. "I'm sorry to hear that, baby. Everything gone be okay."

"I know, but it's crazy. Tweety dies and Tron is still living with his trifling ass."

"Trust me, he's not happy. The man paralyzed. He has a lot to think about and you can believe that."

"I know."

Kilo tightened his embrace. "Just focus on us and our family."

The door opened once more and out walked Jenna and Honcho. "Is she okay?" Jenna looked at her first cousin.

"She will be," Kilo assured her.

Tori looked up with a faint smile and wiped her face. "I'm okay. What's going on?"

"I just wanted y'all to know I'm about to go back to my hotel. I'll be back tomorrow to watch these kids so y'all can head out for that fabulous honeymoon."

Tori managed to muster up a smile. "I can't wait."

"I'm sure you can't, but they'll be out of your hair tomorrow," Jenna smiled and hugged Tori. "I'm just happy to help."

"Thank you for volunteering."

"After everything you did for me, you are more than welcome." Jenna walked away to kiss Torin goodbye.

Next up was Honcho. His smile and big brown eyes were bigger than the Florida sun. "We out, fam. We'll catch up with y'all before our flight leaves out tomorrow for the A."

Tori looked around for Lala. "Where's my girl?"

"In the bed sleep. That's all she do is sleep. My baby gone be lazy as fuck."

Tori managed to giggle despite her mood. "That's not true. I was lazy with Capone and look at his busy ass."

"That nigga just bad," Honcho interjected. "Anyway, we'll see y'all tomorrow."

"A'ight bro, be easy." Kilo hugged his brother.

"Will do." Then he left.

Dazzle and Fresh were the last ones to leave. Eazy and his girlfriend stayed at the house with Kilo and Tori, in the guest bedroom. Once the kids were down, the newlyweds retired to the master bedroom and called it a night.

Kilo snuggled underneath Tori and held her close. "This is what I've been dreaming of for so long and I'm happy you decided to move away and start fresh."

Tori played with his beard. "I would've moved to the end of the earth if you wanted me to. I love you."

"I love you too."

Tori finally had the life she desperately longed for. A loving husband and her babies. It all came at a painful price, but in the end every tear she cried was worth the happiness she retained. Being at the top had its rewards, but it also put her in danger on a daily basis. Now that it was in her rearview, she had new beginnings lingering in front of her eyes.

Lala and Honcho had taken Tori and Kilo's place in the dope game and had Florida and Georgia on the map. They were the new Bonnie and Clyde, and they ruled the south with an iron fist with guidance from Kilo and Tori. In Tori's heart and mind, she would always be "the queen of the trap," until the day she died.

The End

Submission Guideline

Submit the first three chapters of your completed manuscript to ldpsubmissions@gmail.com, subject line: Your book's title. The manuscript must be in a .doc file and sent as an attachment. Document should be in Times New Roman, double spaced and in size 12 font. Also, provide your synopsis and full contact information. If sending multiple submissions, they must each be in a separate email.

Have a story but no way to send it electronically? You can still submit to LDP/Ca$h Presents. Send in the first three chapters, written or typed, of your completed manuscript to:

LDP: Submissions Dept
Po Box 944
Stockbridge, Ga 30281

DO NOT send original manuscript. Must be a duplicate.

Provide your synopsis and a cover letter containing your full contact information.

Thanks for considering LDP and Ca$h Presents.

Destiny Skai

<u>Coming Soon from Lock Down Publications/Ca$h Presents</u>

BOW DOWN TO MY GANGSTA
By **Ca$h**
TORN BETWEEN TWO
By **Coffee**
THE STREETS STAINED MY SOUL **II**
By **Marcellus Allen**
BLOOD OF A BOSS **VI**
SHADOWS OF THE GAME II
By **Askari**
LOYAL TO THE GAME **IV**
By **T.J. & Jelissa**
A DOPEBOY'S PRAYER **II**
By **Eddie "Wolf" Lee**
IF LOVING YOU IS WRONG… **III**
By **Jelissa**
TRUE SAVAGE **VII**
MIDNIGHT CARTEL III
DOPE BOY MAGIC IV
CITY OF KINGZ II
By **Chris Green**
BLAST FOR ME **III**
A SAVAGE DOPEBOY III
CUTTHROAT MAFIA III
By **Ghost**
A HUSTLER'S DECEIT III
KILL ZONE **II**
BAE BELONGS TO ME III
A DOPE BOY'S QUEEN III

Dope Girl Magic 3

By **Aryanna**
COKE KINGS V
KING OF THE TRAP II
By **T.J. Edwards**
GORILLAZ IN THE BAY V
De'Kari
THE STREETS ARE CALLING II
Duquie Wilson
KINGPIN KILLAZ IV
STREET KINGS III
PAID IN BLOOD III
CARTEL KILLAZ IV
DOPE GODS III
Hood Rich
SINS OF A HUSTLA II
ASAD
KINGZ OF THE GAME V
Playa Ray
SLAUGHTER GANG IV
RUTHLESS HEART IV
By Willie Slaughter
THE HEART OF A SAVAGE III
By Jibril Williams
FUK SHYT II
By Blakk Diamond
THE REALEST KILLAZ II
By Tranay Adams
TRAP GOD III
By Troublesome
YAYO IV

Destiny Skai

A SHOOTER'S AMBITION III

By S. Allen

GHOST MOB

Stilloan Robinson

KINGPIN DREAMS III

By Paper Boi Rari

CREAM

By Yolanda Moore

SON OF A DOPE FIEND III

By Renta

FOREVER GANGSTA II

GLOCKS ON SATIN SHEETS III

By Adrian Dulan

LOYALTY AIN'T PROMISED II

By Keith Williams

THE PRICE YOU PAY FOR LOVE II

By Destiny Skai

CONFESSIONS OF A GANGSTA II

By Nicholas Lock

I'M NOTHING WITHOUT HIS LOVE II

By Monet Dragun

LIFE OF A SAVAGE IV

A GANGSTA'S QUR'AN II

MURDA SEASON II

GANGLAND CARTEL II

By **Romell Tukes**

QUIET MONEY III

THUG LIFE II

By **Trai'Quan**

THE STREETS MADE ME III

By **Larry D. Wright**
THE ULTIMATE SACRIFICE VI
IF YOU CROSS ME ONCE II
ANGEL III
By **Anthony Fields**
THE LIFE OF A HOOD STAR
By **Ca$h & Rashia Wilson**
FRIEND OR FOE II
By **Mimi**
SAVAGE STORMS II
By **Meesha**
BLOOD ON THE MONEY II
By **J-Blunt**

Available Now

RESTRAINING ORDER **I & II**
By **CA$H & Coffee**
LOVE KNOWS NO BOUNDARIES **I II & III**
By **Coffee**
RAISED AS A GOON I, II, III & IV
BRED BY THE SLUMS I, II, III
BLAST FOR ME I & II
ROTTEN TO THE CORE I II III
A BRONX TALE I, II, III
DUFFEL BAG CARTEL I II III IV

Destiny Skai

HEARTLESS GOON I II III IV
A SAVAGE DOPEBOY I II
HEARTLESS GOON I II III
DRUG LORDS I II III
CUTTHROAT MAFIA I II
By **Ghost**
LAY IT DOWN **I & II**
LAST OF A DYING BREED
BLOOD STAINS OF A SHOTTA I & II III
By **Jamaica**
LOYAL TO THE GAME I II III
LIFE OF SIN I, II III
By **TJ & Jelissa**
BLOODY COMMAS I & II
SKI MASK CARTEL I II & III
KING OF NEW YORK I II,III IV V
RISE TO POWER I II III
COKE KINGS I II III IV
BORN HEARTLESS I II III IV
KING OF THE TRAP
By **T.J. Edwards**
IF LOVING HIM IS WRONG…I & II
LOVE ME EVEN WHEN IT HURTS I II III
By **Jelissa**
WHEN THE STREETS CLAP BACK I & II III
THE HEART OF A SAVAGE I II
By **Jibril Williams**
A DISTINGUISHED THUG STOLE MY HEART I II & III
LOVE SHOULDN'T HURT I II III IV
RENEGADE BOYS I II III IV

PAID IN KARMA I II III

SAVAGE STORMS

By **Meesha**

A GANGSTER'S CODE I &, II III

A GANGSTER'S SYN I II III

THE SAVAGE LIFE I II III

CHAINED TO THE STREETS I II III

BLOOD ON THE MONEY

By J-Blunt

PUSH IT TO THE LIMIT

By **Bre' Hayes**

BLOOD OF A BOSS **I, II, III, IV, V**

SHADOWS OF THE GAME

By **Askari**

THE STREETS BLEED MURDER **I, II & III**

THE HEART OF A GANGSTA I II& III

By **Jerry Jackson**

CUM FOR ME I II III IV V

An **LDP Erotica Collaboration**

BRIDE OF A HUSTLA **I II & II**

THE FETTI GIRLS **I, II& III**

CORRUPTED BY A GANGSTA I, II III, IV

BLINDED BY HIS LOVE

THE PRICE YOU PAY FOR LOVE

DOPE GIRL MAGIC I II III

By **Destiny Skai**

WHEN A GOOD GIRL GOES BAD

By **Adrienne**

THE COST OF LOYALTY I II III

By Kweli

Destiny Skai

A GANGSTER'S REVENGE **I II III & IV**

THE BOSS MAN'S DAUGHTERS I II III IV V

A SAVAGE LOVE **I & II**

BAE BELONGS TO ME I II

A HUSTLER'S DECEIT I, II, III

WHAT BAD BITCHES DO I, II, III

SOUL OF A MONSTER I II III

KILL ZONE

A DOPE BOY'S QUEEN I II

By **Aryanna**

A KINGPIN'S AMBITON

A KINGPIN'S AMBITION **II**

I MURDER FOR THE DOUGH

By **Ambitious**

TRUE SAVAGE I II III IV V VI

DOPE BOY MAGIC I, II, III

MIDNIGHT CARTEL I II

CITY OF KINGZ

By **Chris Green**

A DOPEBOY'S PRAYER

By **Eddie "Wolf" Lee**

THE KING CARTEL **I, II & III**

By **Frank Gresham**

THESE NIGGAS AIN'T LOYAL **I, II & III**

By **Nikki Tee**

GANGSTA SHYT **I II &III**

By **CATO**

THE ULTIMATE BETRAYAL

By **Phoenix**

BOSS'N UP **I , II & III**

Dope Girl Magic 3

By **Royal Nicole**
I LOVE YOU TO DEATH
By Destiny J
I RIDE FOR MY HITTA
I STILL RIDE FOR MY HITTA
By **Misty Holt**
LOVE & CHASIN' PAPER
By **Qay Crockett**
TO DIE IN VAIN
SINS OF A HUSTLA
By **ASAD**
BROOKLYN HUSTLAZ
By **Boogsy Morina**
BROOKLYN ON LOCK I & II
By **Sonovla**
GANGSTA CITY
By **Teddy Duke**
A DRUG KING AND HIS DIAMOND I & II III
A DOPEMAN'S RICHES
HER MAN, MINE'S TOO I, II
CASH MONEY HO'S
By Nicole Goosby
TRAPHOUSE KING **I II & III**
KINGPIN KILLAZ I II III
STREET KINGS I II
PAID IN BLOOD **I II**
CARTEL KILLAZ I II III
DOPE GODS I II
By **Hood Rich**
LIPSTICK KILLAH **I, II, III**

233

Destiny Skai

CRIME OF PASSION I II & III

FRIEND OR FOE

By **Mimi**

STEADY MOBBN' **I, II, III**

THE STREETS STAINED MY SOUL

By **Marcellus Allen**

WHO SHOT YA **I, II, III**

SON OF A DOPE FIEND I II

Renta

GORILLAZ IN THE BAY **I II III IV**

TEARS OF A GANGSTA I II

DE'KARI

TRIGGADALE I II III

Elijah R. Freeman

GOD BLESS THE TRAPPERS I, II, III

THESE SCANDALOUS STREETS I, II, III

FEAR MY GANGSTA I, II, III IV, V

THESE STREETS DON'T LOVE NOBODY I, II

BURY ME A G I, II, III, IV, V

A GANGSTA'S EMPIRE I, II, III, IV

THE DOPEMAN'S BODYGAURD I II

THE REALEST KILLAZ

Tranay Adams

THE STREETS ARE CALLING

Duquie Wilson

MARRIED TO A BOSS… I II III

By Destiny Skai & Chris Green

KINGZ OF THE GAME I II III IV

Playa Ray

SLAUGHTER GANG I II III

RUTHLESS HEART I II III

By Willie Slaughter

FUK SHYT

By Blakk Diamond

DON'T F#CK WITH MY HEART I II

By Linnea

ADDICTED TO THE DRAMA I II III

By Jamila

YAYO I II III

A SHOOTER'S AMBITION I II

By S. Allen

TRAP GOD I II

By Troublesome

FOREVER GANGSTA

GLOCKS ON SATIN SHEETS I II

By Adrian Dulan

TOE TAGZ I II III

By Ah'Million

KINGPIN DREAMS I II

By Paper Boi Rari

CONFESSIONS OF A GANGSTA

By Nicholas Lock

I'M NOTHING WITHOUT HIS LOVE

By Monet Dragun

CAUGHT UP IN THE LIFE I II III

By Robert Baptiste

NEW TO THE GAME I II III

By **Malik D. Rice**

LIFE OF A SAVAGE I II III

A GANGSTA'S QUR'AN

Destiny Skai

MURDA SEASON
GANGLAND CARTEL
By **Romell Tukes**
LOYALTY AIN'T PROMISED
By Keith Williams
QUIET MONEY I II
THUG LIFE
By **Trai'Quan**
THE STREETS MADE ME I II
By **Larry D. Wright**
THE ULTIMATE SACRIFICE I, II, III, IV, V
KHADIFI
IF YOU CROSS ME ONCE
ANGEL I II
By **Anthony Fields**
THE LIFE OF A HOOD STAR
By Ca$h & Rashia Wilson

BOOKS BY LDP'S CEO, CA$H

TRUST IN NO MAN
TRUST IN NO MAN 2
TRUST IN NO MAN 3
BONDED BY BLOOD
SHORTY GOT A THUG
THUGS CRY
THUGS CRY 2
THUGS CRY 3
TRUST NO BITCH
TRUST NO BITCH 2
TRUST NO BITCH 3
TIL MY CASKET DROPS
RESTRAINING ORDER
RESTRAINING ORDER 2
IN LOVE WITH A CONVICT
LIFE OF A HOOD STAR

Coming Soon
BONDED BY BLOOD 2
BOW DOWN TO MY GANGSTA

Destiny Skai

www.ingramcontent.com/pod-product-compliance
Lightning Source LLC
Chambersburg PA
CBHW070442260626
47161CB00004B/1175